TH
VAMPIRE'S WOLF

By Juliette N. Banks

COPYRIGHT

Copyright © 2022 by Juliette N. Banks. All rights reserved.

No part of this book may be reproduced in any form or by any means, electronic or mechanical, including photocopying, recording, or by any information storage and retrieval system without the written permission of the author, except for the use of brief quotations in a review.

This book is a work of fiction and imagination. Names, characters, places, and incidents are either products of the author's imagination or are used fictitiously. Any resemblance to actual persons, living or dead, events, or locales is entirely one of coincidence. The author acknowledges the trademarked status and trademark owners of various products and music referenced in this work of fiction, which have been used without permission. The publication and/or use of these trademarks is not authorized, associated with, or sponsored by the trademark owners.

Author: Juliette N. Banks
Editor: Jen Katemi
Cover design by: Elizabeth Cartwright, EC Editorial

ABOUT THE AUTHOR

Juliette is a bestselling indie romance author who has taken the genre by storm with her popular vampire series The Moretti Blood Brothers. Juliette has a vast background in consumer marketing and has previously published with Random House. She lives in Auckland, New Zealand, with Tilly, her Mainecoon kitty, and all her book boyfriends.

Official Juliette N. Banks website:
www.juliettebanks.com

ALSO BY JULIETTE N. BANKS

The Moretti Blood Brothers
Steamy paranormal romance
The Vampire Prince
The Vampire Protector
The Vampire Spy
The Vampire's Christmas
The Vampire Assassin
The Vampire Awoken
The Vampire Lover
The Vampire Wolf
The Vampire Warrior

The Moretti Blood Wolves
Steamy paranormal shifter romance
The Alpha Wolf

The Dufort Dynasty
Steamy billionaire romance
Sinful Duty
Forbidden Touch
Total Possession

Realm of the Immortals
Steamy paranormal fantasy romance
The Archangel's Heart
The Archangel's Star
The Archangel's Goddess

THE VAMPIRE'S WOLF

CHAPTER ONE

Kurt Mazzarelli walked through the halls of the Moretti royal castle. His eyes were peeled for… well, you'd think as one of the five Senior Lieutenant Commanders—or SLCs as they were known—in the king's army he'd be looking for threats to the royal family.
Or danger.
Or trouble.
Hell, even keeping an eye out for insubordination by any of the hundreds of soldiers who reported up the chain of command.
There were only two higher than him and the other SLCs and that was Craig, the commander, and Brayden, the captain. Brayden Moretti was also the prince.
Then the king, Vincent Moretti.
Kurt wasn't looking out for any of those things. Well, perhaps he was. He'd been doing this so long it was second nature now.
Which was why he hadn't hesitated when he saw the red, swollen bite mark on Madison's neck when he was in Seattle a couple of weeks ago. He'd ordered a Moretti jet and flown home to Maine with the little flirty blonde barmaid he'd met in the bar.

She was somewhere within these great walls, but he needed to keep away from her. At least when he was on his own.

Three young female Moretti soldiers, dressed in top-to-toe black just as he was, walked past him and shot him blushing smiles. He nodded at them in acknowledgment and continued *not* looking for Madison.

When he got to his room, he shut the door and let out a chest full of air.

Fuck me.

It had been two weeks of physical hell.

No one knew what was wrong with her and, while she wasn't technically in isolation or quarantine, she'd been told it was best if she restrained from any sexual activity.

Well fucking hell, he should have thought of that…

Kurt pulled off his large black boots and kicked them into his wardrobe. Pants, jacket, and a black long-sleeved Moretti t-shirt came next. He threw them on the armchair in the corner of his room.

Unlike some of his colleagues, he didn't do commando. He liked his junk tucked up nicely in a pair of briefs. Leaving them on, he flopped his enormous muscular body down on the bed, face up, and let out another sigh.

Running a hand through his dark hair, his mind, yet again, returned to the flight home with Madison.

They had boarded just before daylight after teleporting to her home so she could pack a few things. She clearly wasn't a wealthy vampire, and at only fifty-five years old, he wasn't surprised.

They'd jumped in an Uber, because teleporting into an airport unless absolutely necessary wasn't recommended with all the security and cameras. Their teams could clean up after them, but it was just another job for them to do. They'd had time, so it was no biggie to order a car via the app.

What he hadn't factored in was his reaction, even just sitting next to her in the back of the sedan. The proximity had set off sparks between them he'd not been expecting, and his fingers had itched to touch her. Instead, he had jammed his hands between his thighs.

When he'd followed her up the steps of the plane and his eyes were glued to her ass, his cock growing ready for action, she had suddenly spun around, and those green eyes had captured his.

"I've never flown before," Madison had said.

"Ever?"

She shook her head.

Kurt had taken a few more steps, her ass now out of his line of sight, and placed a hand in the small of her back.

"There's nothing to worry about. Most people would love a private jet as their first flying experience." He winked down at her. "Come on."

He'd led her onto the jet and the crew had made sure they had all they needed while Kurt unpacked a few of the weapons he had on him and tucked them into a cupboard.

Madison knew he was an SLC, so she hadn't reacted when the handgun and two knives had appeared. In fact, it had been the opposite. Her eyes had glistened with obvious need.

Before he spotted the bite on her neck, just hours before, he'd been about to kiss her. Both of them had built up tension and if she looked down and saw the bulge in his pants, she'd know he was on the edge, too.

They had the entire jet to themselves, with the exception of the crew. Did he go sit on the other side and give her space?

No.

Did he sit opposite her to see where the sizzling chemistry might lead?

Yes.

Given he'd whipped her away from her home and she was in a new territory, he wasn't going to be assertive about it, but Kurt had no intention of making it difficult.

An hour into the five-hour flight, the sexual tension was off the charts.

Madison had asked him about his job with the royal army, and about his training.

"You must work out *a lot* to keep all that going on," she said, waving her hand around in a circle at his body and grinning at him.

"We work out. The job is physical, so there's not a lot of sitting around." He leaned to the side, his head tilting as he took in her lithe body. "What we do is dangerous."

Her eyes sparkled.

Kurt knew this shit got females wet, and he was playing it up.

"Were you on a job in Seattle? Is that why you were there?"

Now that he couldn't answer.

"If I told you that, I'd have to kill you, wouldn't I?" He winked.

She blushed, but grinned. "You wouldn't hurt me, Kurt Mazzarelli. You're one of the good guys."

He let out a snort.

"Oh, sweetheart. I'm not all that good. Don't mistake a warrior for a knight in shining armor. I am no Lancelot."

That was a bit of an inside joke.

Lance was one of the SLCs and had always been a ladies' man. Then when his mate, Sofia, came along, that is exactly what he'd done. Pulled a "Lancelot" and saved her.

That wasn't who Kurt was.

"So, you're a bad boy."

"If what you're thinking is the same as what I'm thinking, then yes. Very, very bad."

She'd bitten her lower lip and his cock had jerked right up. Their eyes had locked and burned as his mind completely stopped working.

"Come here," he'd said.

When Madison slid her things away and stood, Kurt reached to press a button, locking the crew out of the cabin. Then he unzipped his jeans.

Her eyes had shot to his cock as he pulled it out.

"Is this the kind of bad you're looking for?" he asked, gripping one of her hips with his other hand as he began to stroke himself.

More licking of her lips.

"Take off your clothes," he said.

Her eyes had locked with his, nerves beginning to show. He smiled.

"You want to play with bad boys, Madison, you need to be brave. Are you brave?"

She nodded without hesitation and began to undo her jeans. He stood and removed her top, running his hands over her lacy bra.

"We don't need this." He pulled down the straps and she helped him by undoing it at the back. When her breasts were bare, he groaned. "Gorgeous tits."

"Is this what you usually do?" Madison asked. "With females you meet?"

His smile grew as he removed the rest of his clothes. "Did you think I was a virgin, Madison Michaelson?"

He took her hand and planted it on his cock, hissing at her touch.

"No," she replied, lust thick in her voice.

She wanted to know she was special. He was surprised. Humans asked these questions usually, not vampires. But she was young.

Kurt had long ago decided he'd never mate. If he ever met the one, he had a plan. He would move to the Antarctic or some shit so he couldn't bond with them.

That love shit wasn't for him.

He'd seen too many things and lived a hard life since he was young. Love wasn't something he wanted or desired.

Tugging her with him, he stepped back and sat on the leather seat. Without coaxing, she fell to her knees.

One glance at him, where he nodded, and she took him in her mouth.

Oh, yes, fuck!

Her mouth was warm, wet, and not entirely skilled at what she was doing. Yet, it felt incredible. She fumbled away, sucking, licking, stroking, and watching him for a reaction. He was reacting, all right.

When she reached and gave his balls a squeeze, he had to make a decision. Come in her mouth or no.

He decided no.

Gritting his teeth, he pulled Madison off him and up to her feet, nudging a knee between her thighs. She gripped his shoulders.

"Man, you really are built."

"And it's all yours right now." He grinned and her little hands ran over his skin, down to his pecs and over his biceps like she was a kid in a toy shop. His ego, he wasn't ashamed to admit, doubled.

While he glowed under her touch, he slid his fingers along the seam of her panties and then tugged them to the side.

"You wet down here?" he asked, and she moaned in answer, her legs going a little weak. His fingers moved further and struck her creamy moisture, and his mouth watered.

He got rid of her panties and tugged her closer, planting his mouth on her clit. She let out a healthy groan and gripped his hair.

"Holy shit." If he didn't know better, he'd say from all that wetness she'd already come.

He slid more fingers through her pussy and then inside her. She was so damn tight he had the feeling she wasn't all that sexually active despite her flirty bar girl act.

Fuck, she was going to feel incredible around his cock.

He worked her a little more and stared up at her face. She looked like she was in heaven, her teeth clenched around her bottom lip.

God, he could play for hours with this pretty baby vamp.

His cock was impatient, though. It was dark red and leaking, needing to sheath inside her center.

Kurt pulled his fingers out of her and, as she watched him, he licked them slowly.

"Still like a bad boy, sweetheart?"

"Yes," she breathed.

"Good," he said, tugging her onto his lap. "Let me feel you on my cock."

"Go slow. You're bigger than I'm used to."

A sliver of annoyance rushed through him. *Who else was touching this female?*

"We can go as slow or as fast as you want," he had said, lining his cock up at her entrance.

Then Madison had lifted one of her hands from his arm and flicked her hair back.

The bite.

Red, swollen, pulsing.

She tried to slide down onto his shaft. He held her hips firmly.

"Kurt," she groaned, as his eyes had locked onto the wound.

"Fuck, Kurt. I need…"

With vamp speed, he lifted her, dumped her back on her seat and then fled to the door of the cabin.

"Get dressed," he had ordered her.

As he exited the cabin to take a cold shower and change, he heard her questions behind him, but couldn't stop. If he did, he'd plunge into her.

What had he been thinking?

God knows what that bite meant.

The vampire who had bitten her was on the run after they'd assisted his escape from BioZen, a pharmaceutical company who were doing experiments on vampires. Callan had been with them for months after being captured. They had no idea what had been done to the male, but after seeing the wound on Madison's throat it didn't look like anything fucking good.

Until he knew, he couldn't touch her again.

If she ever let him.

And he wouldn't blame her if she didn't. He'd given her no explanation, just let her alone on the plane until they arrived at their destination.

Kurt blinked, coming back to the present, and found his hand inside his briefs, stroking his cock.

Again.

For two weeks it was all he'd done, and it was never enough. Every time he saw Madison his body flared with desire. She barely looked at him, but when she did his fangs ached like a motherfucker.

She was distracting and too pretty for her own good.

And right now, she wasn't going anywhere, so he was going to have to learn to live with her being in the castle.

He jumped up.

There was a female in the castle he shared body juices with from time to time.

Fiona.

It was time to go see her.

One good fuck and Kurt was sure this aching need would subside. He should have done it earlier.

Then he could forget about wanting to sink balls-deep inside the little blonde bar girl once and for all and get back to focusing on his damn job.

CHAPTER TWO

"So, now we have a medical center in the fucking castle." Vincent, the Moretti king, rolled his eyes. "What a fucking time to be alive."

Considering vampires didn't get sick, yeah, it was rather ironic.

Around him, Kurt's fellow SLCs shook their heads and let out a variety of short laughs. But no one thought it was a joke. Especially him.

But that's where they were in their evolution now humans had learned about them. Some bad seeds at a pharmaceutical company had captured a handful of their vampires and conducted experiments on them.

One of the vampires, Callan, had been held by the company for months. No one really knew for how long, as they didn't know his true identity.

Long story short, Ari Moretti, a relation of the royal family had recently met his mate. Sage had worked for BioZen in Seattle and helped Callan escape. That was nearly five weeks ago now, and they were still looking for him. They had been able to get some intel, but very there was very little data about the experiments and what they were using the information for.

Spoiler alert, thought Kurt. It wouldn't be good.

Assholes.

The other captured vampires, recovered from a lab in Italy, had also needed medical support after the scientists had basically tortured them.

Then there were all the royal babies. The queen had recently given birth and the princess was now pregnant.

Giving birth was natural.

Bites that wouldn't heal on a vampire's neck were not.

And no one knew what was next, so the king had ordered a medical center be created.

The space Brayden had hosted his deliciously dirty orgies had now been converted into two areas: a research lab and patient care.

The prince's orgies had been legendary over the centuries, but he was now mated to Willow and a committed mated vampire. Kurt had been a regular attendee and enjoyed the sexual buffet of men, women, and vampires.

Heck, he could do with a taste of the buffet right now.

His visit with Fiona hadn't gone well earlier.

He'd spent half an hour leaning against the doorway talking—*fucking talking*—until she'd finally pulled her top off and he'd stared at her breasts like he was watching some TV advert.

Uninterested.

There hadn't been even the slightest jolt downstairs.

Kurt hadn't wanted to offend her, so he'd feigned being called, telepathically, by the commander and left.

Great.

He was broken and couldn't even fuck his female with benefits, or FWB as he called her.

"So much for being immortal." Sage chuckled. Ari's mate had been a human before the only surviving original vampire had turned her.

This life was all new to her, but for the rest of them, these were troubling times.

It had all started when Stefano Russo, the leader of the vampire rebellion, had tried to take the throne. More than once. The insane—now deceased—vampire had partnered with Xander Tomassi from BioZen.

And he couldn't even get that right.

Xander had sent letters to the President of the United States and global media, under the pen name Ben Johnson, announcing vampires were real to humanity.

It had sent all vampires, including Stefano, into hiding for a period of time.

They'd expected it to happen one day and had procedures in place to protect the royal family. They had fled to a hidden property in Tuscany, Italy, and sat watching social media as their smart-as-fuck communications team had worked diligently to shift the narrative around the world.

Fake news.

Honestly, who would believe vampires existed?

It had worked well thanks to Brianna, who was mated to their commander, Craig Giordano.

Now only a handful of world leaders still knew they existed. The king was now working closely with them, strengthening relationships and building trust. They called their alliance *Operation Daylight*, and their objective was to create a strategy and put in place a plan to announce their existence.

When everyone agreed.

Because the Moretti race was a monarchy and ten million vampires around the world acknowledged Vincent as their king, adhering to some of the human laws in the countries they lived in.

Policing a vampire who had murdered someone, when they could outrun or out-muscle a human cop, was impossible. Plus, vampires were predators. Their own laws represented that.

They'd lived alongside humans for fifteen hundred years and made it work, but it was taking some big conversations to break down myths, fears and build that all-important trust.

And that was with only a dozen people.

Imagine what it would be like when billions learned about them?

That day may just be decades away.

If ever.

Kurt was in no hurry. Especially after what they had already experienced at the hands of greedy and inhumane scientists.

Whatever they had done to Callan was yet to be understood, but they did know, because of the data retrieved so far, that he'd had his DNA altered.

And he'd bitten Madison.

Who else had he bitten?

They were assuming there were more victims and with no way to find the vampire who was still on the run, they were frustrated as hell. It was like finding a needle in a haystack.

Meanwhile, they waited and watched to see how Madison fared.

Kurt was also having blood tests after having contact with her. Not that he'd told them exactly how much.

"The hospital will be of great value," Brayden said.

"Especially with another little royal on the way," Craig said, referring to the prince's mate, Willow, being pregnant.

"Yes." Brayden's smile spread across his face.

"Congrats, man," Kurt said.

"Thank you," Brayden replied, then pushed away from the wall. The prince was the most powerful vampire in the race. Although rumor had it, the ancient vampire, Ari, sitting across the room, now owned that spot.

Or never lost it.

The vampire had been missing for over four hundred years. Or rather, he'd been living anonymously after leaving the royal family when Vincent and Brayden's father was still king in the early 1600s. His identity as a Moretti had been kept hidden and, even now, only those in the royal inner circle and his trusted assassins from The Institute—his private security company in Seattle—knew the truth.

Kurt was surrounded by seriously powerful alpha vampires.

And he was one of them.

He hadn't earned his position as an SLC by being a pussy or a good swordsman. He also hadn't earned it by swinging his big cock around at the orgies.

Or being humble.

Like Marcus, Tom, Lance, and Ben, he'd become an SLC by proving he was a powerful, deadly, skilled warrior and would give his life for the king and any member of the Moretti royal family.

He would, and nearly did, all the time.

His job was not without danger, and he loved it.

Ben was the newest member of the team, and a former assassin from Ari's team. The cheeky yet lethal vampire had mated Anna, a survivor from BioZen, and accepted the king's invite to work for him.

Kurt, Marcus, Tom and Lance had all joined the Moretti army in the early seventeenth century in Italy, when Craig, their commander, had put together his senior team.

Craig was a big mother-fucker vampire and took no shit from anyone. He and the prince bickered and argued like an old mated couple, but their bond was unbreakable and powerful.

All of them were able to communicate telepathically because they'd shared blood.

"I'm eager to eliminate this human threat before my child is born," Brayden said, turning to the king. "I say we stop fucking about and take aggressive action."

The king rubbed his neck. "I understand your concern, brother, but we can't just bomb every BioZen location on the planet," Vincent said.

"I mean, we can," mumbled Craig as he casually lifted a shoulder.

Vincent shot him a frown.

"Vincent is right, we can't," Ari said. "There is real opportunity to introduce humans to our race. It might take another decade, but the work he's doing with world leaders is important. Harming humans, which would be inevitable in those twenty-four-seven operations, would destroy any trust gained. You all know that."

Ari was over fifteen hundred years old, and the last living original vampire. His twin brother Gio had long passed. He had seen a lot of history.

"To them, we're predators who are scary and unknown," Vincent said.

And rightly so.

"We will stop these humans, but killing innocents is not what we do, nor have we ever," Ari said. "Let's not start our relationship with humans in that light."

"We *are* predators, Ari, let's not forget that. It's in our nature to protect our own," Brayden replied.

Vincent let out a sigh.

"I get it. Becoming a father has been the most powerful and terrifying experience of my life. If anything, or anyone, threatens Lucas, my initial instinct is to destroy," Vincent said. "But you would be the first to stop me and tell me to think before acting."

The king was right.

Kurt had seen the prince, time and time again, step in and talk sense into the king when he'd been hot-headed about something. They each had their moments, but it wasn't like Brayden to be so emotional.

Still, a baby… that was a game changer.

If Kurt ever had a child on the way—not that he would, because he wasn't ever mating—he'd destroy worlds to protect a little vamp.

Children needed to be protected.

He wished someone had been there for him, but they hadn't.

"Yeah, fuck. You're right," Brayden said, rubbing his forehead.

"However," Vincent added, "If you can find Callan, and we can get our hands on more data from the vampire experiments undertaken by BioZen, then we can reassess."

Craig grinned. "You mean blow that shit up."

Brayden rubbed his mouth to hide his smile.

"No. I do not mean that, Craig. I mean, I can speak to the Operation Daylight team and form a consensus on how we deal with them."

Operation Daylight was the name given to the team of world leaders who were privy to the existence of vampires. The President of the United States, James Calder, sat on the team, along with a handful of others, including the British prime minister, Jeromy Smithers, South Korea's Chung Lee, and the new Italian president.

Long story short, Ben had assassinated Diego Lombardo, the former president, once he'd found out he was in bed with BioZen and responsible for his mate being kidnapped and experimented on.

"He means blow shit up." Craig smirked and Vincent shook his head.

Ari let out a laugh. "You hired this guy?"

"No. Brayden did," Vincent said, raising a brow.

Kurt smirked at the bickering. Craig was more than the commander of the king's army. He was nearly family.

Brayden had head-hunted him in the early seventeenth century and when the two males mated with Brianna and Willow, the two human best friends, it was as if fate was keeping them all together.

Ari was getting to know everyone again after leaving the royal family four hundred years ago. He had been close to Brayden, from what Kurt understood.

Less so the king.

Now Ari was mated he could create a bloodline all of his own. All other vampires descended from Gio Moretti.

Kurt wasn't sure where they all stood on the matter, but he knew it was a thing. He tried to keep out of all the royal politics, but because he was part of the senior team protecting the king, he needed to be aware of it.

No one truly saw Ari as a threat to the king, but it was a talking point as they found their feet now that they were reacquainted.

"I'm in when you give us the green light," Ben said, kicking Kurt's boots. "You in?"

"I'm always in for blowing shit up," Kurt replied and shared a grin with Craig.

"All right, you fucking animals. Keep your weapons holstered. Find Callan first." The king shook his head. "That doesn't mean we stop looking for Xander Tomassi. If we can get our hands on him, we might find out the information we need with some… gentle interrogation."

Kurt snorted.

So far, the main guy at BioZen had been AWOL after a team had tried to grab him in Italy. They knew—or assumed—he was still in the United States, but so far, he had remained well hidden.

"Any update on the tests you've been running, Sage?" Brayden asked.

Sage tapped away on her laptop, oblivious to the voices around them. She had clearly tuned them out.

"Sweetheart," Ari said, tapping her on the shoulder.

"Huh?" She looked up.

"How are you tracking with the tests on Madison?" he asked.

Sage pushed her glasses up her nose. "Early days. Setting up the lab has taken some time." She glanced at the king. "I'd like to request that Anna continues to assist me. Her vet training is coming in useful. She's very bright."

"And sexy," Ben said, nodding proudly about his mate.

Sage smiled at him. "She's so nice."

Sage thought everyone was nice. She'd befriended Willow, Craig's mate Brianna, Anna and now Madison. He'd had to sit through a lunch one day, with her and Ari, as she raved about Madison being *so* lovely and smart, and how pretty she was.

Like he needed someone to remind him.

He knew.

She wasn't pretty, though. She was fucking gorgeous. At least in his eyes.

The two females had grown up in Seattle, though Sage had been human until recently, and appeared to have bonded over their common love of the city.

"I need to get onto finding an antidote to the product BioZen are injecting in vampires to incapacitate them," Sage said. "I was able to get samples from Kurt and Oliver from The Institute when they were attacked a few weeks ago. I had to put that work on hold when we were called to Maine to help Madison, but it's still important."

"Very," Kurt said. One prick and he had lost all control of his body and vampire abilities immediately.

"Absolutely. That's important. Anna is all yours." Brayden nodded. "And yes, Ben, we know she is yours."

Kurt let out a little laugh as Ben lifted a corner of his mouth. Those stupid dimples appeared. Ari caught Kurt's eye, and they shared a grin.

Ben was way too confident.

"As for the tests, most of it is good old-fashioned observation as we do with humans because I don't have any data to start with," Sage said.

They all stared at her.

"Like a baseline."

More staring.

"There's no vampire healthcare information about our biology for me to compare with what I'm looking at now," Sage clarified.

Ohhh, a few of them said, but Kurt wasn't sure anyone really got it.

Sideways glances and nods.

"It's going to take a lot of time and a lot of testing to gather all we need. For now, all I'm doing is monitoring her."

They nodded.

She waved her hand out in front of her, then looked back at her laptop. "Time. I need time. Madison needs time."

Fucking great.

What he needed was for Madison to heal and go home. He needed the temptation of her to be removed from his vicinity.

"Are you still confident in your decision to not quarantine her?" Vincent asked, and Kurt felt the hairs on the back of his neck prickle.

He hadn't been completely upfront about what he and Madison had done sexually. He told them they'd kissed but not had sex.

Which, technically, was true.

Except he'd had his mouth on her pussy.

And God, it had been sweet and addictive. If only he'd been able to sink deep inside her.

Now he never would.

Because hopefully she would heal and head back to Seattle.
Then he could get his sex life back on track.
And be able to concentrate.
Still, because they had exchanged bodily fluids, Sage was taking his bloods and monitoring any changes in his body.
So far, there was nothing to be concerned about.
Except his needy cock, for one sexy little barmaid.
"Yes. She has access to blood and knows she cannot bite anyone. She reports into the medical center daily." Sage took off her glasses and closed her laptop. "Her wound appears to be healing slowly. It may be that the laboratory did something to Callan, which changed his blood, which irritates vampires and causes a slower healing process. A little like an infection in a human."
Ari's hand slid affectionately over the back of her head.
"This is all speculation at this point," she added. "But there is nothing to indicate she is infectious or there are any behavioral changes."
"Thanks, Sage," Brayden said.
Ari stood and pulled her chair out. "Oh, Kurt, can you stop by the lab sometime tonight?" Sage said.
"Sure," he replied, staying poker-faced, though he wondered what she wanted. When the door closed behind her, all heads turned to Brayden.
"Okay, so we have two main priorities. We are still hunting for Callan. On the ground and through facial recognition tech via our IT guys," Brayden said. "And the hunt for Xander Tomassi continues. If we get him, it's a game changer. Ari, you happy to keep your guys in LA so we can keep visuals on the new BioZen plant?"
It had been built recently and the pharma giant had relocated the scientist who'd experimented on Callan there. They

were extremely concerned about what was going on at that location.

The issue they had with getting inside all these labs was the facilities had been reinforced with Tungsten. The strongest metal on earth and one they, as vampires, couldn't get through.

"Yes," Ari said. "We've set up some cameras so we can monitor the outside perimeter around the clock. If they spot anything, they have been instructed to share with your teams immediately."

"Excellent," Brayden said, "Craig, get your teams out scoping the locations we haven't yet visited. Then when we're ready, we can…"

"Go boom?" Craig said, using his hands.

Vincent cursed, and everyone laughed.

Kurt knew the commander wouldn't be in his job if Vincent didn't trust him. He was one of the most powerful and dangerous vampires on the planet.

When shit got real, he got the job done.

Kurt had fought by his side thousands of times since he joined the Moretti royal army.

"All right, jokes over. Mazzarelli, I want you to stay in Maine in case you're required due to your contact with Madison," Craig said.

Great. Fucking great.

For a moment, he had been going to put his hand up for one of the field tasks. He wasn't surprised by the decision, as it was the right call, but that didn't mean he had to like it.

"Got it," Kurt replied.

"Tom, Lance, Ben, you three prepare your teams for departure in the next few hours," Craig added.

"Marcus, you're still running the end of your training program. Is that right?" Craig asked.

"Yes sir," Marcus replied.

And meeting over in three, two…

"That's all folks. Stay alert." Brayden walked to Craig's desk where the two would dive into more strategy.

Kurt stood, knowing he should head to see Sage, but he was going to delay it as much as he could.

Why?

Because the chances of Madison being there were great.

Plus, every time he visited he felt the weight of his lie.

Hopefully, it wouldn't come back to bite him in the ass.

Or, you know, end his life.

CHAPTER THREE

Madison propped up her feet on the coffee table and grinned at the two faces staring back at her from the wall-mounted screen. She hadn't seen her friends, Selena and Brooke, for weeks and now finally they had found time to do a video call.
Talking on the phone and texting weren't the same.
It was so crazy she was even in the Moretti castle, let alone living here.
Sadly, it wasn't for a happy reason.
"Oh my God," Selena said, waving.
"You guys! I miss you." Madison grinned widely.
"Same! When are you coming home?" Brooke asked. "Not that I would ever want to leave. Are you surrounded by all those Moretti soldiers?"
They had no idea.
Every time she left her room and walked down the hall, there were big muscular males walking around in that sexy black royal uniform. She was sure her hormones were throwing all the blood tests Sage was doing.
"Constantly. It's horrible." She laughed. "And some of them walk around shirtless. I've landed in hell."
They all giggled.

"And Kurt. Is he as hot in real life as he looks online?" Selena asked.

Yes, he was.

Unfortunately.

And he was also a big fat tease. Not to mention he'd ignored her for two weeks.

Madison had seen him in the lab and from a distance, but not once had he inquired how she was or if she was settling in.

Not once.

And fuck him. He'd had his mouth down *there*.

She flushed from the memory, even though she was trying to forget it.

Not that she could.

God, it had been the most powerful orgasm of her life. Her body had not been ready for him to stop when he had, and she could tell he hadn't wanted to stop, either.

But she understood why he had.

What she didn't understand was why he'd had to be so cold and abrupt about it.

Or why he couldn't be civil now.

Perhaps he was just a bit of an asshole. Which was a little heart-breaking as she'd had a crush on the senior warrior since she was a little vampire.

"Yeah. He's huge." She hoped they could move swiftly past this part of the conversation. It had been all fun and exciting to start—even with the bite—but now it was a drag.

She was homesick and angry with Kurt.

Not even one single hello.

"Is he the one who kissed you?" Brooke asked.

Dammit, why did she have to text her friends the night they had stopped at her apartment?

"Yes, but it was no big deal," Madison replied.

"Mads, you totally used to crush on the guy. That is a big deal. Fantasy ticked off," Brooke said. "Did you do more?

Now, wasn't that an impossible question to answer?

He licked me until I screamed. Then dropped me like a hot potato. Every girl's dream.

There was no way she could tell her friends. They'd ask why, and she couldn't tell them about Callan. They had originally seen the bite mark, but Madison had covered it up and the entire thing had been forgotten.

But the thing was, she needed a cover as to why she was in the royal castle, so she said Kurt had invited her to apply for a job. One she couldn't talk about yet.

"No. We're just friends. But a fated meeting as the job could be amazing."

So many lies.

Part of her wanted to warn her friends about Callan, but when the king demanded your silence, you gave it.

"I bet he knows how to make a female scream." Selena smirked. "Let me at him."

Did he ever.

And the thought of Selena with her legs spread as Kurt ate her out sent her straight into a bad mood.

Why?

They could both do as they pleased, and if Kurt and Selena ever met and decided to do each other, it was none of her business.

Kurt would probably love Selena. She'd always been the more vivacious of the three of them. They'd met when they were younger vampires, training to be teachers.

Now Madison was studying once again. She was learning Italian while working at the bar—which she'd had to quit–so she could teach English. Her plan was to move to Italy and fulfill her dream of seeing the country her ancestors were from.

But there was more to it than that.

Her father had died a year ago, which meant her mother didn't have long to live. When a mate died, the other followed quickly behind.

A year was a very long time for her mother to still be with them, but Madison was grateful and, as she lived nearby, she saw her mother regularly.

Still, she knew the day was coming soon.

Her father's death had been a surprise. It had been a freak driving accident where his car had careened into a building site and a pole had stabbed him in the heart.

One of two possible things that could have killed him.

Sunlight or his heart being torn open.

Madison had looked at her life and realized she had been living for her parents. At fifty-five years of age, she had never traveled and always stayed close to her family.

Yes, she was a teacher and had two great friends, but she'd always struggled to get ahead financially and so far, her mate was nowhere to be seen.

Not that she'd gone looking for him.

Her dreams, that she'd never dared to let surface, were so deeply buried she wasn't sure what she would do with her life.

All she knew was she wanted to go to Italy. Teaching English provided the opportunity.

Madison needed something to strive toward because, when her mother eventually stepped into the sun, as all widowed mates eventually did, she'd be alone.

Completely alone.

Brooke and Selena would one day meet their own mates and who knows where that would take them. They could move anywhere in the world.

So, she was making her own plans.

Finish her degree and find a job in Rome, or maybe Tuscany.

Many of the vampires at the castle were Italian, and she loved listening to their accents.

Kurt's was sexy as hell, but she'd die before she told him that.

"I think he's more of a *love you and leave you* kind of vamp." Madison shrugged, responding to Selena.

"Fine with me." Selena chuckled. "I don't need breakfast. Just an earth-shattering orgasm, then lock the door on your way out."

"Selena!" Brooke laughed. "Okay, so can you tell us what the job is, yet? Why do they need a teacher? Is it for the new prince? He's so little, though."

Madison shook her head. "I can't. I'm sorry. I wish I could, but hopefully one day soon."

Probably not.

"When will you be home?" Selena asked.

She shrugged. "I don't know that either. Did you check on Mom for me?"

"I did last night. She's okay," Selena replied, lifting a weight off her shoulders. "So, in other news, it looks like I have a teaching job in Spain."

Brooke and Madison gasped. "No way."

Selena nodded.

"Yes way. I'm just trying to work out if I can fly over at night and get there safely. Or you know, alive."

They all laughed, but it was no joke. Sunlight would turn her friend to ash.

"It's a private family. Homeschooling their kids. I found the job on VampNet," Selena continued, referring to the secure vampire internet which connected over ten million vampires around the world.

It was like a secure company intranet and was owned and run by the Moretti internet technology team.

"That's really exciting. Better than boring old Seattle," Brooke said.

Madison had never traveled further than the outskirts of Washington for vacations in her life. It felt odd and lonely being so far away across the country in Portland, Maine.

It would have been nice to have a friend in the castle, but everyone had their own little cliques.

She'd been intimidated at first by the size of all the vampires. Meeting one enormous warrior was one thing, but walking down the halls with dozens of them all around was daunting.

They were friendly enough, but Madison found herself a little tongue-tied.

She was used to being around hot males—heck, she worked in a bar—but this was taking alpha energy to a whole other level.

The odd conversation got a little friendly, but there wasn't much she could do. Sage had banned her from any sexual activity, and she got the feeling the males who were flirting weren't interested in a tennis date.

Plus, she was still pissed about Kurt, even if she didn't want to admit it. Aside from leaving her hanging—pleasure wise—she hated how he was both ignoring and avoiding her.

Perhaps she'd read too much into their attraction.

She was, after all, just a mere vampire. He was one of the SLCs and had a huge fan base of females—and males—who lusted after him.

There was no doubt he had all the options in the world to satisfy all his needs.

Gah.

She hoped she didn't bump into him somewhere with a female on his arm.

Not that he owed her anything.

Madison just wanted this over with and to get home.

It looked like the bite on her neck, which was now healing after Sage had put some herbal cream on it, was nothing to worry about after all.

However, until they knew one hundred percent, she'd been told to stay in and around the castle. They'd provided her with a lovely room.

She'd also met Sage's mate, Ari.

Being in the male's presence was interesting. He oozed power. Madison didn't know exactly who he was, but Ari was like no other vampire she'd ever met.

But he loved Sage. That was obvious. He was very protective of her and the way the two touched each other and his little Italian terms of endearment declared their love.

She could translate some of the terms.

One day, Madison wanted to be loved like that.

One day.

Maybe she would meet her mate here in the castle? There were thousands of citizens living within the enormous property.

Who knew?

Miracles happen every day, she reminded herself.

She glanced at the clock and her eyes flew open.

"Eek. I have a meeting. I better go." She focused on the chatter going on between her friends.

"Already?" Selena cried.

Madison nodded. "Let's chat again soon. *Arrivederci.*" She waved goodbye and hit the end button after Brooke promised to look in on Madison's mom.

Who she also needed to call.

She hated being so far away from her mom, and every time they talked, it made her cry.

What if her mom died while she was in Maine?

Thinking about it too much had sent her into a panic.

So Madison had found herself avoiding the phone calls.

What she wanted to do was get outside and exercise.

She'd been given full access to the training center, but honestly, working out with a room full of athlete vampires was way more intimidating than she could handle.

And if she had to curtail her sex drive, that was not the place to be hanging out. Twice she'd gone back to her room wet as hell.

She'd told Sage her need for sex had increased since being bitten. Even more so since meeting Kurt. She hadn't mentioned that last part.

Madison wrote it off as not being fully satisfied.

Now wouldn't the vampires of the race be amused to know Kurt Mazzarelli had left a female unsatisfied?

Madison smirked.

She leaped up, pulled on a sweatshirt, woolen hat, and running shoes.

It was time to stretch her legs and get some fresh air.

Maybe that would curb the heat between her legs.

Or perhaps there was only one thing that would do that. Hopefully Sage was going to give her some good news tonight so she could get her wild thing on again.

CHAPTER FOUR

Callan sat on the bus as it made its way along the open road. It was taking more days than he wanted to get across the country, as he and his three companions had to keep stopping and getting off well before the sun rose.

It was a logistical pain in the damn ass.

He twisted and lay down on the back seat, throwing his arm over his forehead. He was wide awake, unlike many of the humans on the bus who had been lulled by the sounds of the engine and road noise.

His eyes darted to three vampires sitting in separate seats in front of him. They were stretched out, chilling just like he was.

Except none of them were really relaxed. There was a tension simmering within them all which, if any of the passengers on the bus fully understood, would have caused a huge panic.

Not least because they were vampires.

And that was the question running through Callan's mind. He didn't know what the hell the scientists at BioZen had done to him, but they *had* changed him while he had been held captive in their laboratory.

He knew that much.

Unfortunately, he hadn't figured it out until too late. After escaping, he had done what was natural. Bite and drink blood.

If his instincts were right, and his body was changing, then it was possible he had harmed others. Which is why he was on his way to the Moretti royal family, who were currently residing in Portland, Maine, on the west coast of the United States.

Vincent Moretti had a reputation for being a fair king, so he'd thought about this long and hard about how to approach him for help. He could have called or emailed, but after being held captive, he didn't trust technology or anyone. He wanted to speak to the prince or king in person and ask for his help.

He wasn't expecting miracles. There was probably nothing they could do for him, but they needed to stop the spread if his bite was harming others.

Callan had tried to do the responsible thing and round up the vampires he'd fed from over the past five weeks. He had found four of them: Noah, Liam, and Ava.

They had been angry.

After explaining that he'd been held captive by humans and sharing some of the painful experiments the scientists had done on him, all four of the vampires had quickly agreed to travel with him to Maine.

At that point, Callan knew they had to get moving. The sensations in his body and following his instincts told him he was running out of time.

For what, he didn't know.

He just knew he wasn't the right person to go randomly searching for vampires and the king would have skilled people on his team to do that. His job was to get himself and the other four vampires to Maine and off the streets.

Or rather, off other vampires' necks.

His body ached constantly and more than once he'd felt his bones crack, then quickly thread back together as his vampire healing abilities kicked in.

It was as if his body was trying to do two things and was fighting against itself.

The pain, at times, was horrendous. As a vampire, that was new to him. He wasn't a warrior used to battle and pain. Most in his species lived a pain-free life.

Whatever was happening to him was nothing good. He knew that.

Noah bobbed his head, white ear pods sticking out as he lifted a bottle of soda to his lips. Callan watched the broody, good-looking vampire. He'd always preferred females, but not exclusively. His new appetite drew him to both sexes equally.

All of them had shared that their bite wound had become infected, then healed slowly. Normally a vampire bite on a vamp would heal in minutes.

Completely.

While he'd bitten these three all within the same two-week period, none of them had experienced any side effects yet. Well, except the increased sexual desire. They weren't having any of the body aches he was.

Ache? No, it was fucking painful.

He'd told them to keep the reason for their trip to the east coast confidential from their family and friends. Callan had expected the king to put out a missing person on him over VampNet when he had first escaped. He knew they'd be looking for him. The scientist, Sage, who had helped him escape, had told him they were waiting for him.

But he'd run instead.

His mind hadn't been clear back then.

So when there was no search notice online, he'd been surprised.

Until he'd worked it out.

The Moretti's didn't want vampires to know what had happened because it would cause widespread panic. Aside from the fact a vampire had been experimented on, which was a nightmare on its own. The real issue, in his mind, was that humans had been able to overpower him.

How had they done that?

Even female vampires were stronger than a well-built human man. There may be a few human men on the planet who could possibly challenge a young female but never incapacitate them as he had been.

If vampires learned about this, it would be very frightening. They may be powerful, but with human technology and their history of destruction and war, all of them lived with the shadow of being discovered.

While he had been in the BioZen lab, Callan had believed humans had discovered them. He had no contact with the outside world.

Now, they were halfway across the United States, and he was eager to get to the Moretti's.

His eyes shot up when Ava climbed out of her seat and made her way to him. He dropped one outstretched leg onto the floor, knowing what she wanted.

"How much longer?" she asked, running her hand over his now stiff cock as she stretched out over him.

Noah turned and shot them a look.

A hungry look.

Callan's eyes drifted to Liam as Ava continued to work him. The vampire's Converse boots were hanging over the edge of the seat, but he was settled. He had to be careful. They were on a public bus with humans.

Vampires were renowned for having a strong sex drive, but this new appetite was a much-heightened sense of desire.

In other words, they were all horny as fuck, constantly. And nothing they did seemed to satisfy the need.

Ava licked his lips before he could answer, and he lifted to nip at hers. A slow smile stretched across her face as she slid her hand inside his jeans and wrapped around his length.

"Want me to suck you off?" Ava asked.

Yes.

He absolutely fucking did.

"Get your mouth on me," Callan replied, pushing her head south as he unzipped his jeans. Seconds later, his cock was sliding deep down her throat. "Shit, yes. That's, fuck. Yup. That works."

He groaned and lay his head back down on his scrunched-up jacket pillow, while Ava's mouth fucked and sucked his cock with the skill of an experienced female.

This wouldn't take long.

He'd been needing a release for hours.

Her hands slid along his swollen flesh, following her mouth and tongue. The latter swirled around his head, then along his shaft, taking him deep.

Her suction was on point.

Hell, it felt good.

Callan bit his lip to stop from calling out and moaning. The last thing they needed was humans seeing them.

He gripped her hair and pressed her down harder.

Yes.

His balls tightened.

"Swallow, Ava," Callan said quietly, thrusting his hips and fucking her mouth. "Good, *fuck*, good girl."

His head threw back in a silent cry as his hot seed shot out. When he opened his eyes, Ava was wiping her face with the sleeve of her sweatshirt and had a twinkle in her eyes.

She pulled her zipper down and displayed her cleavage. Not that he needed encouragement. He knew her breasts were more than a handful and that she needed her release.

"Let me check something," Callan said, pulling out his phone and checking Google maps.

Fifteen minutes until the next stop.

Noah turned around and took in what was going on.

"You want to take over?" Callan asked, indicating Ava.

"No. I'll wait," Noah replied, turning back.

The vampire had that handsome, broody thing going on. It was what had attracted him to Noah when they met. His cock hardened again quickly as he recalled the male behind him, thrusting into him.

"Come here," Callan said, sitting and tugging Ava's skirt up.

She sat on his lap, and he tugged her jacket open and tank top down, so her breasts fell out. He tweaked her nipples and watched the pleasure cross her face.

"Put me inside you."

He lifted her again, and she took control, guiding his cock to her entrance. Then she slid onto his cock.

"Thank God," she said, a little too loudly.

He placed a hand over her mouth and grinned. "Quiet."

Her eyes twinkled at his dominance, then flared when he began to move her up and down his shaft.

"Shit, Callan," she whispered.

Slowly, he removed his hand from her mouth and lifted her so he could suck one of her breasts. His other hand slipped between their bodies and began to strum her clit.

"Ohgodohgodohgod," Ava said *not* quietly enough, gripping his shoulders. "I'm going to come."

Liam cleared his throat loudly.

Shhhh, someone said a few rows up.

Callan's eyes flared and shot back to Ava.

"Come quietly," he ordered.

Her pussy clenched around him as she pressed her lips together. She held his eyes as the orgasm she'd been needing rode through her body. As her mouth opened, his hand slapped back over it.

"Keep going. Good girl. Damn, you are tight."

Callan came again. He felt Ava tremble under his hands as he thrust into her.

"Fuck," Noah cursed quietly.

Callan itched to reach out and have him join them, but this wasn't the place.

Plus, there was no forcing the male. He was stubborn.

Liam sat up, dropping his Converse-clad feet to the floor and shot them a look full of desire.

He lifted Ava off him.

"Ten minutes," he said to Liam and Noah, updating them on their ETA. Both of them nodded. "Unless you want to swap seats with us and play back here real quick?"

The two males exchanged glances.

When Noah's eyes reached his, Callan saw the fire in them. He was reaching his limit. He stood, nudging Ava back to her seat, then sat down next to Noah.

Callan reached over and dug into the male's sweatpants, finding his nice large cock.

Then he began to stroke.

Noah cursed and threw his head back. Callan didn't make eye contact. He simply stared straight ahead and continued working the guy into the release he needed.

Ava leaned over the seat, watching them with greed in her eyes.

"Want some Kleenex, boys?"

CHAPTER FIVE

Kurt pushed through the door, after pressing his thumb against the security panel, and stepped into the lab.
    His body instantly tensed.
    Ahead of him, sitting on the table, was Madison.
    Fuck, she looked gorgeous.
    She had pulled off her sweatshirt and was sitting there in a pair of black lycra pants and a tight white tank top. Her eyes shot to his and then drifted over his body.
    His cock reacted immediately.
    Shit.
    Totally inappropriate, but his eyes dropped to the pebbled nipples he could see even through her sports bra, and he held back his grin.
    "Kurt, thanks for coming so quickly. Is the meeting over?" Sage said.
    "Yes. I wanted to get it over with and then work…"
    He was going to say workout, but it looked like that was where Madison was heading, and the last thing he wanted to do was be in the training center while she moved that damn sexy body of hers.
    It was more than his body could handle right now.
    "Yeah, work stuff." He finished.

"Oh, it won't take long. I promise." Sage slid another needle into Madison's arm.

Madison flinched and his eyes flew to hers, wanting to protect her.

The hell?

He didn't like that she was in pain.

It's a fucking needle, idiot. She's not going to die.

Still, he didn't like it.

"Hi Madison," he said, taking a step closer to her. Her eyes widened.

What's that about?

"Hi," she replied curtly, then blanched as the needle was pulled out.

Kurt narrowed his eyes at the less-than-friendly response.

"How are you?" he asked.

She shrugged.

Shrugged?

She'd indicated, when they first met, she was a fan. Kurt thought the entire thing was stupid. He protected the king. He wasn't a damn Hollywood actor.

Still, the fact Craig was ranked higher was an ongoing humorous competition between them. Neither of them bothered trying to bump into Brayden. The prince card trumped an eight-pack any day of the week.

Plain and simple.

"How's your stay in the castle?" He leaned against the wall, then gestured to the medical equipment. "Aside from all this."

Madison glanced around.

"Yeah, I'm a bit over it," Madison said, and Sage smirked. "No offense. I'm super grateful for your help."

"None taken," Sage replied, dropping the blood sample onto a tray. "One more."

Kurt got a whiff of her blood as the needle pierced her skin and he had to clear his throat.

Everything about this female called to him.

Yet here she was, smiling at Sage and glaring at him as though he was some kind of asshole.

She fingered the butterfly tattoo on the inside of her forearm. He'd barely noticed it before today, but it was a cute little black one with little detail.

And sexy as hell.

Kurt hated how much he desired her.

It was totally the forbidden fruit and all that. If only he could fuck her and get her out of his system.

This was insane.

"Oh damn. I have the wrong unit," Sage said, pulling the needle. "Back in two minutes. Hold this for me, Kurt."

His eyes widened.

What?

"Just press here," Sage instructed him, pressing on Madison's arm.

Fuck.

He walked over and grabbed Madison's arm, pressing the cotton ball into the crook of her arm.

"Be right back," Sage said, going through a side door.

Well, this wasn't awkward at all.

The two of them stayed completely still while the sexual friction sizzled away between them.

Not awkward at all.

Kurt cleared his throat.

"You hate needles." He tried not to run his eyes over the soft, supple skin on her neck.

And failed.

"Until now, I've never needed blood tests. It's not like a vampire bite," she said, shrugging.

The thought of sinking his teeth into her creamy flesh had his cock jumping for joy.

Fuck, this was a nightmare.

He should leave.

For two vampires with such chemistry, it was completely sexual, and he knew Madison knew that.

"Yup. Not like a bite."

She blushed.

Gotcha!

She wasn't immune to him.

Not that he cared. Not that he wanted her to want him. He had just assumed she did.

In one swift move, he could palm the back of her head and slam his mouth on to hers. Then he'd pull down those lycras, spread her thighs and have his mouth back on her pussy.

Where it wanted to be.

She would want it.

He knew she wanted him.

Didn't she?

His thumb rubbed over her butterfly tattoo of its own accord and diluted green eyes lifted to his.

Kurt imagined pulling out his cock and slamming into her moist heat. He would put money on his eyes reflecting back the same need hers shone at him.

They were rich with lust and the need for release.

Shit, shit, shit.

He'd kept away from her for this very reason. They weren't allowed to touch.

A rose blush spread across Madison's breasts, and he knew she was as wet as he was imagining.

The space between them seemed to shrink. Either that or his body had leaned in closer. She swallowed, and he followed the movement with his eyes and then again as her tongue swept across her lips.

God.

Kurt didn't know if he could stand here a moment longer. Heat coursed through his body as the hand under her elbow began to creep up her arm of its own accord.

"I—"

"Madison—"

"Sorry, had to open a new box," Sage said, returning. "Thanks Kurt, you can let go of her now."

Fucking hell.

"Hey. Thanks for finding me," she said. "You know, in case we don't see each other again."

Kurt frowned.

He stepped away and walked to the other side of the room, running a hand over and over his short hair, letting them finish up.

Thank you?

The hell.

And why did she think they wouldn't see each other again? Had Sage cleared her to leave?

"Are you leaving?" he asked.

"She's not going anywhere yet," Sage said. He heard her jump down off the table. "You're up next, Kurt."

Sage patted the table.

His big ass feet moved across the room, his eyes following Madison as she straightened herself and put her sweatshirt on.

"Thanks doc," Madison said. "I know I can't leave *yet,* but am I all clear to resume normal activities?"

Activities?

What the fuck did she mean by that?

Sage laughed. "Let's just wait until I look at these last lot of bloods. Don't let the males here pressure you."

A low growl escaped his throat and Sage raised her brows at him.

What males?

Madison picked up her backpack. She let out a little laugh. "I won't."

"Kurt will help beat them up if you need. Won't you, Kurt?" Sage said. "He has some sway around here."

Madison shrugged. "It's fine."

What the hell?

He'd been keeping away from her to control his desire, but he hadn't stopped to think any of the males in the castle would go near her.

Which was totally his bad because she was fucking gorgeous.

"Who's tried to touch you? Give me their names," he ordered.

"I said it's fine."

"Told you. They're very protective," Sage said.

"Names, Madison. Now," Kurt ordered.

Madison's brows rose, and he had no doubt if they were alone, she would have ripped him a new one. It was a new side to her he hadn't seen.

Then again, he'd hardly seen her.

It didn't matter. No male should be touching her.

If *he* couldn't, those fuckers certainly couldn't.

"Yeah, okay. I'm going for a run." She ignored him and headed for the door.

"Outside?" he asked, but she shot him a look and let the door close.

Fuck.

"She's not a prisoner, Kurt." Sage frowned. "What is wrong with you?"

Good question.One he didn't have an answer for.

"How long is this going to take?"

CHAPTER SIX

Ava skipped off the bus, followed by Liam and Noah. Callan was the last to step down onto the sidewalk and they all stood watching as the bus disappeared down the road.

They were somewhere just outside of Rochester, Minnesota, in a town called Marion. It was three in the morning, but as the next stop had been near six when the sun would be rising, it gave them little time to find accommodation.

Sure, they could use compulsion to stop somewhere else, but a busload of people was a big job.

This was easier, albeit slower.

The moon was bright and high in the sky, looking almost full. But it wasn't.

He knew that because their resident amateur astrologer, AKA Ava, had given them a long rundown on the movements in the sky. Including what astrological sign it was in and what that meant to each of them, depending on their sun sign.

And the rising sign.

Yeah, it had been a long bus ride.

Long story short, the full moon was tomorrow night.

Callan shook his head.

They crossed the road, surveying their new surroundings. The town was quiet, everyone in their beds sleeping like humans did at night.

Crack.

Oh shit.

His back weakened under the voluntary crunch of his vertebrae and he let out a loud curse. He sensed the others around him slow but keep walking as they were in the middle of the road.

His hands landed on his knees in a hunch.

"Dude, come on. A truck could come flying through here," Liam said.

Yeah, and he would hear it first and could teleport.

At least he thought he could. With that level of pain, Callan wondered if he actually could.

He felt the bones begin to heal and then whatever it was that was causing it stopped.

He was calling them *attacks* because that was the best way to describe it. Like his body was attacking itself.

He was given no warning. They just came on suddenly and then stopped.

Callan stood, pointed at the closest motel as he joined the others on the sidewalk. "Let's just go in here. Ava, go see if anyone is at the front desk."

She sighed, but wandered off.

She was a hell of a lot less threatening than three vampire males showing up on the doorstep in the middle of the night.

A few minutes later, she came back swinging a key.

"Penthouse suite." She grinned.

"Yeah, I doubt that." Liam eyed the very run-down motel. "Please tell me there is more than one bed."

Callan afforded himself a small grin.

It hardly mattered.

They'd all end up in a pile of bodies, anyway.

"Two kings," Ava said, handing Noah the key when he held out his hand. "I think I should get one to myself."

Noah snorted.

"What?" she asked.

"You'd lie there for five minutes, then moan, wanting your pussy licked," Noah replied.

She glared at him, then walked off, giving him the bird. "I will pleasure myself."

Noah walked after her at his own leisurely pace. "No, you won't."

No, she wouldn't. They all knew that.

Liam and Callan shared a knowing look.

The dynamics between Noah and Ava were interesting. They'd begun bickering yesterday, and he wasn't sure if the two were extremely attracted to each other or actually didn't like one another.

But they sure knew how to fuck.

They dropped their bags inside the door and began doing shit.

Ava hit the bathroom.

Noah turned on the TV.

Liam opened his laptop and connected to the Wi-Fi.

Callan checked the small fridge and slid the pouches of blood he had in his bag inside to keep them fresh. He'd acquired enough for them all for a week from a blood bank in Seattle.

Enough to get them to Maine.

As he turned, his leg gave way under him and he dropped to the floor.

Pain shot up the side of his leg.

"Fuck." He squeezed his eyes shut.

"Again?" Noah stood, staring at him.

"Yeah."

The attacks seemed to be coming more frequently. But like before, it suddenly stopped. He stretched his body, moving all the parts, and felt nothing. But he felt odd. Like a ticking clock in his head was screaming that time was nearly up.

Callan walked to one of the beds and lay down. "We need some food."

"Doesn't look like there's much around here." Liam glanced up from his laptop. "And they'll be closed. The joy of small towns."

It was why vampires navigated to big cities these days. Late opening hours were a benefit along with employment opportunities.

Thank God for the internet. Many vampires worked online in their own businesses or for corporates. It was much easier living in these times than for many of their ancestors.

"We'll need to help ourselves, but let's make sure we leave some money behind like we did last night," Callan said, tucking his arm under his head.

Ava came out of the bathroom, having showered, wearing nothing but a towel. His body immediately reacted and there was no question in his mind that Noah and Liam had reacted similarly.

"So, this is my bed?" she asked, sitting on the one opposite him.

Liam laughed.

"How long are you going to keep this up?" Noah said, shaking his head and turning back to the TV.

"Longer than you can keep it up," Ava said, taunting him. She shot Callan a wink, and he laughed.

At least they were entertaining.

"You two fuck while Liam and I go get something to eat."

Both of them mumbled something about *no way* and *over my dead body* while he grabbed his backpack and ignored them.

"Back soon," Liam said, and the last thing Callan saw as he closed the door was Ava dropping the towel and Noah's dark gaze running over her body.

An hour later, Callan and Liam headed back down the highway, chowing down on burgers and fries. They'd helped themselves to the kitchen at *Shooters Bar and Grill* and had takeout in their bags for the others.

Liam had also grabbed some sodas, candy bars and potato chips he'd found at the gas station down the road while he had flipped the burgers.

"You think all this sex has something to do with what happened to you at the lab?" Liam asked, his mouth full as they walked.

It had to be. Unless they were some kind of vampire poly family now, there was no other explanation. But vampires mated, and he'd had no desire to bond with any of them.

But he felt something.

Callan was the dominant alpha of their group. There was no doubt about that. As a predator that was normal for them all to sense it. Still, there was a feeling of being responsible for them, and he was yet to understand that.

Was it guilt for biting them?

Possibly.

However, there was something more. He wanted to wrap his arms around them and call him his.

Not as a bonded mate.

And that was confusing as hell.

Callan shrugged and threw his wrapper in a nearby trashcan. "Could be. And again, I'm sorry if—"

Enormous pain laced through his body as hundreds of his bones began to break. He fell to his knees, and then collapsed forward onto his hands, letting out a loud cry.

"Callan?" Liam gasped, dropping beside him. "Shit. This is a bad one."

The vampire's voice sounded like it was surrounded in cotton wool. The pain was all-encompassing, blocking out everything as he worked to hold himself off the ground and fight for his body to heal.

The joints in his legs, arms, and back felt like they were burning from the inside out and he had a sudden animalistic desire to run.

But he couldn't move.

White hot pain lashed every inch of him.

It felt like his body was going to tear apart. Like something was trying to escape him.

What the fuck have they done to me?

"Callan!" a different voice cried.

Ava, he was sure of it.

A strong hand landed on his back. As he lifted his head, he saw Noah's worried but strong and sure face.

"What do you need?" the vampire asked.

Then his neck cracked, and he saw only darkness.

CHAPTER SEVEN

Four minutes and thirty-five seconds after telling Sage to speed up her blood samples, Kurt teleported outside the front of the castle and began tracking Madison.

Why the hell was she off running outside the castle on her own?

There was a completely sufficient training center she could use with the best equipment on the planet. Well, second only to The Institute, which was Ari Moretti's training center in Seattle.

Ten minutes later, he found her running along the lake on the castle grounds.

The moonlight was bright this evening, lighting the path allowing him to easily observe her movements. He was impressed with her pace.

And her ass.

He decided to hang back and keep an eye on her for a few minutes until he began to feel like a stalker.

Which begged the question—just what the fuck was he doing out here?

Something he would answer later.

Right now, his eyes were glued to her ass, and hell, even her calves were sexy as hell.

She didn't need his protection.

The grounds were safe and enclosed in a gate and secure wall around the enormous property. The security team didn't have eyes—as in cameras or guards—on every inch of the grounds, but it would take a very powerful and clever vampire to get inside without being admitted entrance.

Well, there was that time Stefano Russo, their now-deceased enemy, had. But they'd upgraded security since then. If an unknown vampire teleported in, they were notified immediately, and guards dispatched.

Madison stopped running and walked to the water's edge, placing her hands on her hips.

She stared out across the water.

Kurt slowed and walked to stand next to her.

"I wondered when you would notice me," he said, knowing that's why she had stopped.

She shot him an irritated look. "Why are you following me?"

Good question.

"Instinct." He shrugged.

She finally turned to face him, and his cock did a little jump. Tiny beads of sweat covered her forehead, and her cheeks were pink. Her chest rose and fell as she regulated her breathing.

He nearly had to look away. She was so sexy.

Nearly.

Instead, he let his eyes run over her body and enjoy every single inch of it.

"Am I not safe here?" she challenged him.

"Yes—"

"Then can I please have a moment to myself away from all of this?" She gestured at his body. "Stuff."

His lips curled. "Stuff?"

She sighed.

"Not all of us are used to living in Testosterone Castle."

He snorted.

"Officially, it's Castle Moretti, but sure, we can call it that."

Then a thought hit him, and he suppressed a growl.

He turned and placed a hand on her arm, turning her into him. "Madison, are my males acting inappropriately toward you?"

Her brows bunched. "No. And even if they were, I work—worked—in a bar, remember? I can handle myself."

His heckles rose.

"You shouldn't have to handle yourself. No one should be touching you."

She turned away.

"Well, maybe I want them to." She began to walk off.

What?

"Maybe you do." He cringed, knowing he had no right to say anything about that. "But if someone you didn't want to touch you, did..."

Jesus, he sounded like her fucking father.

Which wasn't creepy at all, given his other thoughts.

"Kurt, I'm fine," she said, rounding on him. "Look, I don't need your protection. I said thank you for finding me. I am truly grateful, but let's just leave it at that, okay?"

Grateful.

That's how she felt about him?

Bullshit. He'd felt the chemistry between them earlier. She could pretend she wasn't interested all she wanted, but as his eyes dropped to her nipples, they told a different story.

Dude, you have been keeping away for a reason. Leave.

"I didn't find you. We were hooking up." He growled.

It was true.

"Yeah, well, look how that worked out," she muttered, turning away again and then jogging.

Kurt raised his brows and joined her. "Excuse me?"

Madison didn't answer, simply continued her jog along the path.

"Forget about it. All of it," she said. "Go home."

Go home?

The fuck?

And yeah, there was no way she was forgetting about what they had done. No way he was letting her get away with that. Her orgasm had been off the charts.

They both knew how frustrating it had been not being able to finish.

"I doubt very much it was all that forgettable for you." He grinned, jumping over a large branch laying on the track, and with one hand on her lower back, guided her around it.

She stopped dead, hands back on those sexy slim hips.

"Are you kidding me? How does your ego fit inside that big head of yours?" she snapped, her eyes blazing, then her hand flew to her mouth.

Kurt pulled her hand from her mouth.

"Please, speak your mind. It's very sexy." He smirked.

Madison shook her head. "I'm not trying to be sexy. That's the very last thing I am trying to be."

They stood staring at each other, panting, the air thick with sexual tension. Then he noticed the stress around her eyes and the small scar still on her neck.

A reminder both of them shouldn't be together.

"I know. But you are. Sexy, that is." He brushed a curl from her face, then lifted his eyes to look over the lake behind her. "I shouldn't be here. With you alone."

When he glanced down, he was expecting to see the same desire on her face.

Instead, Madison crossed her arms and glared at him.

What the hell?

"I don't think there's anything to worry about. You seem to have fantastic self-control."

Was she joking?

The hell, he did.

His brows bunched as he took a step closer. That same tantalizing energy sending a vibration of desire through this body.

"You have to be kidding me. Why do you think I've been keeping a distance?"

Her shoulder lifted in a shrug. "Obviously, because you got what you wanted."

He laughed lightly and shook his head once. "All I got was a taste of your pussy and the pleasure of seeing you come, sweetheart."

Her cheeks turned red as her mouth parted. He reached out with his thumb and pressed it inside her mouth, running it along her bottom lip.

"If not for my job, I would have sunk deep inside you and fucked you for hours, Madison," Kurt said, his cock encouraging just that very thing as it pressed against his clothing.

When he removed his thumb, she swallowed in a gulp.

His hand gripped her hip, bringing her closer.

"Would you like that?" he asked. "Would you like me to pull you onto my lap, so you could ride my dick while I twirl your pretty nipples between my fingers, then make you come?"

Kurt pulled her against his body, knowing he shouldn't be doing this, but God, he wanted her.

He just couldn't stop.

"That's rather descriptive," she breathed, still looking annoyed.

"Do my words make you wet?" He smirked. "*Are* you wet, Madison?"

She took a step back.

He tilted his head, surprised.

"You know, I understand why you stopped on the jet. I really do. But ignoring me for weeks? That was mean. I didn't know anyone here, and it was pretty scary finding out about Callan. So, after *licking my pussy* as you so crudely put it, it would have been nice to have a friend while I found my feet."

His eyes widened.

Holy hell, this woman had spice.

He liked it.

"Am I wet? I guess you'll never find out, Kurt Mazzarelli." She spun and ran off. "And stop following me!"

He grinned.

She was totally wet.

And hell, Madison Michaelson just got a whole lot sexier.

CHAPTER EIGHT

Xander Tomassi tapped his pen on the desk, wanting to get the phone call with the Russian over with quickly.

"I'm flying over to the United States," Nikolay Mikhailov said. "We will have dinner together and then visit the labs where you're creating my products."

Oh, hell no.

Nikolay was an investor, not his boss. Hell, he was a senior executive at BioZen Pharmaceuticals. He wanted to tell the man he was unavailable, yet Xander had to tread carefully.

Mikhailov was the head of the Russian mafia. As in, the most dangerous mob boss on the planet.

Saying no was not on the cards.

Still, that didn't mean Xander didn't feel a little murderous. Not that he'd do it. He had people for that.

But he needed this man.

He needed his money.

Plus, Xander was pretty sure the Russian was more dangerous than the vampires. Despite being powerful beings, they at least seemed to play by ethical rules.

More fool them.

Nikolay didn't have the same scruples. That was widely known. It was heavily rumored he'd killed his father—a man he had appeared to love, respect and fear—with his own bare hands, which is how he had been promoted.

Clearly not.

Initially, Xander had been happy to bring him into their top-secret project as an investor in return for a certain number of their products.

They were making hybrid soldiers from the research they had done on Callan. His DNA and bloods, of which they had a lot, were being blended into humans, creating the most powerful humans on the planet.

Their clients? Governments, of course.

Now he was beginning to think he'd made a bad decision selecting the powerful foreigner as an investor.

Okay, fine, it was *fucking* stupid.

Nikolay was unreasonably demanding and didn't like the word 'no'.

Still, he had given them a trillion-dollar idea. If he stayed alive long enough to enjoy it, that would be a bonus.

He had asked them to create a vampire vaccine. Which was ridiculous. From what they'd learned from Callan in their US labs—and a few of the others in their Italian-based lab—the vampire bite changed a human, and there was nothing that could stop the process once it was underway.

Still, nobody knew that.

Once knowledge of the blood-sucking race's existence spread around the world, there would be insane panic. Then, boom, BioZen would announce the vaccine and people would line up for miles waiting to get their completely useless medicine.

He smirked to himself.

Knowing their competitors, they'd figure out the product was full of chemicals which did nothing—well, there would be a few side effects but that was business—and create their own just as ineffective product to get out into the market as quickly as possible.

CDC approval? Forget about it. Fear would override any need for that red tape.

Even if it didn't work, it wouldn't matter. With no other solution, people would keep demanding it. In fact, Xander was already considering a recommendation for a series of injections. They could claim protection built up over two, three or four shots.

It was the perfect plan.

By the time people realized it didn't work, it was more than likely the Moretti family would begin a PR campaign to eliminate the fear.

Good luck with that, vampire.

Who would believe them?

A race who had lived amongst humans for thousands of years and lied to them? One who could, with one bite, kill you?

Good damn luck.

Right now, Xander was waiting for his director to get the vaccine approved. The problem was, the other directors at BioZen were not informed of their little side hustle—or Project Callan, as it was formally called. Cash Waltmore, Director of BioZen, had been the one to oversee that budget, so they'd been able to keep it discreet.

He'd approached the man when he first learned about vampires and, after securing interest from a number of governments, they had proceeded to set up the lab and research.

Manufacturing a line of new products was a different kettle of fish. It would require a different budget and include many more people and departments across the organization.

It was a sensitive situation.

Cash said he needed to advise the entire leadership team and get them on board. They had talked through it for hours, deciding whether or not this was the right path to take.

One question on the table had been whether they had a choice with a mob boss demanding it.

Probably not.

Xander was now back in Seattle and had moved some of his team over after doing an internal restructure. One of those roles was the finance manager of his division.

Elizabeth.

It spoke volumes that Elizabeth, who had worked in their Rome office, had accepted the relocation and pay increase.

Clearly, she had missed him and their little *arrangement*. In fact, he was in a hurry to get this call over with because she was next in his calendar. His cock stiffened inside his black suit pants, so he pressed his hand on it, giving it a rub, then opened his bottom drawer to ensure he had everything prepared for their meeting.

Dildo, tick.

Spare necktie, tick.

Custom-made nipple rings with a clit clamp attached. Tick!

She was going to love it.

"When are you coming?" Xander replied.

"Tomorrow."

Jesus.

"Nikolay, do you recall me telling you we do not have any product samples of the super-soldiers yet? Nor do we have approval by the board to create the vaccine," Xander said calmly. "It will also take months to manufacture. Perhaps you should delay your visit."

Deathly silence.

He swallowed.

"There is a long road ahead of us as we get ready for launch, meanwhile creating the narrative to announce the new species on earth," Xander added.

Surely the Russian understood the complexity of this entire project and investment. Not to mention it wasn't just him involved. They had very important government clients.

"Hardly new from what I understand," Nikolay replied darkly.

No, they weren't new. Not even close.

One thing Xander wasn't going to do was share anything he knew about the vampire race.

That was sensitive BioZen data.

Knowledge was power and all that.

"Regardless, I am heading to America, and we will meet," Mikhailov added.

Not a request.

God damn it. He had no choice. He would need to meet with him and act as host while his investor was in town.

"I look forward to it," he replied, ending the call. "Safe travels."

Xander slammed his fist down on the desk.

Dammit.

He leaned back in his seat and loosened his tie.

What he needed was a new strategy. He hadn't gotten this far in his career and plans with BioZen to let some Russian asshole derail him.

The guy had inherited his position. Xander had cleverly manipulated humans and vampires to get where he was.

If Mikhailov wanted to underestimate him, he could try.

Was he nervous?

Fuck yes, but that only served to drive him… and it made him horny as hell.

A knock at the door sounded, and he grinned. "Come in."

Elizabeth entered, and closed the door behind her.

"Good afternoon, Xander." She walked to the two sofas that sat facing each other with a coffee table between them. She held a stack of files and her laptop, which she dropped on the table.

"How are you settling in?" he asked, sitting on the opposite sofa and placing the dildo, necktie, and other toys on the cushions beside him.

There was little reason to hide them.

Her eyes dropped to them as she sat down.

She swallowed slowly.

He never truly knew if she hated their agreement or enjoyed it. The fact Elizabeth was sitting here told him it was the latter. But he honestly didn't care either way.

"Well, it's cooler here, and the pasta isn't as good." She smiled, lifting her eyes to his. "But it's a lovely city."

"Excellent," he said. "Now, pull off your panties, lift your skirt up and spread your legs for me, please."

Her nipples hardened under her white blouse.

"Now?"

He nodded.

"But…" She turned to the door, which they both knew was unlocked.

"Yes, we could be interrupted." He grinned. It was highly unlikely, but he'd be interested to see his secretary Miranda's reaction if she did. She might like to join them.

But that could be his ego.

He rolled up his sleeves and watched her make a decision as he lifted the little box containing the nipple clamps.

"I have a four o'clock meeting, Elizabeth, so please remove your panties." He spoke more firmly.

They both knew it wasn't a request.

By the time he walked around the coffee table, moving it out of the way, she'd done as he asked. He sat down, widening her legs so he fit between them.

"Open your blouse and pull out your breasts.," he said, his Italian accent thickening. As she did, he removed the nipple clamps and untangled the chain attached to them.

"We do have those numbers to go over," Elizabeth said as his mouth lowered, and he sucked on her nipple harshly.

She liked it hard.

Her following gasp confirmed it.

Xander added the little clamps onto both nipples and reveled in the control he had over her.

"Hands," he ordered, and tied the spare necktie around her wrists, behind her. "Love when you shove your tits into my face like this, Elizabeth."

Then he sat and ran his hand up her thigh to her nicely shaven pussy.

"Oh, God."

He frowned.

"You're not very wet, young lady." He looked up into her flushed face. "Do we need to change things up a little?"

"I've just been stressed."

"Lean down and suck me while I prepare you," he ordered, running out of patience. Xander undid his fly, pulling out his long, hard cock. Her mouth wrapped around him, and he let out a groan as her tongue did miraculous things to his body.

This was what he needed.

Fuck coffee.

A good blow job was far more uplifting.

Especially from a woman who was willing to be tied up and clamped.

He turned on the vibrator and touched it to her clit, circling it as she moaned around his member.

"Suck harder, Elizabeth." He pressed his hand on the back of her head, and as his cock slid further down her throat, he nearly spilled into her as she gagged.

He wasn't ready.

He wanted more than just five minutes of entertainment to break up his stressful day.

"Legs apart." He pulled out and dropped between her thighs. He slid his fingers into her pink flesh and smiled. "Now we're talking. Look at all this creamy goodness." He spread the moisture around her pussy with the vibrator and tugged on the nipple clamps. Elizabeth fell back against the sofa, her breasts in the air due to her hands being tied.

She cried out in the little moans he was familiar with from her.

Xander leaned in and helped himself to her sweet goodness. Lapping with his tongue, he swirled it around and pressed the vibrator inside her a handful of times until he was confident she was ready for him.

He dropped the toy and undid the necktie.

"Are we finished?" she asked, surprised.

Yeah, see. She loved it.

"No. I want you bent over the sofa arm. Like this." He pushed on her lower back, knowing the nipple clamps would hurt deliciously as they rubbed against the sofa. "Legs wide."

In one thrust, he filled her.

Elizabeth cried out, but it was muffled from the cushions.

"Yes, fuck, exactly what I needed," he gritted out, quickly readying to come. Today he was feeling generous, though, so he leaned down and thumbed her clit. A dozen more strokes and they both cried out their pleasure.

He really did treat his employees well.

CHAPTER NINE

Ari bounced Lucas Moretti in his arms as he stood on the large balcony overlooking the rear of the castle grounds. Below them was a beautiful rose garden he planned to take Sage for a walk through later.

She had been busy since they'd arrived in Maine a few weeks ago, but she was happy. In fact, she was more than happy. Sage was glowing.

A bride-to-be's glow.

He'd seen it a million times over during his fifteen hundred years on earth.

Finally, that bride was his.

Vincent walked out with glasses of whiskey and placed them on a nearby table.

"Gaga," Lucas said, stretching out his arms for his father.

Without a word, Vincent took his son and kissed his forehead. The infant nuzzled into his father's neck, content and safe.

"I remember when you were born," Ari said to Vincent. "It was the happiest I ever saw your father."

To someone not familiar with the fact they were vampires, the conversation would have seemed odd. They both looked like thirty-something year old men. Brothers even, because they were so closely related.

Except Ari was five hundred years older than Vincent, and was his great-great uncle.

"He was happy at the end," Vincent replied. "They both were."

Ari shook his head and stared back out across the grounds. He had his own reasons for not being *terribly* unhappy about Frances's death. The former king had been his nephew—his twin brother's son—and part of the reason he had become estranged from the Moretti family.

His family.

If Gio and Frances had only seen reason and realized Ari was no threat to their line of succession—as in the entire vampire race on earth—things may have been different.

For one, he'd never mated, so was unable to procreate. And yet the fear had been so rich and irrational.

Now he had Sage.

Fucking finally.

Growing up, Vincent and Brayden hadn't known he was their uncle. By then his identity had been so hidden by Gio and then Frances, no one knew who he really was.

Until one day, around four hundred years ago, he had left the Moretti castle, where he was the captain of the army, and never returned.

Everyone had thought him dead.

And for a long time, he had felt dead inside.

Ari had never wanted the throne. These were Gio's vampires, and he had loved his twin brother. He wanted his own line, and yet as each century passed without meeting his mate; it looked less and less likely.

But what didn't change was the fact he was an original Moretti vampire. The power of their blood ran through his veins. More powerfully than any other vampire.

He wondered if the king realized that.

It taken many decades, but eventually Ari had landed in Seattle and created The Institute, a private training and security company. It was only a few months ago he had revealed to his nephews that he was still alive.

"One thousand years of love between your parents," Ari said. "Perhaps it is more than any of us can ask for."

"Perhaps. As their children, Brayden and I see it differently," Vincent said. "I'm still angry with them."

Frances had turned his human mate into a vampire without her permission. Ari had been living with him at the time and they'd all been subjected to Guiliana's loud howls. For many weeks.

In the end, as it turned out, the king and new queen had made a secret pact. He promised her they would end their lives together after one thousand years. She had been opposed to immortality, and apparently the agreement between them had been enough to appease her.

They had loved each other, as mates do, and lived a happy life.

None of them understood it, but Ari had lived a long enough life to realize it wasn't for anyone else to agree with. People could choose their own paths.

Even kings and queens.

"Understandable," Ari replied, turning, and crossing his arms. "I loved your father, but in the end, we weren't close. I think you must know that."

Vincent blinked at him a few times and he recognized the vampire was telepathing.

Kate, his queen, swept in.

She was a graceful looking woman with eyes full of kindness, strength, and wisdom.

"Hello, Ari. Hello my little angel, come here." She took Lucas from Vincent, kissing his lips, then smiling at Ari.

"*Ciao*, Kate," Ari said in greeting. One thing he never did was greet any of the royals with their official titles.

Now more than ever, he wouldn't.

It was time to draw a line in the sand.

"I will leave you both to speak," she said, intuitively picking up this was an important conversation.

"Gah," Lucas said, reaching out his hand over his mother's shoulder as she retreated.

When the door closed, the two powerful vampires turned to one another.

"Let's sit," Vincent said.

A part of Ari wanted to lead this conversation, to take control and show his great nephew he was the most powerful vampire. But with a long life came wisdom.

Vincent knew that as well as Ari did. He wasn't a young vampire himself. Physically, Brayden was more alpha than Vincent. Ari was more powerful than both of them.

Vincent was a bright vampire. A strategist. And he knew how to play the modern game.

These things also made a male powerful.

The difference was, Ari was the full package.

Not arrogantly. But one knew themselves very well after living for fifteen hundred years.

But today was about creating a new future for him and Sage. Not fighting.

He was no longer willing to hide who he was.

Simply by existing and being alive, Ari had a right to *be*. To be whoever and whatever he chose.

Like every living being on earth.

And he was a Moretti.

He had his reasons for allowing what had transpired to take place, but today he was done.

"I've looked through Frances' and Gio's archives, diaries, and every type of record. I still cannot find a reason why they were so threatened by you," Vincent said, getting right to the heart of the matter.

Ari nodded.

"My father said you wanted the throne, but then you left. When I questioned him, he never answered me directly." Vincent shook his head. "Then I was told you were dead, and it was likely because you were unhappy in your endeavors for power."

"You?" Ari asked. "Only you were told this?"

"Yes. Brayden was not included in these conversations. Plus, Father knew how close the two of you were. The prince was... unhappy."

Ari's chest tightened as it always did with the guilt of having left Brayden.

It was his only regret.

Vincent was right. The prince didn't know he was his uncle, but the two of them had been close. Ari had trained him since the time he was an eager little warrior. There had been no stopping the little future alpha.

When he first returned, Brayden had been furious. Ari had listened with sadness and compassion, understanding his pain. He had hated being separated from the prince. Now they were re-building their relationship.

"He may not have known," Ari said. "Frances, I mean. Parental influence is the most powerful in our lives. Gio was full of fear, always worried I would overthrow the throne. It's likely he brainwashed your father while he was still alive."

He knew that's what had happened. He'd lived through it, but he was softening the blow for the current king.

"And yet you didn't," Vincent said, his eyes not wavering from his face.

Ari held his gaze for a few beats.

He'd waited hundreds of years to have this conversation.

"No," Ari said, firmly. "It was never my goal or desire. It was an irrational fear on Gio's part. No matter what I said or did, nothing could change his mind."

Vincent sat listening, not interrupting him.

"When my Gio and his mate died, there was only Frances as the sole remaining heir," Ari said. "The crown was never more vulnerable. That would have been the perfect opportunity to act. You must know I am more powerful than your father ever was."

Vincent stared.

"I helped your father find his mate. It was an important time," Ari said. "Now there have never been so many Moretti's alive."

Vincent nodded, lifting the glass of whiskey to his lips.

"And you have no interest in becoming king now?" he asked.

Ari shook his head and let out a laugh.

He realized these questions needed to be asked and got out in the open, but after centuries of it, he was sick of it.

"First, I'd have to kill you, then Brayden and Lucas. If you truly thought I was a threat, I wouldn't be sitting here right now, and I most definitely wouldn't have been holding your son a few moments ago."

Vincent placed his glass on the table.

"Then tell me why Gio never trusted you. Why did he have such fear?" Vincent demanded, his tone firm.

Despite the situation Ari felt a moment of pride at Gio's grandson showing such strength. His brother would have been impressed with the male.

Brayden chose that moment to enter the room. He sat down on the other end of the sofa from his brother.

"Hey."

"Brayden," Ari said, nodding his way.

"I missed the good bit, didn't I?" the prince asked.

Ari's lips curled.

Brayden's playful nature, when he wasn't being the powerful warrior that he was, always brought Ari joy. But it didn't matter how old Brayden was, he would forever be the little prince trying to fence with him with a battered wooden sword.

He watched as Vincent telepathed Brayden and got him up to speed. Brayden smiled, emotion in his eyes, then he blinked hard.

"Gio was a complex man, even as a human. When we became vampires neither of us knew what we were doing," Ari said, standing to refill his drink. He turned, staring down at the two Moretti brothers. "You cannot imagine being human one moment, and then suddenly becoming a vampire with no one to guide you."

He let that sink in, then continued.

"The unnatural desire to consume blood and the willingness to kill for it was shocking. We had no control over our powers and hurt many people."

"Yeah, fuck, that." Brayden shook his head.

"We were only told to stay out of sunlight before being let loose. We tested that once on the first day of our new lives—my damn small toe–and clearly never had to do that again."

Fortunately, vampires healed fast, and his toe had regenerated, but had it been his entire body he would have turned to dust. Forever.

"How did it happen?" Vincent asked. "Gio was dead before we were born, and our father never told us of our origin."

Both sets of eyes held his.

"It is unlikely that he knew. But that is a story for another day," Ari said, sitting. "Tonight, let's stay on topic."

Vincent nodded, as Brayden stretched out his long muscular legs and a flicker of disappointment crossed his face.

With no one to collaborate his story, it was a difficult one for Ari to tell. It sounded like fiction even to his ears, despite living it.

He may take it to his grave, or he could share it with Sage. He'd told her his entire life story, but not how he'd become a vampire. She'd asked. That inquisitive scientific mind of hers wanted answers. Yet, even to him, after such a long time, it sounded like fiction.

"Back to why Gio was as he was," Ari said. "He populated the race over the next one hundred years. We were told we both would, but I never did. There were no love matches with these women and Gio. Our role was to grow the population. After one hundred years we were told our mates would arrive. Gio met your great grandmother Caterina, and later Frances was born."

Ari turned and walked to the door, looking outside. Talking of these early days was difficult. He missed Gio. How could he not? They had been twins. But it had been a rocky road for them after they became vampires.

Even more so in the years that followed as Gio became more and more unstable.

"It was no secret during that time I was furious I had never impregnated one female. Not a vampire or human. Why Gio and not me?" Ari said. "I became angry during sex, not treating females with the respect they deserved. It was simply a transaction."

He returned to the sofa.

"Meanwhile Gio was building the race and becoming a king. I was beside him the entire way, supporting him and sharing my disappointments. That didn't mean I wanted his throne."

"You were brothers. You should have been able to tell him how you felt." Brayden shrugged.

They were more than brothers.

They had always told each other everything. Ari had never stopped to think that his words were being translated incorrectly.

His brother had turned into a powerful king, and like many, he was thick with fear of losing that control and power.

"One day those words backfired on me. I hadn't seen his growing unrest and concern. He had everything and I had nothing. In his eyes."

Ari tossed back the whiskey.

"I never saw it like that. I had him—my brother—and what we had created together. A new species on earth. I thought we were a family." Ari shook his head at the memories and feelings that were coming up as he recalled the arguments. "While Gio was busy worrying I would steal his fucking crown, I was training vampires to protect him."

Brayden frowned.

"Just as I do."

"Yes," Ari said.

"Gio didn't do all that alone. You helped him build the royal structure, along with the infrastructure such as many of our castles," Vincent said. "Just as I rule with my brother alongside me."

He had a feeling the king would understand once he began to share more. Vincent was different from Gio and Frances. Giuliana, he suspected, had passed on some good genes. She had been a wonderful queen, mother and confident to him over the years.

In private.

Frances had not liked their friendship all that much. But Guiliana loved her mate and never crossed the line.

"Correct," Ari said, nodding.

Vincent stood. "I get it. I've seen enough family cycles amongst humans to see how it repeats."

Brayden glanced between them, but Ari didn't miss the subtle look. The prince was nervous. Being back in each other's lives was important to them both. But Ari had to be clear on what his future held.

His and Sage's.

"I meant what I said, Vincent. Your throne is safe. I do not want it, nor will my future offspring." He carefully spoke the words he'd been curating in his mind for a while. "However, when I walk out of this room tonight, my identity will no longer remain hidden."

The king crossed his arms and the prince watched him.

"You're not asking my permission," Vincent said.

"No," Ari said firmly. "No one had a right to take it from me and while what's done is done, I am taking my birthright back. Right now."

Brayden turned to his brother.

"Vincent—"

The king held up his hand, in a rare gesture to silence the prince. Brayden's eyes darkened.

He didn't want this to destroy any more relationships but enough was enough. Like he'd said, he had a right to be who he was.

Aristide Moretti.

"You're right," Vincent said. "No one can change who you are, Ari. However, just by your very existence you will always be a threat."

He shook his head.

"You are wrong, Vincent. I strengthen your reign." He stood. "Sage and I, from this point on, will be known as the House of Moretti. We are not royalty—we are a different bloodline. What happens when we breed, will be ours to determine over the centuries."

He let that piece of information simmer.

Nothing was going to happen in a hurry. Ari knew that better than any of them. He'd lived through every single damn day of the creation of the existing race.

"What happens if I disagree?" Vincent asked.

Ari smiled at him.

He'd never voiced this.

Not to his brother and not out loud to himself.

But it was time the entire truth was spoken.

Truth that would change everything.

"Nothing. You are not my king. I am not a vampire of the current Moretti race. I am my own vampire. The original power of the blood runs through my veins. No one else wields that power."

As in, he was the only vampire alive with pure Moretti blood.

Brayden's eyes widened as he stood, and if Ari hadn't been so astute, he would've missed Vincent doing the same.

"You can be my friend or foe, Vincent Moretti, but we both know I am far more powerful than any living creature on this planet," Ari said, casually sliding his hands into his pants pocket. "It is my hope we both choose the former."

All three powerful vampires stood staring at each other for a moment, then he let out a sigh and walked to the door.

"I'll await your decision."

As the door closed behind him, he heard Brayden curse.

Ari teleported to his quarters where Sage was scrolling through her phone. She saw the look on his face and ran to him. He wrapped his arms tightly around her waist and buried his face in her hair.

He may be a powerful and ancient vampire, but those boys were his family. He'd lost them once. He just hoped he wouldn't have to do so again.

But if he had to, he would.

It was way past time he put himself and his own line first.

CHAPTER TEN

Madison lay staring at the ceiling waiting for the shutters to open. She'd slept fitfully all day and was exhausted.

Her mind had gone over the conversation she'd had with Kurt during her run a million times.

Aside from being incredibly attracted to him, she was horny as hell. This wasn't a problem she was used to having. Working at a bar meant there was no shortage of opportunities. But for a vampire, Madison wasn't as highly sexual as some of her friends.

Like Selena.

Feeling like this was strange... and it seemed to be triggered by him. But Kurt Mazzarelli could go to hell. After his arrogant comments last night, she wasn't interested in fueling his ego. That she wanted to climb him like a tree was beside the point.

Sexy men aside, that wasn't the only thing keeping her awake. Her body had been aching, which was a new sensation for her.

At first, she had thought it was because of the blood tests.

Clearly, she was no doctor.

When she really thought about it, it was no different to being bitten and sharing blood.

She knew she should tell Sage, but Madison just wanted to go home. She was missing her mom, her friends and even the dumb bar.

She wished she could talk to her mom, but even if she could talk about the top-secret information, she wasn't that type of mom. They weren't *not* close, but they just didn't talk about girl stuff.

Plus, her mom was only just hanging in there. Now her dad had passed, Madison would never bother her mom with her problems.

Madison had called her this morning before she went to bed.

"Hey Maddy, how's your holiday?"

"It's not a holiday, Mom. I told you I'm at the Moretti castle in Maine."

Silence.

"Oh. Yes. You did, sorry sweetie. Is it fun?" she'd asked.

Fun?

No, it wasn't fun.

It was weird, strange, and lonely. She was outside her comfort zone, and while at times she found parts of it exciting, she would go home in a split second.

This was the furthest she'd ever traveled from home, and in a private jet no less.

"Yeah, it's great. This place is huge," she said instead.

"When will you be home?"

And there it was.

Madison knew her mom was unhappy with her being away. She'd always lived for her mate and daughter, and never really had her own interests or hobbies. It had created a sense of obligation within her to stay close to her mother.

She knew it was why she had never traveled or gone far from the nest. It was embarrassing in some ways.

Worldly vampires like Kurt would never be interested in someone like her.

Not as a mate.

Not that she was thinking of him like that.

He was a rude vampire.

Even if he was hot as sin.

Soon, her mother would pass on. Then she'd have all the freedom in the world. It was mildly terrifying, while being exciting.

But she wasn't in a hurry for her mom to go.

Not ever if she had her say.

"Not sure, Ma. Hopefully soon. Brooke will visit tomorrow, so bake her some of those chocolate chip cookies she loves." Madison knew her mom enjoyed baking for them all and it would give her something to focus on. "I'll call you again in a few days."

Fortunately, they hadn't talked long as she felt guilty being away and not being able to say why.

Madison stepped into the shower and sighed as the force of the water pressure massaged her shoulders. As she sponged her body with soapy suds the sensation only made her body more sensitized.

"For crying out loud," she said as her nipples hardened to the point of aching. Her fingers slid between her legs and circled her nub as Kurt's face came to mind.

She spread her legs further and increased the soapy friction, palming her breast and tweaking the hard pink bud. Desire soared through her in a rush that had her wobbling.

"Fucking hell," she cried as an orgasm struck out of nowhere, nearly dropping her to her knees.

Jesus.

Madison stood staring at the shampoo bottles as the water flowed over her. That was one hell of an orgasm.

Perhaps her sex drive as a mature vampire was finally kicking in? She couldn't wait for Sage to lift the ban so she could try it out with someone.

Someone, not her fingers.

In the meantime, she could line up a few of the friendly warriors in the castle.

It was a great idea.

After all, she wasn't going to be at Castle Testosterone forever and Brooke and Selena would kill her if she didn't make the most of it.

Thirty minutes later Madison walked into the social room and made her way over to the mini kitchen. She lifted a glass from the rack and poured herself some fresh blood. She had some in her own fridge, supplied by the Moretti's, but this was a good excuse to get to know more of the citizens and soldiers who lived and worked in the castle.

They seemed to hang out here, play pool, and drink coffee and blood as she was. There was a buffet down the other end of the room which was supplied twenty-four-seven due to the round-the-clock nature of the shift workers.

Madison tucked her hand into the back pocket of her jeans, her old Levi's t-shirt fitted tight across her breasts and her short wavy blonde hair scrunched and styled more than usual.

Oh, and her lip gloss was on point.

Her ankle boots clicked as she walked slowly across the room, taking in the few dozen or so vampires who were currently milling around.

She could tell who was finishing or starting a shift by their energy. Or maybe it was just that some vampires weren't afternoon vamps, like her. That's why she liked the early shift at the bar. She could take her time waking up, then go for a run before starting. Then have the rest of the early morning free to see her friends.

While humans snoozed.

"Hey, Madison. You're still here," Darnell said, wandering over to her.

She'd met the gorgeous dark-skinned male when she first arrived, and he'd been more than flirty with his bright cheeky eyes and deep dimples. He wasn't as tall as Kurt or the other SLCs, but he still towered over her.

Which was damn sexy.

"I'm still here," she grinned, cocking a hip. "And going a little stir crazy."

His slow smile said he had picked up on her hint. "That so?"

"Uh, huh. I'm thinking of joining the royal army. Put in a good word for me?" she teased.

His eyes widened, then he laughed.

"Well, we'd need to test out your fitness and see if you fit before I can do that."

"Fit?" she asked.

He grinned.

"Yes, ma'am. With the team. How about you join us later at Max Bar, then we can assess your suitability?"

She'd heard of the bar, which was located within the castle. It sounded like a popular spot where many of the vampires went to socialize and… hook up.

Because they had to blend in with humans, it was rare to be able to be so openly sexual in public. Madison had never been in a vamp-only bar. The idea seemed so naughty and…exciting.

And how typical she could only watch.

Before she left, she would make sure she visited it one last time. It would be wrong not to.

Castle Testosterone was like a vampire Disneyland.

"I'll bring my A-game." She winked. "See you there."

"I think you might be trouble, little M," Darnell said, laughing as she walked off.

Little M.

He'd called her that a few times since she'd arrived, her petite stature standing out amongst the enormous males. Even the females here were tall and strong.

She felt very average in comparison. At least Sage and Anna, who she'd only met once or twice, were around her size.

She shot Darnell a final seductive glance over her shoulder, then turned and walked straight into a wall.

Or rather, a huge wall of muscle.

Oomf.

Dark chocolate brooding eyes glared down at her.

"Having fun?" Kurt asked, an unimpressed set of brows raised.

She removed the hands she had laid on his abs to defend herself and slowly nodded. His eyes lifted and he glared over her shoulder.

"Lieutenant Reed," Kurt said tightly.

"Senior lieutenant commander Mazzarelli," Darnell replied, saluting him.

"At ease," Kurt replied. "I see you've met Ms. Michaelson."

"Yes, sir."

Marcus, who she'd met when she first arrived at the castle, stepped into the room next. He looked chirpier than his fellow SLC.

He smiled when he saw her. "Hey, Maddy. How's castle life?"

"Hey," she said as Kurt raised his brows even higher and mouthed *Maddy?*

Ugh, why was he standing so close?

She ignored him.

"It's boring, honestly." She answered Marcus.

"Want to come out catching bad guys with us?" Marcus asked, winking.

Kurt growled.

"She's not going anywhere."

"Dude, it was a joke." Marcus laughed, but Madison didn't miss the look he gave Kurt that asked *WTF*. Then he glanced up. "Darnell, you good, man?"

"Yes, sir."

"Good training circuit today. Keep it up," Marcus said, slapping him on the shoulder and walking into the kitchen.

Darnell thanked him and turned to Madison. "See you later on."

Dammit.

"Sure will. Bye." She bit her bottom lip, knowing what was coming next.

She could feel the emotion rolling off Kurt's body as the vampire left the room.

"Okay, well nice seeing you again Kurt—" she started, but he repositioned his body so it towered over her and seemed to suck all the oxygen from the room.

"Making friends, I see." He glowered at her.

Yes, because you're an ass.

"Well, *most* people here are nice." She raised her brows a little in challenge. "Some people even want to hang out with me."

He let out a dry snort and lowered his eyes to her breasts. "I think we both know why."

Madison slammed her hands on her hips.

How dare he?

"No. I don't know why. Why don't you enlighten me?"

They stood glaring at each other for a long minute until Marcus joined them. He glanced between the two of them. "What did I miss?" he asked.

"Kurt was just going to explain—"

He grabbed her arm and pulled her out of the room, calling over his shoulder. "Tell Craig I'll be a few minutes late for the meeting."

"Tell him yourself, dick," Marcus yelled after them and Madison let out a laugh, which was immediately silenced as Kurt teleported them down the hall to a door.

"Ugh, don't do that. And let go of my arm," she said, tugging repeatedly and getting nowhere.

Kurt kicked open the door, which led to a private outdoor patio where he finally let her go.

Madison rubbed her arm while Kurt ran a hand through his hair.

"What do you think you're doing?" he hissed at her.

Her mouth parted, unsure how to answer.

Kurt took a step closer, and she tried to back away, but her boot caught on the cobblestones. He reached out to steady her and was now far too close.

Madison swallowed and cursed at her body for reacting to him.

"Fuck," Kurt's eyes glowered at her as his hands remained firmly on her hips.

They stood staring at one another for a few beats, neither moving.

"You should…" she started.

"I know what I *should* fucking do," Kurt growled quietly. "And I know what I want to do."

Their breathing became heavy, and she could hear his increased heart rate. Or was it hers?

"The question, Ms. Michaelson, is whether you want *my* mouth on you, or someone else's mouth."

Damn him.

Her panties were toast—soaked from his words and the way his huge muscular body enveloped her with such pure sexual dominance.

She suppressed a quiver and cleared her throat.

"Your mouth had two weeks to seek me out," she said with as much credibility as she could muster.

It was a poor effort, and they both knew it.

Part of her wished he'd stop talking and just kiss her and the other part wanted to walk away with sass. She just wasn't sure she had it in her.

He was too intoxicating.

Kurt's fingers tightened on her hips in a crush. She flinched and he let go of her, taking a step back.

"You know as well as I do why I've stayed away." He leaned in. "You smell different."

Okay?

"I'm using the castle body wash," she replied, confused.

"No, its…forget it," he said. "When are your test results back?"

Madison shook her head. "Tonight, I guess."

His hand cupped the back of her neck, his fingers threading through her hair, sending shivers down her spine.

"I want to fuck you properly, Madison. Correction. I am *going to* fuck you properly."

Tell him no.

Tell him he had his chance.

The words were on the tip of her tongue but wouldn't venture out.

Then she lost all ability to breathe as his hand slid down the side of her breasts, over her hip and then between her thighs. He pressed against the denim in just the right spot and, dammit, she let out a groan.

Body, you are a traitor.

He smirked.

"You can play and pretend all you want, but I know you want me. My mouth, my touch, my cock," Kurt said, his hand now on her breast, taunting her hard nipple.

She'd lost all sense of time and space, existing only in his rich chocolate eyes laced with the same desire she felt.

When her lips parted, his thumb swept over hem. "I want this mouth on my cock. Sucking me as you kneel before me."

God, he was an asshole.

But a really fucking sexy one that had her locked in some kind of aroused hypnotic state. He tugged her in closer and she could feel his erection against her stomach as she arched to hold his gaze.

She was aiming for a rebellious female who wasn't at all influenced by his predatory sexuality.

She had a feeling he wasn't buying it at all.

"I'll make sure you're completely pleasured this time, and the entire castle will hear you scream my name."

Ugh.

Such over confidence.

God, I wish he would fuck me right now.

Traitor.

Kurt's body was on fire as he held Madison against him. He could feel her slight tremble at every touch point, which only served to make him harder.

His lips were inches from hers.

His self-control was slipping by the second.

He could see her defiance, but whether she liked it or not, her eyes were begging him to touch her.

And God, he wanted to give it to her.

One tiny taste was all he wanted.

Liar.

You want to consume this female.

Yet he couldn't, and neither could Dar-fucking-nel. There was no way Kurt was letting any of them touch Madison.

She was… *not* his. But while she was here, she was under his protection. He would make that clear to anyone who tried to get close.

Kurt could smell her carnal desire for him. It was unlike anything he'd scented before. It was taking more willpower than he possessed to stop from ripping her clothes off and plunging deep inside her.

His hand slid under her t-shirt and tugged her bra down to reach her bare nipple.

"Kurt," she moaned.

His eyes burned into hers as desire rippled from her.

"Do you want more?"

"Yes. Dammit. No. Yes." She moaned, pressing harder into his hand.

They shouldn't be doing this. He needed to step away from her. But surely if she was able to walk around the castle and...

Fuck it.

His control snapped. He undid her jeans with vamp speed and tugged them so he could slip his hands into her panties.

"Oh, shit," she cried, her body turning to jelly.

Jesus.

"Madison, holy fuck." He growled. "You are soaking."

Angry eyes shot to his. "Well, that's what happens when... oh God, yes, do that more."

Fuck. She was on fire. And so was he. Hunger didn't start to describe their need for each other. He tugged her jeans a little further, allowing him to press his fingers inside. Then he plunged deep as she dug her nails into his pecs, panting.

"Fuck my fingers," he ordered, gripping her face with his other hand. "God, I want to kiss you."

Madison glowered back at him, her rebellion never slipping even as her mouth slid open and her body shook, completely at his mercy as her orgasm built.

Need that mouth on mine.

He'd kissed her before and was still alive.

His mouth salivated with the need to taste her. All of her.

"Madison," he ground out, his eyes darting between hers and her mouth.

"Yes. Yes!" she replied, but did she know what he was asking?

His mouth grazed hers.

"I need to kiss you." He moaned. "Be sure."

"Yes, fuck it. Fucking kiss me."

Thank God.

His mouth slammed down on hers, their bodies crushing together as he awkwardly continued to slide his fingers through her pussy.

"Oh, God." She cried into his mouth. "This is—"

Kurt swallowed her words, his tongue slipping inside, demanding her full attention. Her hands gripped his thick biceps.

Suddenly, her mouth ripped from his as her pussy clenched around his fingers. His thumb dashed over her clit, doing its best within the restricted movement it had. But it didn't seem to matter. Madison was on fire, and he felt her body vibrate and shudder against him as her orgasm erupted.

He slid his hand out and held her as she flopped against him.

Holy hell.

CHAPTER ELEVEN

Blaa, blaa. Baddies. BioZen, blaa, blaah.
Fuck, how long was this meeting going to last?
Although Kurt was as happy as everyone else to hear that Xander Tomassi was back in Seattle and that their teams had eyes on the pharmaceutical executive.
They had even been able to put a tracker on his vehicle as he was driven home from work one evening. And had surveillance at his home address.
Things were looking up.
In other more important news, Kurt needed to get to the lab to speak with Sage. Not that he was worried about what he'd done with Madison earlier tonight, but knowing their blood results would put his mind more at ease.
He'd been unable to stop thinking it.
Her.
It wasn't just his mind that needed to settle the fuck down; he was still semi-hard. Thank goodness he had his Moretti jacket which was laying across his lap.
Not that every vampire in the room hadn't seen his cock at one point in time over the past few hundred years.
Well, except Ari.
He'd only met the ancient vampire in recent months.

They'd all seen each other during one orgy or another. Now, all of them were mated except him and Marcus.

The two least likely to ever mate. Kurt would flee the continent if he got a hint his mate was nearby.

His find flew back to Madison.

Which was totally unrelated.

But damn, watching her come had been an experience.

He wanted to see her do that again while tied to the posts of his bed. For that, he needed Sage to clear them both for, in Madison's words, *activities.*

He smirked.

Sexy times aside, Kurt was concerned Callan was still out there biting vampires with no support. Bites that left an infection of some kind.

That wasn't right.

It was great Madison's neck had cleared up. It wasn't great it had happened it the first case.

It wasn't normal.

And how many other vampires had he bitten?

They needed to find the male.

"Do we have an identity for Callan yet?" He suddenly blurted out. The room stilled and all turned to him.

Brayden narrowed his eyes. "Not yet, but hopefully we will soon."

"You okay?" Craig asked, studying him.

Kurt ran a hand over his head a few times.

"Spill," Marcus said.

Dammit.

They all knew each other far too well.

They were a tight team. They needed to be in order to protect the race and the royal family.

Then add in a little fact like fornicating with a sexy little vampire who'd been bitten by a rogue vampire with altered DNA, and you got watched.

Yes, he'd do the same if he was them, but it was fucking annoying.

Kurt blew out a breath.

"Does this have something to do with Madison?" Marcus asked, crossing his ankle as he shouldered the wall.

Here comes the therapy session.

But this wasn't about him. Not completely.

"It doesn't *not* have something to do with her. She was bitten. I kissed her," he answered. "But we need to find him. He's out there likely biting more vampires and possibly suffering. I think we need to up our game."

A bunch of heads nodded.

They were all feeling the pressure to help Callan, whoever he was, and ensure the safety of their race.

If Callan had never met Madison, they wouldn't know of the increased risk, but now they did and were able to monitor the effects on both her and Kurt. It was giving them more information.

And more pressure to find him.

"Sage will have your blood results for us in a few hours," Ari replied. "If there is anything to be concerned about, you'll be the first to know."

Kurt did that nodding, shrugging-guy thing.

He didn't want this to be about him, but that was simmering in the background. He felt fine, aside from being a little obsessed with the sexy minx he'd just brought to orgasm like it was her very last.

"And" Brayden pointed to the screen. "I'm going to assume you just had a mini nap because we're talking through our strategy on finding Callan, right now."

Oh.

Fuck.

They'd moved on from BioZen and he hadn't heard a thing.

◆

"Shit, sorry. My mind must have wandered," he confessed. Although it was pretty obvious.

As an SLC you didn't have an off day.

That could get a vampire killed.

"You good?" Marcus asked, as he sat down in the chair next to him. Brayden continued with his presentation and Kurt shot his colleague a look.

"Yeah. Bad sleep today."

They both knew he was bullshitting. He was a strong, resilient warrior and a poor sleep—or, hell, even no sleep—wouldn't interfere with his job and performing at the level he needed to be at.

What the hell is wrong with me?

"The king has given approval for us to go public. The comms team are putting a notice on VampNet," Craig said, dropping his feet down off the desk. "To answer Mazzarelli's earlier question, both Sage and Madison have worked with our artist to sketch a likeness of the male."

"What are you going to say?" Kurt asked.

"Obviously not the truth," Craig answered. "We'll just say he's missing and wanted. No details need to be given."

Kurt slowly nodded his head in response.

People would assume he was a criminal, which wasn't a bad thing if it kept him from biting anyone else.

It could even piss the guy off and encourage him to make contact.

Whatever it took to bring him in.

Callan needed help. That was clear.

"If we get a proper photo from someone, we can start tapping into face recognition technology and speed up our search," Brayden said, crossing his arms, his Moretti t-shirt stretching tight and bunching around his biceps. "We'll find him. Eventually."

Meanwhile, Madison would remain in the castle and the two of them would need to keep their hands off each other.

He hadn't thought clearly.

She was like a drug, pulling him in and making him choose poorly.

Good one, asshole. Blame her.

He began to wonder how she'd feel when she realized she was going to be here a lot longer. She'd snapped at him and said she had felt alone when she first arrived, and a sliver of guilt ran through him.

He thought he was doing the right thing, keeping away.

You know, instead of fucking her.

The truth was, he had no idea who she had left behind in Seattle. Did she have family, friends, a boyfriend—some vampires had casual relationships at times—or a hobby?

Nothing. He knew absolutely nothing.

He'd uprooted her, and rightly so, and flown her across the country where she was unable to leave until they worked out the effects of being bitten by a guy who'd been a science experiment.

She must be fucking terrified.

Yet those sassy eyes of hers were full of courage.

He wondered how much of that courage was real.

Movement around him snapped him out of his thoughts.

Again.

"Busy week ahead," Brayden said. "Craig, I'll leave you to manage your males and execute. Call me if I'm needed."

"Got it," the commander replied.

"Ari, assuming you're staying here with your mate?" Brayden added.

As if any male would leave his mate, least of all Ari. The newly mated couple were inseparable.

"Of course," Ari replied, and Kurt noted a slight tension between the two vampires that wasn't there yesterday. "If you need more bodies, I can lend you a few of my assassins."

Kurt had recently spent time at The Institute and was highly impressed with Ari's team members. They were highly trained and skilled.

He had traveled to Los Angeles with Oliver, the head assassin, and Ben, who was a former member of the team. It was after they'd returned to Seattle that he had met Madison.

"Stick around after and we can look at the numbers," Craig said, which got him a nod from Ari.

Brayden glanced over at Kurt, and he could see the concern in the prince's eyes. All of them were watching him with the same look. Since he'd returned, they were waiting for him to grow another head or fucking something.

He was fine.

Just horny as fuck.

Though he wasn't going to say that.

"Tom, Kurt, I want you guys to connect in with our Italian team and find out what the rebels are up to," Brayden said. "With Stefano Russo removed from the picture,"—he meant dead as they had assassinated him—"it may have slowed the rebellion, but let's not make the mistake of thinking they've all packed up and gone home."

The prince knew they wouldn't do that. The rebellion had been around for centuries. As far as he knew, every Moretti king had held a healthy respect for their existence.

It was unnatural that everyone would think alike and agree. However, the vampire race wasn't a democracy and there would always be someone who wanted to overthrow the throne in a kingdom.

Human history showed that.

The difference was the Moretti royal family had been born and procreated to establish their race. No one had sailed to a land, shoved a flag in the ground, beat their chest and claimed to be a king.

Then again, no one said the rebels were smart.

Just power hungry.

"We haven't," Tom said.

His fellow SLC had mated Lucinda, Stefano Russo's sister, over one hundred and twenty years ago. She'd left the family, having never been aligned with the beliefs of the rebellion, and served the king ever since.

Kurt knew it had been difficult for them both, while her family had been public enemy number one.

Brayden respectfully nodded at the male. "I want a report to take to the king by the end of the month."

"Got it," Kurt said.

Basically, he was being benched because of his connection with Madison. Tom often stayed in the operations room because of his technical abilities.

Kurt was an action man.

He said nothing.

At the end of the day, the prince could do what he liked.

"One final thing," Brayden said. "I want to expand our team. This team. With life throwing us some serious bullshit these last few years we've been stretched. Hence, Ben joining."

It had been a change having Ben on the team, but he had fit right in. Vampires lived a long time, so they were used to change, but the four SLCs had been together a long time.

Now they were five.

"We have some real potential in the lieutenants who report to you. But let's not restrict our search. Who else do you know who could be a potential?"

Interesting.

Kurt lived and breathed castle life. He didn't have friends outside their circle. The sort of skill they would need was unlikely to be found elsewhere.

Except...

"Let me talk to my team and see if anyone is looking for a career change," Ari said.

Craig snorted. "Not much of a change. We're not crunching numbers here, Moretti."

Ari smirked and shared a look with Ben. "No comment."

They all knew Ari's team did very dark black ops work. Their clients were top secret—humans obviously—and frankly Kurt would rather not know.

So Ari was right. There was a difference.

The Institute crew were assassins, trained and recruited to kill.

For the most part.

Whereas the Moretti army was focused on defending the vampire race and royal family. They were all warriors, but their objectives and modus operandi were very, very different.

The fact that some of the assassins, such as Alex, Jason, and Oliver from The Institute, had worked with them recently, and that Ben had transitioned over so easily, spoke to it being a great source of new blood.

No pun intended.

Kurt smirked.

"Okay, anything else?" Brayden asked, clicking keys on his laptop and the screen on the wall turning black.

Heads shook and chairs scraped as everyone headed off to their allotted tasks.

"Kurt," Craig called out, indicating with his head to stay back.

He'd half expected it.

Craig missed nothing.

Kurt stood with his hands in the side pockets of his black Moretti jacket and waited. When the room emptied and Craig had packed up his laptop and shit, he glanced up.

"Talk."

Kurt nearly laughed.

Craig was no Dr. Phil, but even that was a poor effort for the enormous vampire.

"Well, I have this rash on the inside of my thigh. It's near my b—"

"Asshole," Craig said, shaking his head. "What aren't you telling me?"

Kurt stared at him for a long moment.

Sharing what he'd done with Madison wasn't on the top of his to-do list, but the guilt had been eating at him. He knew he should tell Sage, but honestly, the last thing he wanted to do was talk about eating out Madison's pussy with Ari's mate.

Or anyone.

"I've never seen you so distracted," Craig said. "I'm going to assume this is to do with Madison."

The huge vampire crossed his arms.

"Are you having symptoms? Because if you are, you better start fucking talking, Mazzarelli."

"No. None."

Except he couldn't stop thinking about her and seemed unable to fuck anyone else. In his world, that was a very serious side effect.

Craig frowned at him.

"I want her, okay?" Kurt spat out, angrily. "Like all day, all night. I want to fuck her. It's driving me insane."

Craig's brows were through the roof.

He continued.

"And I can't fuck her. Obviously. And apparently The Incredible Hulk doesn't want anyone else."

Craig's brows shifted direction and bunched. "Did you just call your cock, The Incredible Hulk?"

Kurt smirked.

"I mean, it's not green but…"

"Okay, I cannot have this conversation," Craig said, shaking his head. "You need to talk to Sage."

Kurt shook his head.

"That wasn't a request," Craig added.

Yeah, so about that…

"Shit man, I can't. I… You see, I…"

Jesus, now he was mumbling like an idiot.

Craig had picked up his laptop and froze. "What aren't you telling me?"

A lot.

Probably.

It was confession time.

"I more than kissed Madison on the jet that night. I know I omitted the truth but, fuck, I don't know why I didn't tell Sage."

"You fucked her?" Craig growled.

"No, I didn't fuck her. I stopped, but…"

Craig raised a brow. "Suddenly you're a blushing virgin. Spit it out, for fuck's sake."

It felt wrong talking about her to anyone. Kurt clenched his fists and cursed.

"I went down on her. Licked her pussy. Made her come." He closed his eyes as he shook his head.

Craig might be a mated male, but he did not want him thinking about Madison's body. Certainly not the space between her legs.

Or her breasts.

Or any damn part.

"Christ's sake. Was that so hard?" Craig replied. "Go tell Sage. She needs to know. Meanwhile, keep your mouth and cock away from anyone else."

Obviously.

Except he hadn't.

"Right."

"We'll talk about this once all this shit is sorted but Kurt, don't ever fucking lie to us again." Craig stared at him, then walked out of the room.

Fuck.

CHAPTER TWELVE

"I wish we knew what you were having, then I'd know whether or not to keep Lucas' clothes for you," Kate said to Willow as she bounced the little prince on her knee.

Vincent rolled his eyes across the room at Brayden, but he could see the king's pride.

The Moretti family was growing.

With the birth of Prince Lucas, Brayden mating Willow and pregnant with their first child, Ari back in their lives, and now mated to Sage, it ramped the Moretti family numbers to seven.

The largest number ever in their family history.

Soon it would be eight.

Brayden had been thrilled when he and Willow learned of her pregnancy. She'd been very—as in overly—emotional when Kate had given birth.

Now they knew why.

She'd been pregnant.

But he'd also been stunned.

No one had ever heard of a vampire getting pregnant so quickly after mating. Usually, it took somewhere between fifty and one hundred years.

They had mated less than two years ago.

Sage had added that fact to her growing list of things to research about their race.

"I think Brayden can afford to buy his child some new clothes, Kate," Vincent said.

She frowned at him.

"Go and do king stuff. We females are talking," Kate chastised him, while Willow failed to hide her amusement behind her hand.

"Hand-me-downs are a thing, Vincent," Willow said, rubbing her stomach. "This child will want for nothing but imagine knowing you wore the future king's onesie."

Their eyes connected, and Brayden felt her familiar and powerful love flow through their mating bond. Her fiery spirit had calmed to a steady simmer since falling pregnant, and she was glowing.

If it wasn't for the danger his race currently faced, he would feel the same. He wasn't *not* happy. He had his mate, a female he loved more than his own life, and a child on the way.

He was just feeling a lot of pressure.

There was one thing that would make him happy, and that was peace between his brother and uncle.

The bomb Ari had dropped still made him shake his head.

You okay? Willow asked through their bond.

Yes.

"Do king stuff? What kinds of kingly things would you have me do, my love?" Vincent asked, ignoring Willow as he often did.

Brayden rolled his eyes.

"Dadaaa," Lucas cried out and Vincent squeezed the little prince's knees, which sent him into a raft of giggles.

"You might want to start by acknowledging the princess just spoke to you," Kate said, and picked up the toy Lucas had dropped.

"Hmmpf," Vincent mumbled. "Fine whatever, our kids can wear each other's underwear."

"It's not underwear, for God's sake," Willow said, shaking her head. "Gross. Do you have no filter?"

As Vincent opened his mouth to speak, Brayden shot him a telepathic message.

Pregnant. Let it go.

Is she going to use that argument for nine damn months? Vincent asked.

Probably.

Six. He smirked, and Vincent snarled at him, but he knew his brother wasn't serious. His mate and brother may never be the best of friends, but the king respected Willow for her strong personality.

He'd walk all over a meek and mild female.

"All right, let's discuss the purpose of this family meeting," Vincent said, his tone letting them know this was serious.

And it was.

"The prince and I met with Ari Moretti yesterday," Vincent said. "Some of the things we discussed I was expecting; others were a surprise."

To say the least.

"I have my thoughts on the matter, but I wanted to give you all the opportunity to tell me how *you* feel before I make a final decision."

Brayden sat beside Willow and lay his arm behind her. She melted into him and draped her hand over his thigh. He'd already shared the conversation with her and knew Vincent would have done the same with the queen.

"Can you recap for us, darling? Just so we're all clear on what Ari said, and what you want our input on," Kate said, grappling to keep Lucas on her lap.

The prince was one wriggly worm these days.

Willow jumped up and took him from Kate, and the two females exchanged a look of gratitude.

"Lowbuba." Lucas smiled and grabbed for Willow's hair.

Why he called her that, no one knew, but it was as if he knew his Aunty Willow, or *Lowbuba*, was having a baby.

Which was, of course, ridiculous.

Willow grabbed a toy and snuggled into his side again. Brayden rubbed Lucas' soft head and smiled at his nephew.

Then he gave the king his attention.

"Ari has, rightly I might add, reminded us he is not of our Moretti bloodline," Vincent said. "Therefore, there is no requirement for him to pledge allegiance to me as king."

Which was a mindfuck.

Why they hadn't put two and two together before, Brayden had no idea.

And he still wasn't sure why Ari hadn't said the same to his father or grandfather.

But then again, his uncle was an incredibly loyal man who considered them all family, regardless. Brayden had only discovered Ari was his uncle since his return to their lives a few months ago but, if he was being honest with himself, Ari had always felt like family.

They'd had a close relationship that his mother encouraged and his father tolerated.

Now it was very clear why.

Still, Ari had put a stake in the ground that he couldn't come back from, and right now they had to decide how they wanted to proceed as a family. The final decision was Vincent's because he was king.

Brayden ran a hand down his face.

"It's crazy. If Ari had created his own progeny, there could have been two royal families. Or they could have ruled together as a democracy."

Vincent stood and walked to the drinks cabinet, pouring a whiskey. "Doubtful. It's more likely they would have battled for power and dominance. Potentially ruling their own lines in different parts of the world."

Willow's eyes shot to his.

"It is possible, or they may have done things differently. It's all speculation." He rubbed his shoulder. "Going back to the original point, Ari has established he has no obligation to acknowledge Vincent as king and he is correct. What we are assessing today is if we consider that a threat."

"Ari has only just mated. His first child may not be born for many decades," Kate said.

Willow frowned. "Wait. So how did they populate the world with vampires to start with? The math doesn't add up."

Brayden looked at Vincent for a response. One only he could give.

There were a few Moretti secrets.

One was the power of their blood. Only those with the Moretti blood running through their veins knew about it. It made them far more powerful than any other vampire. And it was a highly guarded secret.

Ari had hinted that he was the purest. Brayden suspected he was telling the truth.

An issue for another day.

The other secret was how the two human twins had become vampires in the first place. Ari was the only being on the planet with that knowledge.

Unless he'd told Sage.

Brayden wasn't sure whether he had, but if he was going to tell anyone, it would be her.

He hoped his uncle would share the knowledge with someone and not leave them with no knowledge how they all came to be. It was something he had often wondered about, just as humans questioned their existence, he supposed.

As to how the world had become populated with vampires so quickly, given how long it took them to impregnate their mates, that was something only the king knew.

And Ari. Obviously, Gio had told his son, Frances, who had told Vincent.

Who had told him, but that was during a weak moment when they were the two remaining Moretti's on the planet after their parents had died.

Brayden often felt Vincent had regretted telling him so they never spoke about it. But he was glad he knew. And in fact, Ari had openly spoken to them about it during their conversation. The old days of secrets by kings did need to end.

As a Moretti prince, he deserved to know his family history.

Of course, it was confusing why they had been able to procreate so fast in those first one hundred years. And that was why he very much wanted to know how Ari and his great grandfather had become vampires in the first place.

A mystery to solve one day.

Vincent's eyes moved from his to Willow's.

"That, princess, is something only Lucas Moretti will ever know," Vincent said firmly.

Willow's eyes shot to Kate, who shook her head and shrugged.

Interesting. He hadn't told the queen either.

"Why?" Willow pressed.

"The knowledge is passed from king to king. That's just the way it is," Vincent replied.

"Stupid," Willow muttered, and Brayden's body shook with silent laughter.

And agreement.

Kate bit her lip.

"So anyway, Ari has spent his life in the shadows, his birthright unacknowledged." Brayden moved the conversation on.

"His own choice," Vincent said.

"Was it? I don't think so." Brayden shrugged.

"You are letting your feelings for our uncle shroud your judgment."

Brayden's anger rose.

He'd had enough of this nonsense. It was time to put his cards on the table.

"Because he's our fucking—sorry Kate—ducking uncle! He's no threat to you, Vincent. No threat to this family. He's shown his support in many different ways these past few months."

And he'd been up front about his position, rather than using his vast power and influence to do anything nefarious.

Why was it not obvious?

"What exactly is he asking for?" Willow asked.

"He didn't ask. He told." Vincent tossed back his drink.

"Well, you aren't his king, so..." Willow shrugged and got a dark look for pointing out the obvious. "I'm just saying, if you aren't, then you aren't. He is free to do as he pleases. I agree with Bray, it doesn't look like he's out to take your throne."

Kate turned on the sofa to look up at the king, who was standing behind her.

"I have to agree with the princess. Sage is lovely. Ari is lovely. They've worked with our teams collaboratively for months and I've seen him with Lucas. He may claim you aren't his king, but he loves this family."

Brayden's heart swelled at hearing the queen's words.

"As the captain, your brother, *and* the prince of this family, if I thought he was a threat, I'd be the first person to say so. You must know that."

"I do," Willow shrugged.

"Slightly biased," Vincent said, shaking his head.

"Guilty," she retorted.

They sat in silence for a few beats, all of them with their eyes on the king.

Brayden understood both sides. Ari was not a male to be underestimated.

He was powerful and could be a great threat. But that didn't mean he would act. His openness and honesty spoke volumes.

Yet, as king, it was Vincent's responsibility to take care of over ten million vampires as well as his family. And for that reason, Brayden didn't push. He had faith that, as always, Vincent would be a fair and reasonable king.

More so than their father had been. He had been far more bloodthirsty.

Though, they were now living in different times.

"Ari's request for independence is his birthright and I cannot—and do not—disagree with that," Vincent said. "But I have to consider the repercussions. What if other vampires decide they want to become independent of the crown?"

They couldn't.

All vampires in existence, except Ari, and now Sage, were of Vincent's bloodline.

It was a moot point.

"They have no grounds," Kate said.

"We already have the rebellion trying to do that." Brayden shrugged.

"Yeah, and as a monarchy with one ruler," she said, using Lucas' baby hand to point at the king, gaining her a giggle. "You. So, you have the right to say no to them. With Ari, you do not."

Vincent winked at his son.

Then the king's eyes met Brayden's.

"The harsh truth is Ari has told us he's going public with his identity, and he will be known as the House of Moretti. We could do a dual announcement and show our support, or he does it alone and it will raise a ton of questions."

Vincent nodded.

"Cool name," Willow said.

"You don't know what you're talking about, Willow," Vincent snapped. "You've been a vampire for about five damn minutes."

"Brother, be careful," Brayden growled, his fangs creeping out.

"Okay, settle down," Kate said, using her queen voice, and they all did. The female was graceful and had a huge heart, but when she wanted, she was a force of nature. "Do we really believe Ari is a threat? Surely his inaction over fifteen hundred years proves otherwise?"

Vincent stared at him across the room. Their eyes held for a long moment.

Brayden looked away first. "No."

The king sighed.

"No. I don't. But trust me when I say there will be consequences. I'm just not entirely sure what they are." Vincent rubbed his face.

Brayden nodded slowly.

Nothing was ever without consequence. The two of them had been alive long enough to know that.

Still, he believed the benefits outweighed the risk.

At this point.

Ari was a powerful ally and would be a dangerous foe if he chose.

That was what none of them had voiced.

And he hoped they never had to.

Vincent walked around the sofa and sat next to his queen.

"I know you all see me as the ogre in this conversation, but you need to understand my position. I am the king. Over ten million vampires rely on me to keep this monarchy working." He shot Willow a look. "Rightly or wrongly. Vampires are predators, and a structured system with a strong ruler works to keep us safe and living within the rules we have set for our society."

His brother was right.

Without a strong ruler, who knows if vampires would have survived living in a human society? They could have ended up as caged animals *or* they could have eliminated the human species.

Brayden didn't know for sure, but he suspected Gio and Ari had no desire for that to happen. With vampires' inability to live in daylight, humans had been important for their survival in some ways, and the evolution of modern-day life.

Now humans had become a threat.

But only a handful of them.

It was a time of standing strong together, not fighting internally. Certainly not with family. And not with a family member as powerful as Ari.

Vincent reached for Lucas and Willow handed him over. The baby nestled into his father's powerful arms. The king stared down into his now sleepy face and nodded for a long while.

"Then the decision is final. But have no doubt, family, this will create changes we cannot foresee. *Yet*," Vincent said. "Aristide Moretti *is* an original vampire; therefore, I have no right to stop him declaring his identity, nor carving out his own path under our shared name."

Brayden held his brother's gaze when he lifted his head. Both brothers' eyes were rich with emotion.

They were all quiet as the reality of that sunk in.

"I'm sorry," Willow suddenly said, and all sets of eyes shot to her. She was staring at the king.

Vincent looked a little terrified, if not humored.

"About?"

Willow rubbed her tummy even though there was barely a bump. "Well, this will impact my child one day and you're right. I'm a new vampire and barely understand all of this king stuff."

Vincent's brows shot up. "I think I might like pregnant Willow."

She snorted. "Take a photo as it's probably never going to happen again."

Kate let out a laugh.

Brayden leaned over and kissed her forehead. "It's going to be fine. Ari would never let harm come to anyone in this family."

Vincent didn't comment.

"I'd like to propose an idea. An olive leaf of sorts. A public show of support," Kate said. "Sage is researching wedding venues. Let's invite them to marry here."

Willow whooped and clapped.

Vincent groaned. "Fine. But they're getting married at Christmas. You either get a wedding or reindeer. Not both."

There was a moment's silence and then Kate and Willow both broke out into loud laughter. Then Lucas woke and began crying, creating even more laughter from the females.

Brayden smirked.

They all knew there would be both.

CHAPTER THIRTEEN

"Wake him up, Ava," Liam whisper-yelled.

"You wake him up," she snapped back.

Wasn't the whole point of a whisper that you were quiet? Well, they had failed. Their voices had in fact woken him, but Callan wasn't ready to open his eyes.

The pain.

It had hurt like a mother fucker, and he was reluctant to move. And he wanted a minute to digest everything.

What the hell had happened?

Actually, when he had first begun to wake, Callan had thought he was back in the lab where he'd learned quickly to feign sleep. Sometimes those few moments were the only peaceful ones he had.

Then he'd scented Ava, Noah, and Liam.

His mind had gone back over the events of the past few hours.

Pain.

Darkness.

Liam crying out.

Noah lifting him.

Callan's eyes flew open, and he sat up abruptly.

"Jesus!" Noah cried, and they all jumped back.

"Freaking hell. Are you okay?" Ava asked as Liam lay a comforting hand on her shoulder.

Callan looked around the room. They were still in the motel room.

"What happened? Were we attacked?" He swung his legs off the bed.

Noah stood and made room for him.

"No, man. You collapsed. Your bones were cracking for a good five minutes," Liam said in answer.

Callan glanced at the vampire and saw the deep concern on his face. He knew they were all worried that the same thing would happen to them and he didn't blame them.

He felt guilty, but he didn't have time to dwell on that. Something was happening to him. He could feel it in every cell of his body.

Yes, he had pain.

Yes, he wanted to fuck more than a rabbit.

But he felt different in a way he couldn't describe. Like the very essence of who he was had changed and was still changing.

The urgency to get to the Moretti's was increasing. They would arrive tomorrow if they kept moving. They had helped him escape, and he trusted the king would help him.

"I'm going to have a shower. Let's get packed up and ready to leave." He glanced toward the windows. "In about an hour."

"Aren't you going to tell us what happened?" Ava asked, and he could hear the disbelief in her voice.

A little of his restraint slipped.

He turned at the bathroom doorway. "I don't fucking know what happened, Ava. I was experimented on. Tortured. I hope like hell I haven't hurt anyone else, but right now, we just need to keep moving."

There was silence as he closed the door and turned on the shower faucet.

CHAPTER FOURTEEN

"Can I get you to—"

"Sorry." Kurt pushed away from the bench.

"You know, these results won't be here any faster by following me around the lab." Sage shot him a look as she carried a tray of something gross-looking across the room.

He was totally unaware he'd been doing that, even though she'd asked him to move several times.

Okay, maybe he had been in the way.

He'd been making small talk, something he never did, working up the nerve to talk to her about Madison.

Or rather, what he'd done with Madison.

And said nerve was nowhere to be seen.

When had he become a prude?

"I get the feeling you have something on your mind," Sage added. "Are you worried about the results? Because you look fine to me. I don't think we need to be concerned."

Well, that was a good sign.

If it was up to him, he would have taken that as a sign to leave and hope she was right for a few more days. But oh no. He'd had to confess to fucking Craig, so now he was obligated to speak to Sage.

About his sexual experiences with Madison.

Jesus, he needed to man up.

"I went down on her." He spat out the words.

Sage's eyes flew open. "I'm sorry, what?"

Shit.

"Madison. I ate her out."

"I know what that means," Sage said, putting the tray down.

Right.

God, he was an idiot.

"Yeah, of course you do. Not that you... what I mean is, I'm sure Ari... shit." Kurt ran his hand over his face.

What the hell was wrong with him?

He was never this awkward.

Never.

The door clicked and both of them turned to see Madison walking in.

"Hey," she said, and then her smile faded. "What's wrong? Is it the results?"

Sage looked at him.

Great.

Just fucking great.

"I think you both should sit down," Sage said, pointing to the table on the other side of the room, and a minute later Brayden walked in.

"Hey team. Just popping in to see about the blood..." Brayden slowed his walk across the room to a stop.

Oh, just fucking excellent.

"What is it?" he asked, his voice now a demand, and planted his hands on his hips.

"That's what I would like to know," Madison said, her eyes flicking between him and Sage.

He let out a sigh.

"I fucked up. I'm sorry," Kurt said, shooting a look at Brayden. "I should have told you all what happened on the plane. The whole story."

Madison's face turned red, and he wished he could have done anything to save them both the embarrassment. But he also had a prince to answer to and despite his feelings for Madison, lying to the royal family was unacceptable.

"Why are you just telling us now?" Brayden growled.

Kurt could only imagine how Madison was feeling. He shot her another look, but she glanced away.

"I don't know." He answered truthfully. "In some ways, I was trying to protect her dignity."

Madison shook her head.

"Oh great. Blame me." She stood and pushed her chair away.

"Stay here Madison," Brayden said calmly, but firmly.

She sat back down and glared across the table at Kurt, but he quickly turned back to the prince. Madison would get over her embarrassment. He may lose his job.

"Sage, do your tests show anything irregular?" Brayden asked.

Sage shook her head.

"Not so far, and it has been two weeks of testing. That doesn't mean we're in the clear. DNA altering of one person won't necessarily pass on to another, but the fact his bite created a reaction in Madison is the concern," she said. "Kurt has had no side effects."

He coughed.

All eyes shot to him.

"Well. There's something." Brayden's angry expression encouraged him to just spit it out. "I am overly attracted to Madison."

"Excuse me?" she asked, her brows shooting up.

Brayden tilted his head. "You what now?"

"Overly?" Sage asked. "Can you elaborate on that, please, Kurt?"

He glanced at Madison and tried to send a bunch of telepathic *sorry's* her way, but they hadn't exchanged blood—

thank God—so he couldn't. Plus, she was now throwing daggers at him with her eyes.

He didn't blame her.

Not after what they had done.

But this was a thing.

A real thing.

He'd never wanted only one woman this much.

So clearly, something was wrong.

"Well, since we flew home and did those things on the jet—"

"He went down on me," Madison said and he shot her a surprised look.

Brayden cursed.

"I stopped though," he snapped.

"Oh, I know. Remember, I was there." She curled the side of her lip.

"Anyway... since then I have not, um, been able to... fuck... have sex with anyone else." Kurt said the last bit really fast.

He shot to his feet and pointed to Madison. "This has never happened. So obviously I am infected."

Madison gaped at him.

"The hell. Because you want to fuck me?"

Sage began to wave her hands to calm them down, but Brayden took a few steps close to them and they all shut up.

He looked mildly amused.

"Okay. Let's not jump to conclusions, which I am sure Sage was about to say."

"Yes. Thank you, Brayden," Sage replied.

Kurt shook his head.

What else could it be?

"Have you had any... side effects, Madison? Like Kurt's?"

She lifted her iPhone off the table and nervously twisted it. "I've had some aches which could be from all the extra exercise I'm doing. I don't have a gym like your training facilities."

"Fair enough.

"And," Kurt prompted.

Because that wasn't what they were asking about, and she knew.

Please fucking tell them so I don't have to.

She shot him a glance. Not a friendly one.

"I've been a little hornier than usual," she said. "But it's been about a month and..." She shot a dark glance his way. "Someone left me hanging, so I figured that was why."

Well, then.

All the cards were on the table. Except their last encounter, which he didn't feel needed...

"Plus, I've been told not to have sex." Madison interrupted his thoughts. "But I'm sure I could," she added, and he shot her a glare. She lifted her chin and kept talking. "Then Kurt finger-fucked me earlier this evening."

Okay, so *now* all the cards were on the table.

"Fucking hell." Brayden stared at the ceiling.

Sage crossed her arms.

"For goodness' sakes, you two! Which part of *don't be sexually active*, did you not understand?" Sage asked.

Both Madison and Kurt pressed their lips together, with no answer.

"They could be mates," Brayden said.

"What?" Kurt cried.

"No," he and Madison both chimed out together.

Kurt began to pace.

"Okay, you know what? I'm done. I just wanted to get this all on record. For your research. I'm sorry I withheld this information."

Sage tapped her pen on the table.

"It's possible. And I don't think there is anything to be concerned about. The blood exchange is the greatest concern, I believe. Other bodily fluids? Not so much."

Kurt crossed his arms.

"That's a hypothesis, however, so keep your lips—and fingers—to yourself. Both of you," Brayden said.

"Got it." Madison stood.

Brayden stared at him.

"Got it." He nodded to the prince.

They all began walking out of the lab.

"Craig knows," he said to Brayden as they opened the door for Madison.

"Before today?" the prince asked.

"No, I told him about an hour ago," Kurt answered.

"We will talk about this later." He teleported away.

Madison dipped under his arm, which was holding the door open, and began to march away.

"Madison," he called out.

"Leave me alone," she replied, continuing her march down the hall.

The vamp sped in front of her, and she stopped. "Look, I'm sorry. We both know we had to tell them."

She wouldn't look at him, and he could see she was embarrassed.

"Well, we have, and it was awkward. And clearly you are dying of some disease that makes you attracted to all of this." She indicated her body. "Because what else would it be?"

Oh, shit.

"That's not what I was saying." He shook his head. "Don't you feel it, though? It's insane."

She went quiet.

"I should have told them when we got back. I suppose I thought I was protecting you," he said, and then knew it was a lie. "No, that's not it. I didn't like how I felt."

She squinted at him. "What does that mean?"

He glanced up and saw all the vampires walking around them.

"Come with me so I can explain," he said when she began to shake her head. "Just to talk."

"Fine. Five minutes." She crossed her arms.

He pulled her against him and teleported away before she could change her mind.

CHAPTER FIFTEEN

Madison wasn't used to someone teleporting her, so she wobbled on her feet when they landed in what she assumed was Kurt's quarters, despite the fact he held her.
   His rooms were much fancier than hers. And larger.
   Great, I'm in his damn bedroom.
   Still, he thought his attraction to her was a medical issue. Idiot.
   It was unlikely he'd make another move on her. She would listen to his explanation and then leave.
   While she'd been furious and embarrassed earlier, Kurt had been right to speak up. Madison had been surprised to hear he was as attracted to her as she was to him.
   She knew why *she* was feeling it.
   Personality aside, he was a gorgeous vampire with a warrior's body and rich chocolate eyes that screamed of sex. While he was larger than ninety nine percent of the vampires in the castle, many of them were incredibly attractive.
   Yet, Kurt was the only one she had the same physical reaction to.
   "You all right?" he asked, steadying her.
   "Yes. I don't teleport often. Or with someone, without warning."

"Sorry about that."

"So you keep saying." She frowned and walked over to the sofa, taking a seat. "Okay, talk."

Madison heard him open the fridge as she glanced around. His home was filled with trinkets and photos from all over the world. One wall had what looked like a Persian wall hanging, and the other a large painting which she suspected was worth more than the one she had purchased recently at the markets.

A lot more.

But then again, being one of the king's senior warriors, probably paid a little more than a barmaid. Who also had a student debt.

"Da Vinci," he said, handing her a bottle of water.

"Really?" she asked, surprised. Madison loved art and knew many of the master's works, but she'd never seen this Da Vinci.

It was also a reminder of how old Kurt was. Well over five hundred years, as Da Vinci had died in 1519.

"It's not finished, but I offered him some coins for it, and he said it was mine as long as I never sold it." Kurt shrugged and sat opposite her. "So, I never have."

She stared at the landscape painting filled with flowers and sky. "It's truly beautiful."

When she turned, Kurt was studying her.

She sighed and relaxed into the cushions around her.

"You were right. Sage needed to know," Madison said. "You don't need to protect me."

Kurt propped his leg over his knee and took a sip of his water. "And yet I can't stop it."

Why does he have to be so hot?

She drank her water to give him time to explain. That's why he had asked her here, wasn't it? Kurt stared at her some more and it began to get awkward.

"Look—"

"I want to know why I'm so attracted to you. Despite not being allowed to sleep with others, I have no interest. You must agree this isn't normal."

"Yet it's hurtful."

"We're not mates," he said.

"I'm not saying we are. But I have feelings," she snapped, shaking her head. "Forget it."

He cursed and scrunched the water bottle in his hand until it was a bunch of plastic. Her eyes glued to his taut forearms.

She swallowed.

Stupid damn hot vampire.

Even when she was mad at him, her body wanted him.

"I'm not trying to offend you. I just want to make sense of this," Kurt replied. "I'm not short on female offerings. I could have—should have—controlled myself with you every single time. But I didn't. And can't."

She bit her lip.

"Fuck, don't do that," he said, shaking his head.

She tried to keep her face expressionless, but she quite liked that she was affecting him.

"I'm sorry. Do you need some medicine for that?"

He glanced down at his erection and shot her a raised brow.

"Minx."

"Well, seriously. You think I infected you and made you like me? That's so offensive."

"It's not just *like,* Madison. Don't you feel this?"

Yeah, she did, but she didn't want to sit here and tell him how hot he made her. The vampire had an ego the size of the Atlantic Ocean.

"I mean—" she drawled.

"Honesty, Madison." Kurt growled. "The reason I've kept away from you is because all I want to do is sink deep inside you."

"Not helping," she said, crossing her legs at the growing heat. Now he was playing unfairly. "Maybe I should go."

"Fuck," he cursed.

Madison drank the rest of her water and dropped the glass on the coffee table.

"I need to know if this is because of Callan," he said. "This reaction to you, our attraction, is very strong. Sage is guessing and we both know that."

She shrugged. "I guess."

"Do you always come like that?" he asked.

Wow. Did he really just ask that?

Kurt let out a groan and ran a hand over his cock.

"I wish you would stop blushing. It makes me so fucking hard," he ground out.

"Then stop asking me questions with such graphic wording."

He leaned forward. "I had my fingers inside your pussy a few hours ago. Now you can't handle me asking you a question about it?"

"Yes. Because it's different."

"No, it isn't. Answer the question. Do you always come like that?"

Her body lit up from both embarrassment and arousal. Her nipples hardened and she crossed her arms.

Kurt's eyes dropped to her chest.

"Madison," he insisted.

"No," she replied. "That was intense. All-consuming." Her eyes lifted to his. "I'm sure it's nothing. I feel fine. I mean, I'm aching."

"Aching?"

"My back. It could be—"

"Vampires don't ache," he interrupted; his eyes narrowed.

She nodded.

Why was she nodding?

"Well, it comes and goes. I'm fine right now," she said.

Kurt leaned back against the cushions and cursed. "This isn't good. How bad is the pain?"

She shrugged.

"Madison. How bad is it?"

"Bearable."

The arousal in her body suddenly dampened. He had hit her soft spot. She'd been worried for weeks about the pain coming and going, but she knew it was wrong.

What if there was something more serious going on in her body? What did that bite do to her?

She had no one to talk to. Kurt only wanted to fuck her. Everyone around her was a stranger. They were kind enough, but she dared not get close to anyone to build any friendships.

Hopefully, she'd be going home in a few days.

Or…

What would happen?

Was she going to die?

She felt the emotions rush to the surface. Including the one she had been trying to ignore.

Fear.

She was scared.

Which was entirely reasonable, given the situation. But she couldn't talk to anyone. Not her friends or her mom. And her poor mom had already lost her mate. What if Madison left her alone in this life as well?

What if Madison never got to travel and see the world?

Or really live?

Or love?

Oh God.

She wiped away a tear and Kurt was across the room a half second later.

"What's wrong?" He turned her and placed his hand on her hip.

God, he was huge.

She blinked away the tears and felt entirely dwarfed by his body. It made her feel ridiculously small and girly. That familiar lust sizzled within her again as she realized he could snap her in half without breaking a sweat.

Except he wouldn't.

He was gentle with her.

Firm in a protective and sexy way, but as if he was responsible for looking after her. Even though she had told him he wasn't.

His fingers pressed gently into her hip, as if to remind her he was there. But what she needed more than his physical comfort was someone to talk to, and she suspected that wasn't his sort of thing.

"I'm fine. This is all just a bit much, you know?" she sniffed. "God, I'm so stupid. Sorry."

His eyes burned into hers, concern lining his face.

"Just being here is a big deal. I know it's your life, but most vampires never get to meet the royal family, let alone live in the castle with them."

"Yeah, I guess I never looked at it like that."

Her eyes darted away, then back to him. "And Kurt, we could die. Who knows what happened to Callan? We don't know. You can't find him... and we could die."

Tears poured down her face as the floodgates burst open.

"Shit." He pulled her into his arms. "We're not going to die, Madison. I can promise you that."

They both knew he was lying.

He couldn't promise anything.

She melted into his large, warm chest and let the emotions she'd been holding back pour out as his hand ran up and down her back.

"I'm sorry you've got caught up in all this." He lifted her chin to look at him. "What do you need?"

She blinked at him.

"I mean it. Tell me what you need."

Another sniff.

"Just this. Someone to talk to, I guess." She wiped her eyes. "I can't tell my family or friends. I don't know when I'm going to be able to leave. I'm not allowed to have sex." They both shared a small smile.

"Yeah, I feel you on that part." He smiled wider.

"I suppose I'm asking a lot, but I need a friend." Madison shrugged.

"I can do that," he said, taking her wrist and running his thumb over her black butterfly tattoo before lifting his eyes to hers. They were full of heat.

"Can we, though? Without wanting to rip each other's clothes off?"

"No. I still want to do that," he said, wiping the remaining tears from her cheek.

Madison gave him a wet smile.

"Still, how different are tears to semen?" she wondered out loud.

"Oh, crap." Kurt stood, then shook his head. "Jesus, we are useless at this."

Then they both did something completely unexpected.

They burst out laughing.

Kurt shook his head as he took a number of steps away from the addictive sexy vampire before him. Seriously, they may as well just lick each other from head to toe and infect each other.

Which he may have already done.

Surely, if they were at risk, the line had already been crossed. He'd kissed her, eaten her pussy, fucked her with his fingers and now run his hands over her tear-stained face.

But he'd promised the prince.

His loyalty trumped everything.

Except this female, it seemed.

When Madison had begun crying, his need to comfort her had overridden everything including his sex drive. Without thinking, he'd flown to her side and held her in his arms.

What he'd found as he comforted her was a sense of calm he'd been searching for, for weeks.

She was safe.

She was his.

His to look after. Not for life. He didn't do that. But he would look after Madison. For some reason she was his responsibility.

No matter what happened, he'd get her home safely.

What that meant, he didn't understand, but she needed him, and he was going to do what he was trained to do.

Protect her.

Would they die, as she feared?

He fucking hoped not.

He'd do whatever he could to stop that happening and knew the king, prince and the entire Moretti team would do the same for both of them.

Until they found Callan, no one knew what they were dealing with. Even then, they may not.

For now, he would be her friend. He'd been a real asshole, just dropping her off and letting her fend for herself in this huge overwhelming place.

Kurt saw that now.

No wonder she'd been drawn to Darnell and his charming fucking smile. He was a good soldier, rising up in the ranks, but the tall, dark-skinned vampire needed to keep his mitts off Madison.

They all did.

Why?

Medical situation aside, that was not why he was being so possessive of her.

"Okay, friend." He smirked, standing a few feet from her and digging his hands into his denim pockets. "I have to get back to work, but I'll stop by afterwards and we can talk and stuff."

She wiped the remaining tears from her face and smiled. "Can we go to Max Bar?"

Can we fucking not?

Max Bar was the local watering hole where many of the vampires who worked and lived in the castle hung out. The SLCs didn't venture in there, nor did the royal family, for the sole purpose of giving their employees a place to relax and have their own space.

It wasn't like he couldn't go.

His presence would be very noticeable, and Kurt wasn't sure that was the kind of attention Madison wanted. Still, he got it—she wanted to socialize and have some fun.

And he kind of owed her one after deserting her.

The alternative was taking her out of the castle to a human bar, which he was reluctant to do. Or to a Moretti event with the family, which wasn't ideal either.

He'd make it work and try to look discreet.

All six foot four, two hundred and twenty pounds of him.

"Sure, we can do that. I'll pick you up after I've finished."

No big deal.

"I'll meet you there. I promised Darnell I would have a drink with him, and I want to keep my promise."

God damn it.

His jaw tensed.

"Sure," Kurt nodded, knowing he couldn't stop her.

When she smiled at him, looking happier than he'd seen in days—well, except when she was coming earlier tonight—his heart swelled.

Yeah, he liked that smile on her.

And he planned to see more of it.

Then, when all of this was over, he'd make sure she got back to Seattle and on with her life.

After he'd tied her to his bedframe and took his sweet time fucking her until she screamed his name.

Several times.

CHAPTER SIXTEEN

"We should get off here," Noah said, his broody tone becoming more familiar to Callan.

After blanking out the night before, he was feeling more vulnerable than ever. It wasn't just the fact he'd lost consciousness; it was the pain and not knowing what was going to happen.

And he knew the others were feeling it, too.

Ava was quiet.

Liam kept shooting him looks.

Noah was sticking close.

And he couldn't do a damn thing to ease their concerns. Or his own.

He looked out the window, then leaned over to get a better view of Noah's phone. He had Google maps pulled up and was pinching the screen to zoom in and out.

They were about a day's bus ride from Portland, where the Moretti castle was located. It was already four thirty in the morning, so they needed to get off.

After checking in to a motel, the four of them took a moment to relieve the pent-up sexual energy. Liam had sat on the bed, Ava dropping to her knees and sucking him off.

Noah had walked up and pulled his cock out, and stroked it. Then Liam had taken over.

Callan wanted them all.

He'd nearly come just watching them.

Instead, he'd knelt on the floor, tore off Ava's panties and slid his fingers through her wet heat. Then, after listening to her moan around Liam's cock, he'd thrust inside.

As she'd cried out, Liam had pushed her head back down to his cock, and taken Noah's cock in his mouth.

"Fuck," Noah had moaned.

Minutes later, they had all come simultaneously as he'd leaned over Ava's back and flicked her clit. Then the little minx had lain on the bed, sliding her fingers through her pussy and grinning. Noah had growled, then sunk inside her.

Liam had taken one look at him and both had hardened immediately. Next thing Callan knew, his cock was in the vampire's mouth.

It was just one big damn orgy for over two hours.

Not a bad way to live.

Except they all knew their appetite was way over the top and there would be a reason for it.

One they may not like when they found out.

Four showers and a meal later, they were all in bed scrolling on their phones with Ava giving them updates on the astrology.

"Full moon in twenty-five minutes," she said. "Seriously, this is an important one. It's in Scorpio. No wonder we're all rutting like rabbits."

"What does that even mean?" Liam asked, more in judgment than wanting an actual answer.

But Callan knew they were all going to get one.

"Scorpio is the sign of death, rebirth, sex and dark secrets," Ava shared and continued rattling on.

Callan tuned out.

His back was aching and his jaw felt like it was going to snap. Even his gums were killing him. He popped his fangs out and back in again.

Noah shot him a concerned look.

Shit. He was trying not to worry them all further. He kicked off the sheets and walked to the fridge, mostly for something to do because lying still was becoming painful.

He grabbed a bottle of blood and lifted it to his mouth.

"Jesus. Is this stuff off?" He almost gagged, spitting it into the sink and quickly rinsing his mouth with water.

It had smelled rotten.

"Since when does blood have a use-by date?" Noah asked. "What's wrong with it?"

"Tastes like shit." He put the bottle back in the fridge, but Noah had joined him and grabbed it from him.

He sniffed it. Took a sip.

"Tastes fine to me." He gave Callan another concerned look. "Are you going to collapse again?"

Callan leaned against the bench.

"Maybe. I'm not sure."

"Why don't we ring the Moretti's? They'll come and get us," Ava said.

Callan spun.

"No. Don't!" he snapped.

Shit, the last thing he wanted was to alert anyone digitally to their location.

Those scientist fuckers might find them.

"Dude, I think she's right," Liam said.

"No. If those scientists have any way of tracking us, they will. There's no way I'm going back there and if any of you got captured, I couldn't live with myself."

They all stared at him.

A strange thing had been happening over the past several days. He'd formed a connection with the three vampires. Sure, they'd been shagging like rabbits, but it wasn't that. Vampires were sexual by nature. It didn't mean, like it did with humans, that they formed bonds. This was different. Callan felt protective of them. Like it was his job to look after them and guide them.

He figured it was guilt.

"I've been having some pain in my back. Nothing like you're experiencing, Callan," Liam confessed. "But I think it's arthritis."

Noah raised a brow and snorted. "How do you know? You aren't human."

Liam gave him the bird. "I looked it up, asshole. The pain and sensations feel exactly as they describe it. Joint pain, stiffness, swelling of the joints. I think that's what this is."

That was exactly what it felt like.

Except not mild.

Perhaps BioZen had injected him with diseases to see how his body reacted to them?

Was that what he was suffering from?

Severe arthritis?

"That describes my pain, but about a thousand times worse," Callan said. "Maybe we should get some human medicine."

He bent over again as another bolt of pain shot through him.

"It could be worse because vampires have no pain tolerance. You know, because we rarely experience it," Ava said, "Over time you may grow—"

Callan let out a roar and dropped to the floor.

Crack.

"Shit." He heard Noah yell.

Snap.

Crack, crack, crack.

"What the hell is happening to him?" Liam asked, his voice now closer. "Callan!"

All the bones in his body felt as if they were crumbling and collapsing. He heard himself screaming as the pain roared through his body and the ends of his fingers burned.

Fire laced through all his digits as he felt them shift and change.

Then his cheeks ripped open, and his jaw snapped.

Mother fucker!

Suddenly, his eyesight changed.

It was blurry at first, and then he felt the skin around his eyes stretch and rip. He tried to lift his hand to his face but couldn't. His back continued to crack and arch, no longer under his control.

He felt *wrong*.

Then Callan felt his body try to heal itself. It was like a war. One part of him wanted to break apart, the other tried to heal.

One part of him would crack and then it would heal.

Rinse and repeat.

After what felt like hours, the pain and exhaustion finally depleted his energy and he let himself go. As soon as he stopped fighting it, the pain lessened as his body shifted in a shimmer of energy.

Then suddenly all the pain was gone, and he blinked. The world looked different.

"Holy fucking hell," Ava cried, and she jumped up on the bed as the males backed away from him.

He looked down and saw he was on his hands and knees.

"Stay away," Noah said, holding his arm out, keeping the others away from him.

"Whaa... waww." Callan tried to speak and couldn't. An animal sound escaped his mouth.

He tried it again.

Louder this time, but what sounded like a howl ripped from him.

He looked down at his hands. They were paws.

He blinked.

Clearly, he was losing his mind.

When he moved, his body felt heavy, changed, powerful but wrong. He turned his head and the world wobbled.

When he tried to ask what was wrong with him, all that came out was *waaohhee ahh awhooo.*

Great. Now he spoke dog.

Dog?

He looked down at his hand again.

Still a paw.

What the fuck?

Callan lifted his, er, paw, and collapsed, then scrambled to his feet. All four of them.

"Jesus," Ava cried. "Is that is going to happen to me? To all of us?"

"Fuck me," Liam said, staring at him.

"Holy fucking shit," Noah said, running his hand through his hair and gripping it. His eyes were wild and wide.

Callan tried to talk again but failed and now he was just fucked off. He moved his paws—*Jesus*—and padded to a mirror.

Then let out an ear-piercing scream.

Correction. He howled.

He wasn't a dog.

He was a goddamn *wolf.*

A huge black wolf with blue eyes.

CHAPTER SEVENTEEN

Madison made her way to Max Bar.

She had no idea what time Kurt would finish work or if anything would come up, but it had been nice of him to say he'd join her tonight for a drink.

As friends.

If he showed, great. If not, she'd just have to keep being strong.

If not, she had to just keep being strong.

Who was she kidding? She wanted to climb all six foot four of his black-uniform-clad body.

Would he want to relieve their tension if they got clearance to have sex? Damn, just thinking about what he might do to her as she walked through the castle had her biting her lip.

Madison snapped herself out of it.

A friend was what she needed.

At least she now felt a little less alone and a bit more supported. Kurt had surprised her with his compassion.

It was a reminder she didn't really know him.

Sexy time aside, they had never sat and chatted.

She hoped they could do more of that tonight.

The night they'd met at her bar, he'd flirted with her until she finished her shift. Even then, they'd never shared anything personal about themselves. She had no idea if he had any siblings or who his parents were. Or if he liked his job—she guessed he did—or his favorite ice-cream.

He'd never asked her anything either.

Aside from wanting to know if she was wet.

And usually when he asked, ten seconds later, she was. Especially with his thick, deep, Italian accent and those chocolate eyes sparkling back at her mischievously.

Despite her outburst of emotions earlier, the sexual attraction between them had remained strong. Kurt had walked her back to her room afterwards and winked at her as he said goodbye.

She rubbed the tattoo on her forearm and let out a small laugh. Talk about a visual reminder of how he made her feel. A million butterflies had appeared out of nowhere and had a rave party in her tummy.

Like a damn teenager.

How on earth was she supposed to curtail her desire for him when she'd had a crush on him since she was a young vamp?

It was much easier when he was being a complete dick.

She smiled at the Moretti soldiers walking past. Two of them were females, a fact she loved. In fact, there were more females in the castle than she'd expected.

It wasn't that females were considered weak, but they were, compared to males. It was just a biological fact.

These females had a lot more power than she did. She'd seen them lifting weights in the training center.

Madison was strong compared to humans, and toned, but not powerful. And she was okay with that.

Turning the corner, she saw the sign above the door of Max Bar.

She caught her reflection in the glass doors and fluffed up her short, wavy blonde hair. Then she rubbed her lips together, hoping her lip gloss was still on form.

She'd opted for a pair of black jeans, a black crop top, ankle boots and a black leather jacket. It seemed to be the popular color around the castle, so she figured it would help her blend in.

With her phone and credit card in one hand, she pushed through the doors and immediately felt the warmth of the busy bar.

A sense of comfort came over her.

She knew bars.

Royal castles, not so much.

Glancing around, she took in the moody vibe. The music was a decent level so you could talk, and the beverages and what she thought was smoke from the odd cigar drifted over her.

"She made it," a voice drawled.

Darnell.

"Hey," she said, smiling and walking over to the tall bar table where he sat with a handful of vampires.

"Madison, this is Casey, Charlotte, Will and Tristan," Darnell said, and a bunch of eyebrows, glasses and hands were raised in hellos.

It was obvious they were all soldiers by the way they held themselves and the power emulating from their bodies.

Casey and Charlotte were at least five foot eight and both had long, dark hair. Charlotte's hair had more wave in it, while Casey's was in a long pony.

Will, Tristan and Darnell were all built and ranged, she guessed, from six, to six foot two. And they were all muscular, with bulging biceps.

Madison looked around her at tables full of warriors. All gorgeous vampires with strong sexy bodies.

And yet, not one of them grabbed her attention like Kurt Mazzarelli.

"You owe me twenty dollars," Charlotte said, holding her palm out to Tristan.

Lord, he was hot. His silvery blue eyes and mop of dark curls would have Brooke tripping over herself. She was totally taking a group photo so she could send it to her friend after.

They would be so jealous.

If only they knew she was unable to partake in any of the goodness on offer. Even if she could get past her desire for Kurt.

"Please tell me you were considering standing this douchebag up." Tristan smirked and slapped the note into Charlotte's palm.

"Um, no." Madison laughed and shot Darnell a grin.

"Ignore these idiots. Get you a drink?" he asked, climbing off his stool.

"I'll get it," Madison replied.

"I like her. Independent," Casey said, nodding as she lifted her bottle of beer to her lips.

Was she?

Or had she worked in bars long enough to know the drill? Let a guy buy you a drink and it meant you were interested. It didn't guarantee sex—no fucking way.

If a woman said no, she meant no.

End of story.

But she'd put out major vibes earlier, and Madison could hardly explain her medical situation to them. It was easier to just hang as friends. Plus, Kurt had kindly taken the edge off.

And then put it back on, but… semantics.

"I like her too." Darnell winked.

Madison laughed and turned to go to the bar when her ankle weakened, and a crack sounded.

Fuck.

Darnell caught her elbow, holding her from falling.

"The hell was that?" He stared down at her.

She shook her head, cringing from the pain.

"Damn shoes. Wobbly heel."

Shit, shit, shit.

"Right," he replied, obviously not believing a word of it.

She stretched out her leg and felt it click back into place. The pain was bad but nothing she couldn't handle. It was the unknown that had her freaked out.

"See. All good."

An hour later, the bar was busier, and Madison was on her second vodka dry when she felt a shift in the room. And a voice over her shoulder.

"Enjoying yourself?" The husky tone breathed along her neck.

She turned.

Crack.

Shit.

Her hand flew to her neck.

Kurt and Marcus stared at her with wide eyes.

"Hi. Hey. Shit." She rolled her neck as pain shot up over her head to her temples.

"Was that your neck?" Marcus asked as Kurt continued to study her. Then his eyes darted around the table.

"What's up?" Kurt asked, lifting his chin.

"SLC Mazzarelli," Darnell said, and the rest of the table of vampires greeted the two SLCs formally.

Except Charlotte, who seemed to be glaring at Marcus.

"Relax. Enjoy yourselves. Forget we're here," Marcus said, leaning against a pillar and plugging a hand into his jeans pocket.

Charlotte snorted, but didn't look impressed.

"Here we go," Kurt mumbled.

Madison rubbed her neck and watched the dynamics between the two.

"'Scuse me?" Marcus asked, raising a brow.

"Nothing. I'm just surprised you've finished torturing your subjects long enough to have a drink," Charlotte said, taking a swig of her beer.

Kurt turned sideways to hide his smirk and winked at Madison.

"Is this normal?" she asked quietly.

Kurt nodded. "Normal and irritating." He shook his head. "I wish they'd just fuck. At least they can."

"Yeah. Right." Madison nodded knowingly.

"One day you'll thank me," Marcus said, seemingly unperturbed, but Madison sensed he was simply well practiced at the antagonism between the two of them.

"Don't hold your breath," Charlotte snorted.

"Give it a rest, Char," Tristian growled. "You do know he's an SLC, right?"

"Not in here, he's not," she snapped, and finished her beer. "I'm out. See you tomorrow."

Whoa.

Madison was surprised at the insubordination from the vampire. She couldn't imagine anyone talking to one of the king's warriors like that.

Marcus shook his head and watched her leave.

"Sorry, Marcus. I'm not sure—" Casey began.

"Do not apologize for her," Marcus replied. "I've been hard on Charlotte for a reason. She'll either step up or fail."

Oh, so she reported to him.

Holy heck.

Madison couldn't imagine giving that kind of attitude to her boss. She'd be fired in an instant.

"You need to sort that out," Kurt said quietly, though Madison could hear.

"Yeah, I know. Fuck it." Marcus glanced around the room and let out a long sigh. "You know, I think I'm going to head out."

Kurt slapped him on the shoulder and the huge vampire left.

"Is he going to fire her?" she asked.

He placed a hand on the small of her back and she wondered if he was aware he was doing it.

"No," Kurt replied. "Now, what the hell is wrong with your neck?"

Oh, that.

Casey jumped down off her stool and began dancing with Will and Tristan.

"I'm getting another beer," Darnell said, pushing away from the table. "Want anything?"

The world spun.

Her body began to tremble like there was something inside her scratching to get out. She placed a hand on Kurt's arm. "I think I need to leave."

"Really? You've only been here for a little while. More of the gang is coming later," Darnell said., as her eyes lifted to Kurt.

Something wasn't right.

Crack.

His eyes widened as her back arched with another loud crack, and she cursed.

"What the hell is happening, Madison?"

"I don't know," she whispered, feeling scared. "Get me out of here now."

"Fuck." He growled.

Kurt scooped her up, and they were out of the bar in a flash.

CHAPTER EIGHTEEN

"Charlotte!" Marcus called as he marched down the hall. He'd caught the back of her as she turned the corner and knew she'd seen him.
Damn frustrating female.
As he rounded the corner, and she was gone. *Damn it!*
She had teleported.
He knew where she was.
Where she always was.
If she kept this up, she would burn out and be no good to anyone.
Marcus teleported to the SLCs office in the training center and ripped open the door.
Remain calm.
He ignored all the vampires who were lifting weights, running on treadmills and sparring. He walked past the room where a yoga class was taking place and leaned against a wall near the female changing rooms.
And waited.
A few minutes later, a slim, toned vampire walked out.
He cursed to himself.
Try as he might, he couldn't ignore his reaction to her body.

Her long dark wavy hair was pulled up in a pony, her perfect booty clad in a pair of tight black exercise shorts—short that should be fucking illegal.

Charlotte fidgeted with her top, which finished above her midriff, showing off her toned abs.

Abs, he'd seen her work damn hard to create.

She walked past him. "I'm off the clock."

He pushed away from the wall. "Then why are you here?"

She whirled on him. "I'm sorry. Are you my mother?"

He smirked.

The things he wanted to do to her were not maternal *at all*.

Fuck. *Stop thinking about that stuff.*

He wiped the smile from his face.

"No, but I told you before, if you work your body this hard, then you'll go backwards," Marcus said. "Rest is as important as diet and exercise."

She shook her head and suddenly changed direction and walked off.

"I've asked to be reassigned," she called over her shoulder.

What?

He vamp-sped in front of her and planted his hands on his hips.

"Explain," he demanded.

She frowned. "You know why."

Sure.

But that had been once.

One kiss.

It had never happened again.

Un-fucking-fortunately.

Marcus lifted his eyes and saw the side door. He pulled her outside.

"The fuck?" she said, ripping her arm away.

"Don't be an idiot. There is an opportunity for you to get promoted. You know I'm the best person to train you," Marcus said, not arrogantly, but because she had been on his team for years.

Changing coaches would set her back.

Charlotte had enormous potential. She was fast, strong, and smart. But she didn't have as much experience as some of the others and her skills needed more work.

He'd been working her hard the past few months and together they were making good progress.

As a lieutenant, Charlotte could be someone he recommended to the prince for one of the new SLC positions.

But there was that little thing about the kiss.

Marcus wasn't going to let that get in the way of her success. The fact they had such sizzling chemistry was a job every day to ignore.

"Maybe I don't want it."

He raised a brow.

"Okay, fine. I'm interested. But someone—"

Marcus stepped closer, and she went silent.

"Don't," he said quietly. "What happened won't and can't happen again. If you want this job, we can only ever be colleagues."

Never anything more.

She swallowed, her mouth slightly opening, and his eyes dipped down to her lips.

She pressed them closed.

Good girl.

"You'll need to show you can work with all of us. That includes me. Forget what happened. Drop the attitude and go follow your dreams, Charlotte."

"I kissed you," she confessed.

He nodded. "I know."

"I'm so mad at myself." She cursed. "Such a fucking stupid—"

He pulled her against him and slammed his mouth down on hers.

God, he'd wanted to do that again for damn weeks.

When he released her, she glared at him.

"What the hell did you do that for?"

"Because now we are even. But we can never do it again."

Marcus stared at her for another beat as her fingers touched her lips, then he turned and walked away.

"Go home. Rest," he called over his shoulder. "You are going to need it."

"Asshole," she muttered.

If she knew what he wanted to do to her, what he imagined doing to her when he stroked his cock in the shower, *then* she'd think he was an asshole.

But he was going to help her achieve her dreams.

Which might mean spending every day for the rest of his life working alongside her.

And if he didn't find a way to stop desiring her, it would be a fucking nightmare.

CHAPTER NINETEEN

Kurt stopped outside the bar, with Madison in his arms, considering whether he should teleport her to the medical center. The way her bones were cracking, the last thing he wanted to do was reassemble her damn atoms.

He telepathed Ari. *Send Sage to the medical center. Something is wrong with Madison. Urgent.*

We'll be there in one minute, Ari replied.

He messaged Ben next. *We need Anna. Urgent, buddy. Medical center.*

On it.

Anna, Ben's mate, was a veterinarian and while she wasn't a medical doctor, her knowledge may be of some assistance.

He'd accept any help right now.

The king had organized a doctor they all knew and trusted from Los Angeles to work for them. He was wrapping up his practice and moving to the castle. But he hadn't arrived yet.

Murphy's damn law.

"Kurt, what is wrong with me?" she asked, clinging to his shirt.

"I don't know," he replied darkly.

Crack.

Jesus, it sounded like she was breaking on the inside.

Kurt methodically moved to the other side of the castle using vamp speed in bursts. One, to check she was okay, and two, so he didn't create havoc in the busy hallways.

By the time they arrived at the medical center, Sage, Ari, Anna, and Marcus were there.

"I saw Anna on the way," Marcus said, glancing at him and Madison. "You okay?"

She shook her head.

Crack, crack, crack.

"Get her on the table," Anna said as Sage removed some folders that were lying on it.

"Oh, my God!" Madison cried out as more cracking sounded from her body.

Fuck.

Kurt thrust his hand through his hair. "What the hell is it?"

"Step back, Kurt," Ari said, a strong hand on his shoulder. Anyone else, and he probably would have punched them.

Marcus took a step closer to him. Both of them were letting him know they would intervene if he lost it. They were protecting the females.

Un-fucking-necessarily.

As if he would hurt them.

Fucking hell.

Anna pulled out a stethoscope and attempted to listen to Madison's heart, but she could barely lie still.

"I think it's safe to say it's beating really fucking hard. Can you not hear it?" Kurt said.

Ari shot him a warning glance and then read out some numbers, and Anna nodded at him.

"Dude, stay calm. She'll be okay," Marcus said.

"You don't know that," he growled.

Madison lifted her head, and her eyes met his. Full of pain and pleading for help. He tried to take a step closer, but two strong hands landed back on his shoulder.

"Let them do their job," Ari said firmly.

Brayden burst into the room.

"Update now," he ordered, as Craig joined him a second later.

"Can we all just calm down, please?" Sage said, shooting Ari a look asking for support. "We need to take care of Madison and find out what this is. We've been here three damn minutes."

Ari attempted to move him away.

Kurt turned his head to look at the ancient vampire. "You need to let go of me. With all due respect, Ari, take your fucking hand off me."

Ari stared at him for a long minute and then looked at Madison, who still had her eyes locked on Kurt.

He nodded.

"Give the females room to check her out. If you harm my mate in any way, I will kick you outside under the sun faster than you can form an apology," Ari said calmly.

Deadly.

Jesus, had he been that aggressive?

"Is that fucking necessary?" Craig asked, glancing between them.

Thank you.

"Look at his eyes," Ari said, dropping his hand.

Craig and Brayden stared at him, but he just shook his head, not understanding what the guy was on about.

His two superiors cursed.

He ignored them all.

Madison was his responsibility. He'd found her and now it sounded like her entire body was breaking into pieces.

He gave her his full attention.

"I'm here. I'm not going anywhere."

She nodded.

Anna gripped her head and used a device to look into her eyes, mouth, and ears.

Then suddenly Madison's entire back arched and as she took one last look at him, and screamed as her entire body turned to jelly and she collapsed.

Kurt leaped forward and caught her. "Either I'm staying here, or she's coming to my place where I can keep an eye on her."

"You aren't a medical professional," Anna said, her hands on her hips.

"And you have a job to do," Craig said, pointedly.

"Consider me on leave." He growled.

The door opened and Willow poked her head in. "Is Madison, okay? I heard what happened."

Brayden's arms uncrossed, and he was across the room in a flash. "The fuck, Willow. Do not come in here! Jesus."

Her eyes flew open. "I heard she collapsed with broken bones."

A deep growl escaped the prince. "The damn baby. Craig, sort this out," Brayden said, and the two of them teleported away.

Kurt glanced at Craig, and they shared a knowing look.

It concerned all of them. All of it. What the hell had they done to Callan?

And what had Kurt brought into the castle?

"You both stay here. Leave and there will be consequences," Craig said to Kurt and Madison, his tone one Kurt knew was final.

CHAPTER TWENTY

Madison blinked awake, taking in the now familiar walls of the medical center.
Why was she asleep in here?
She began to stretch and felt the edges of a small bed.
"Hey," a gruff voice said. "Anna, she's awake."
Madison looked up into Kurt's worry-lined face and nodded. "I'm awake. Why am I—"
Oh.
The pain.
All her memories came flooding back. The noise, the cracking of her bones, the feeling of her body restricting itself in the most excruciating way. The look of fear in Kurt's eyes as he'd been held back by the Moretti team.
She had needed him. Wanted him to hold her and stop the pain.
Then, when all she could hear was voices in a fuzzy tunnel, her spine had felt like it snapped in half, and she'd blanked out.
At least, that was all she could remember.
"Are you in pain? Do you—"

"Kurt, can you please let me do my job?" Anna said, frowning at him and shaking her head. "Madison, ask this damn alpha male to step aside and let me look at you."

He growled.

Madison blushed and gave him a small smile. "What she said."

"Fine."

He took a step away. Or more like a half step, which bought him a sideways glare from Anna.

Another step was taken, and Madison giggled.

"Well, that's a good sign," Anna said, smiling. "How do you feel?"

She cleared her throat. "Fine. Thirsty."

Anna handed her some water. "Drink slowly. You have been out for nearly a day."

She sat up, splashing water over herself. "A whole day?"

"Nearly," Kurt said.

"You passed out from the pain," Anna said, and glanced to her right as Sage joined them. "While you seemed to heal just as rapidly, we took some bloods and Sage is going to get them urgently processed elsewhere in a few hours when it's dark out."

Sage walked into the room. "Ari and Craig are taking me. We'll have to break into a facility in Portland. I should know by midnight."

Madison nodded.

They must be really worried if they were putting that much resource into getting results back.

"Are you in pain?" she asked Kurt.

"No, sweetheart. I'm not." He lay a hand on her leg.

Sweetheart?

"Can I take her home?" Kurt asked.

Home?

Sage and Anna exchanged thoughts.

She didn't know if the two had imbibed each other's blood so they could telepath, but it was probable.

"We'd rather you didn't leave," Anna said, talking directly to her, "But keeping you in here seems pointless when Kurt appears to be willing to babysit you. He can call any of us immediately if something happens. Don't leave your room—whichever room you go to."

Madison glanced at Kurt for confirmation of said babysitting services.

"Absolutely." He nodded.

"We still don't think you're contagious as Kurt is showing none of the symptoms you are, but let's not dance with the devil," Sage said.

Madison let out a silent sigh of relief.

She would hate if she had passed on whatever this was to Kurt.

Or anyone.

The entire episode had been more pain than she'd ever experienced in her life.

"Also, the last bloods we took show they are normal. Which is strange," Sage added. "We have more questions than answers."

Okay, not so good.

Kurt helped Madison climb off the bed and stood restlessly watching her put her boots and jacket back on. She kept shooting him odd looks.

"Thanks ladies. I promise to be on better behavior next time." He smiled, then added, "Hopefully there won't be a next time."

"I'll let you know when I have the results," Sage said, nodding at him.

"I'm going to get some sleep. Wake me if you need me," Anna said.

He had wanted to swap blood with the two females so he could call on them directly if something happened, but that wasn't possible while they waited to see if he was sick.

Words he never thought he'd think.

And yet life had surprised them over the last few years.

Just as they were walking out the door, Madison stopped and turned to the two females. "There will be others out there like me. Going through this. We have to find them."

Anna's face paled.

Oh shit.

"I know," Anna said. "Trust me, I know."

"The team are looking for them," Kurt said as Sage rubbed Anna's arm. "We will help them."

Madison shot him a look of confusion at the female's reaction. He didn't want to speak on Anna's behalf, so he turned to her in question.

Anna nodded.

"I was one of the kidnapped vampires taken by BioZen. I was lucky. The Moretti's got us out. But Callan was in there for a long time," Anna said, her Italian accent heavy as she shared the memory.

Hardly lucky, but the female had an incredibly positive attitude.

"Sage helped Callan escape," Anna said. "So we are all part of this."

"Oh, my goodness. I'm so sorry," Madison said, her hand flying to her mouth. "That must have been horrible."

Of course.

Madison knew the bare minimum about what had been happening these past few months. Well, it was time he updated her on the history.

"I'll explain everything," Kurt said.

She was a part of their story now and deserved to know what was happening.

Even though it would likely terrify her more.

CHAPTER TWENTY-ONE

Kurt led Madison back to her room. When they had privacy, and she was settled on the sofa, he began to explain.

"A few months ago, about a dozen vampires were taken by the same pharmaceutical company who had Callan. We were able to find out their location in Italy and retrieve them."

She shook her head sadly.

Like all vampires, it was the worst-case scenario. It was what they had nightmares over. That, should humans discover them, they would experiment on them like lab rats.

And it had happened.

Well, only a bunch of politicians, scientists and conspiracy theory bloggers knew about their existence—the latter of which they were keeping a close eye on—but that was all it had taken.

"Thank goodness," Madison said.

He shook his head.

"Well, it's not that simple and far from over. They were all traumatized by the event, and it's been a long road to recovery. If it ever will be," Kurt said. "Anna mated with Ben. He's an assassin and… well, long story short, he got his revenge on one of the men responsible for Anna's suffering."

Madison's mouth dropped open. Then snapped shut. "I mean, good. But really, Ben is an assassin?"

Oh, yeah, she'd met him when she first arrived.

"Former. But yes."

Once an assassin, always an assassin, the vampire had told him once.

Actually, twice.

The second time when they'd had a disagreement, and he was telling him to watch his six.

It had been said in jest, but Kurt knew the guy was totally capable of deadly means. As they all were. Ben's techniques were just a little more covert than the Moretti original team.

"It's such a different world here." She leaned into the cushions.

Kurt studied her.

He didn't know how to look after a sick person, but they'd all been around humans and watched enough TV to know a little.

"Do you need a blanket or soup?" he asked, rubbing the back of his neck.

She narrowed her eyes. "For what?"

"To feel better?" He shrugged.

"I'm healed."

"Some blood then? Plasma?"

"Plasma," she replied. "Oh, I don't have any left."

Kurt telepathed the kitchen with a food order. She could pick and choose what she felt like. "The café will deliver some in about twenty minutes."

"Can I have ice-cream?" she asked.

"Yes," he laughed, adding it to the order, then dropped his elbows to his knees, rubbing his face.

He was tired.

It wasn't so much the loss of sleep, but he'd been overthinking everything for nearly twenty something hours.

He'd seen enough vampires bond with a mate over the past few years to know what was going on. Replaying the looks shared between his fellow vampires recently, Kurt knew what they were thinking.

Hell, Brayden had even said it.

Kurt had laughed it off as ridiculous.

Now he was beginning to wonder if they were right.

Was Madison his mate?

There were signs he couldn't ignore, such as his overwhelming need to look after and protect her. Possessiveness was right up there.

Darnell was lucky to have a damn head on his shoulders. All he'd done was talk to Madison.

Then, of course, there was the sexual attraction that even now buzzed statically between them. A little glance. A smile. The semi he always seemed to have around her. Unless she was in pain.

He knew she was aware of it.

The way she licked her lips and the flash of heat that warmed her cheeks told him she craved what he had.

Would they ever be able to satisfy this need?

Last night, his brain had gone full steam worrying she was his mate.

He had promised himself he would never mate. Not after what his father had done to his mother.

And him.

He would leave his job and move continents if he had to. You didn't live through his childhood with a violent father without knowing you weren't mate material.

He was a deadly warrior.

Having a soft female in his life who trusted him to keep him safe—from him—wasn't his path in life.

If Madison was his mate, he'd need to keep his distance from her before they bonded. But first he had to fuck her.

They both deserved and needed the fulfillment it would give them.

He wouldn't deny them that.

So he'd created a four-step plan.

First, if she wanted, he was going to fuck her.

Second, he'd make sure she got the care she needed and someone to look after her.

If it looked like she was going to remain in the castle, he would leave. Or he would ensure she was returned home and safe.

All before they bonded.

If they were mates.

They may not be.

But if they were, step four would be Kurt alone, knowing he had dodged the mate bullet and carry on with his life.

Unbonded

He was pleased with his strategy.

There was just one slight glitch.

He seemed incapable of leaving her side right now and if he was told she was about to die from whatever the fuck was wrong with her, he'd destroy the fucking world.

Starting with Xander Tomassi.

But he was currently looking to mitigate those wee issues.

I'm fucked.

His mind fled back to those moments when Madison had held his gaze, pleading for his help and comfort.

They had to find Callan.

He wanted to strangle the vampire, but the guy didn't deserve his anger. This was on Tomassi and all those fuckers behind this. Blowing up BioZen would go a long way to curbing his fury.

Fucking humans.

"You didn't sleep," she said, standing to walk past him.

His eyes followed her as his body flared to life. Without thinking, he reached for her, and she fell in his lap.

"Kurt," she gasped.

The feel of her in his arms, on top of his cock, was like a long cool drink.

Finally.

"I know." He understood the meaning in her gasp, and dropped his forehead to hers.

Her body relaxed and melted into him. Her hands were hot on his pecs.

"I thought you were going to fucking die last night." He growled low in his throat.

"You did?" One of her hands lifted to the side of his face, her eyes softening.

"Yes, God damn it. You were cracking like a God damn firecracker. It was terrifying," he said, his eyes drifting down to her lips.

Just one little…

"Kurt, you could get sick."

His thumb ran along the edge of her bottom lip, teasing them both as it caught and tugged her skin. She let out a little sound and his cock twitched.

"Will I?" He was starting to not care. "I need to kiss you. I need to taste you." His thumb slipped inside. "And I think you want that, too."

A guttural moan escaped her, and that was all he needed. His mouth dropped to hers as he pulled her hard against his body. Madison's arms wrapped around him as they finally let all their pent-up frustration and arousal loose on each other.

Like it was the last kiss of their life.

Which it could be.

His tongue slipped inside, his hand on the back of her head, demanding more as he stood. She pulled back and for a split second they panted, staring, and then she claimed his mouth.

He carried her into the bedroom.

"I really fucking hope I don't break you." He growled.

"I'm not that small," she replied.

"Yeah, you are." He smirked, dropping her on the bed and pulling her jeans off. "But I don't mean that."

"Oh."

"If you hurt in any way, I want you to stop me," he said. "Tell me you will."

Madison nodded.

"Say it," he said, removing his own clothes.

"I will." She lifted her crop top off, leaving only a pair of turquoise lace panties.

And Jesus, those breasts.

"Fuck you're gorgeous." He stood and stroked his cock as his eyes ran over her body. She lay down on the pillows and stared up at him as if he was a god ready to service her.

And hell, yes, he was up for it.

The strange thing was, while his usual sexual appetite leaned toward the wilder and more adventurous, all he wanted to do was slowly make every inch of her feel incredible.

If it took all night, then so be it.

He wouldn't be using his silk ropes. Or clamps. Or any devices. Madison would know his mouth, his hands and his cock and every other inch of his body.

Her lithe petite body would be his and feel only pleasure.

Slowly.

"You need to stop doing that or I'm going to come just watching you," she said.

"Show me." His hand tightened around his cock. "Remove your panties and show me how wet you are."

As she scrambled to do that, his need to have her mouth around his cock overtook him.

When her panties landed on the floor, he stepped closer. Madison spread her legs and swept her fingers through her pussy.

God.

She lifted them to her lips and when her tongue reached out and tasted them; he thought *he* was going to come right there and fucking then.

"Jesus, female." He cursed, taking her face and lining his cock up with her lips. "Suck me now before I embarrass myself."

"Yes, sir."

Holy fuck.

He was not going to last.

As her mouth surrounded him, Kurt threw back his head and let out a loud curse to some God he'd never heard of. She moved fast, sucked hard, and was cupping his balls like she owned them.

And right now, she did.

His eyes ran over her naked, perfect body while his cock was being caressed in her wet, hot, skillful mouth. Her moans drove the heat through his body and made his cock swell and thicken.

He reached for her pussy, his long arms a blessing, and groaned out a *yes* as he felt her moist pink folds. His other hand cupped a breast and loved the hard nipple he tweaked over and over.

Her eyes shot to his, desire thick and wanting.

"Will you come if I do this?" he asked, circling on her clit.

Her mouth fell off him. "Fuck," she cried.

Now his cock was out, he had to have his mouth on her. He grabbed her body, spun her and sunk down onto her pussy.

"Kurt, fuck!" she cried again.

God, she was heaven. Just as he'd remembered from weeks ago on the jet.

Sweet honey and nectar of the gods.

His tongue lapped as he sucked and slipped inside her. His hands gripped her hips as she shook with pleasure.

"Don't come," he ordered her.

"What? I have to." She gasped.

"No," he said firmly.

Lick.
Lap
Suck.

His fingers slipped inside her, his eyes on hers. "I want you to come on my cock. Hold off for me, sweetheart."

"God, Kurt."

"Grab your breasts," he said, licking as his eyes continued to hold hers.

"Mphff." She cried out as her nipples were pinched.

When her shaking became a tremble and his cock was screaming to be inside her, only then did he sit on his knees and pull her down to him.

"Lift your arms," he said. "Now grab the headboard and don't let go."

"I want to touch you."

Yeah, if she did that he was going to explode.

"Do as I tell you, sweetheart." His mouth dropped to her breast.

Time was up.

He had to get inside her.

Kurt gripped his cock and aligned it with her entrance.

"Thank fucking God." He moaned, as he slid inch by slow inch inside her.

Madison cried out, attempting to arch, but he held her hips firmly as he continued to go deeper.

"Take all of me, baby." He cried. "Yes, fuck, yes. Christ, you feel amazing."

"How am I going to come already?" she gasped, her body convulsing around him.

And she did. She came.

Jesus.

He hadn't even thrust yet, but her pussy gripped him as it vibrated around the waves of her pleasure.

Kurt dropped down over her, his mouth taking hers and, as their bodies connected in the way of lovers, a feeling rushed through him.

Mine.

No.

Fuck.

Yes.

Her hands let go of the headboard, but he didn't care. When she wrapped her arms around him, it felt right. Two beings couldn't be more connected than they were right now, and he never wanted to let her go. Not just physically.

God damn it.

When he lifted his mouth from hers and their eyes met, Kurt knew, as he spilled his seed inside her.

Madison was his mate.

But he couldn't bite her to bond.

That was the blood exchange he wouldn't risk.

His fangs edged out as he threw his head back and cried out his orgasm.

CHAPTER TWENTY-TWO

Xander walked down the steps of Nikolay Mikhailov's private jet and stopped when his feet hit the tarmac in Seattle.

The tall, square-jawed man with strong brows and short dark brown hair followed. He lowered a pair of dark glasses, covering the pair of deadly and sharp crystal blue eyes.

How anyone could smirk and scowl at the same time, he had no idea. But Nikolay had the art perfected.

Frankly, it was unnerving.

Meeting the mob boss in person had been a stark reminder to Xander exactly who he was in business with. A powerful and dangerous individual with more money than God, it seemed.

He'd done further researching knowing the Russian was heading to the United States and learned he was the fifth richest person in the world. Apparently. Either way, he had a shit ton more than Xander had.

Which meant power.

A language Xander spoke.

And respected.

And feared.

His security team stood around him—which seemed to amuse Mikhailov—waiting to escort him to the black SUV parked alongside the enormous black Russian jet.

Or maybe the guy just had resting-smart-ass face.

He'd seen enough of it today.

After enduring a long lunch with him and five of his *family* members—family my ass, or maybe they were, but Xander wasn't that familiar with the whole Russian gangster family tree—Nikolay had insisted he fly them to Las Vegas.

He'd been unable to hide his shock.

Very few people knew about the second location they had built in the desert city.

"Are we going gambling?" he had asked, feigning ignorance.

"Don't fuck with me, Tomassi. We're going to see your new plant. I have a feeling there might be some shiny new things I would like to buy," Nikolay had said, then blown his cigar smoke in his direction with the arrogance of someone who knew no one ever said no to him.

And Xander wasn't going to be the one to test him.

But it was a problem. He was juggling a lot of powerful people and their corrupt money.

As they got closer to delivering on the vampire enhanced soldiers, everyone wanted to be first.

And they couldn't be.

"Looks like you're further ahead on production than you've been letting on," Mikhailov continued darkly. "Let me make it easy for you. When I leave the United States, it will be with one of the new products, or your ashes."

Tomassi had felt his face pale.

"The decision is not purely mine," he had replied. "Nor are they ready."

Fuck you.

How had he known about Las Vegas?

While Xander had tasked his head scientist, Dr. Phillips, with creating the new lab in Los Angeles, the other plant had already been in production.

Las Vegas was his top-secret production line. He'd even kept it from Dr. Phillips.

While the scientist had been on board with learning about vampires and seeing what was possible when you paired their DNA with humans, Xander knew his morals would restrict them from moving forward with speed. He'd sensed his reluctance and realized he needed an alternative.

Not just because of Phillips, but because of the vampires. He knew they had been investigating BioZen and staking out their sites.

He needed to go off the books with this one. And sometimes as a leader, you had to find the right people for the job. So, a small team of new scientists had been provided with the research and data and they'd recruited trainers who were currently testing on volunteer soldiers.

These former soldiers had been let go by the US Army for a range of different reasons. Some of them were dropouts. Some rejects. They had no direction or hope and were looking for fast cash and a purpose.

BioZen had provided it to them.

Well, technically, Xander had.

Only the director and the small Las Vegas team knew about the plant.

So how the fuck did Nikolay know?

The Russian had merely shrugged. "Then your ashes it is. Shall we go?"

So, they had flown across the States, and he had shown him around the top-secret location, which was an hour out of the main city.

The building itself had a number of different areas, including accommodation for their test subjects and those rostered on to monitor them, training areas, and the laboratory where they did testing and research.

"I want to see one of them in action. Give me a demonstration," Mikhailov had said as they walked through the training area.

Xander had turned to Brian, the manager of the site, and nodded.

Not that he had a choice.

Not with five large Russian fuckers standing around like they were in an eighties movie, ready to pull out a bunch of Uzi's and let loose.

"I can bring Kane out. He is available. The others are undergoing treatment or asleep right now," Brian said.

"That's fine." Fury had roared through his veins as Brian had left to get one of the enhanced soldiers.

"Excellent," Nikolay said and had wandered around the room with his hands behind his back.

Cool as a fucking cucumber.

Xander had remained vigilant, his security standing stiffly nearby.

"Tell me who else will be receiving this product," Nikolay ordered.

Everything he said sounded like an order.

Xander crossed his arms.

"You know I can't tell you. I would be a dead man by morning."

The Russian smirked. "You might be. When you play in a dangerous sandpit, that is what can happen."

Fuck you.

The man then shrugged. "You can tell me, or I will find out."

How? How the fuck was he getting this information? There must be an insider. It was the only explanation.

Brian had chosen that moment to re-enter the room and interrupt the growing tension with one of the enhanced soldiers.

"This is Kane, otherwise known as subject seven. He had recently completed the treatments—DNA and blood transformation—and has started the testing phase," Brian shared. "He and all our subjects will require ongoing treatments. At least that's what the testing is showing right now."

"What's up?" Kane had said, eyeing the powerful men around them.

He had been confident, and it was deserved. In theory, he was over twenty-five times stronger than a human.

"Show us what you can do, Kane," Mikhailov had said. Ordered.

Fucking asshole.

In the corner, there had been a pile of concrete slabs. Kane had walked to them and lifted one.

"Impressive," one of the Russians had said. "But I can do that."

And he did.

Kane had winked at the guy and dropped his slab back on the pile. Then he had lifted two of them.

The huge Russian had rubbed his hand over the scruff on his chin and followed suit. He lifted them both, but with a lot more effort than Kane had.

"Impressive." Kane had grinned, taunting the guy. "Drop them."

He did and Kane had reached down, taking all seven of the slabs in his hands, and lifted them up to his chest.

"Impressive indeed," Mikhailov had said, now standing beside him as the men around them all cursed out their surprise.

Xander had seen the smile on the dangerous but stupidly good-looking Russian.

God, he hated him.

"Consider him sold, Xander. Pack up six months of the medication he needs. I will return for the rest soon."

Brain had turned, his mouth falling open. Xander had shaken his head at him.

"There is a lot more testing to be done before we can release them. These subjects are lacking in self-control and respect for authority. They are dangerous."

Mikhailov studied Kane, then turned to Xander.

"Is he immortal?"

"That is untested. Obviously, we haven't tried to kill one yet," Xander had said, keeping his voice low.

Nikolay had shrugged. "We will figure it out."

The fuck?

"You're paying millions for each subject. Are you just going to shoot him?" he had asked.

The dark smirk on his face was chilling.

"Unless you're my financial advisor, I don't think that is for you to worry about. Pack him up and have him ready for collection. I will return tomorrow." Then he had slapped Xander on the shoulder and turned, sending his men into action, opening the door for them to leave.

Now, back in Seattle, Xander felt one step closer to getting home. He'd never been so happy to see the Emerald city. "I have some business to attend to this evening." He spoke as the door to the SUV opened and Elizabeth stepped out.

Ah, yes. He'd asked her to meet him at the airport so they could '*go over some numbers*' on the drive home. This time, he had given her the choice. Not instructed her.

He smiled, pleased she had chosen to come.

He turned back to wish Mikhailov an enjoyable evening and froze when he saw the fire in the man's eyes. Eyes that were running up the length of Elizabeth's body.

Nikolay walked slowly and deliberately toward her and held out his hand. When she, looking mesmerized, lifted her hand, Xander watched as he turned it and brought it to his lips.

His jaw clenched.

"What is your name, angel?" Mikhailov asked in a smooth, low accented voice.

"Elizabeth," she replied, a blush hitting her cheeks.

Oh, hell no.

This was not happening.

"Elizabeth is an employee. We work *closely* together," he over pronounced.

Mikhailov didn't move. He continued to stare down at Elizabeth and ignore his very existence. Something Xander would have enjoyed just moments ago.

He cleared his throat.

"We should go. I will see you tomorrow, Mikhailov," Xander said, his arm on Elizabeth's shoulder, guiding her to the SUV.

Then she did something he wasn't expecting.

Something that infuriated him.

"What is your name?" she asked the Russian mob boss.

Nikolay held her gaze with such dark lust Xander had to fight the urge to look away.

"Nik," he replied, his accent thick as his lips almost curled into a smile. "You can call me Nik."

Ah, so he didn't want her knowing who he was. Xander's lips stretched into a small smile and the Russian's eyes slid over to him and narrowed.

"Xander will bring you to dinner tomorrow night," he said.

Dinner?

Anger rolled through him. How dare this man order him and his employees around?

There had been no plans.

He was just about to make excuses for them both when the man continued.

"I will expect your director to be there as well," Nikolay said to Xander, then turned back to Elizabeth. "Wear red."

Her mouth parted.

The fuck?

See that mouth, you prick? It will be my cock inside it in the next twenty minutes, not yours.

"A moment, Tomassi," the Russian said, basically dismissing Elizabeth.

She nodded and climbed back into the car.

Mikhailov took a step closer to him, the man's height overbearing and causing him to arch his neck.

"Lay one finger on that woman and I will slit your throat with one of the many knives on my body." He growled in warning. "She is no longer yours."

It was then Xander decided he was going to find a way to kill the man.

Because Elizabeth was *his* toy.

CHAPTER TWENTY-THREE

Ari squeezed Sage's hand as they walked through the castle halls toward the royal wing where the king and queen resided. It wasn't far.

Ari and Sage had been given a very nice suite near Brayden and Willow.

"I'm fine," Sage said, smiling up at him. "I think you're more nervous."

"I don't get nervous," he replied and glanced down as she giggled. He smiled privately to himself.

Love.

It did wonderful things to a male.

Despite the road he had just paved them, he'd never been happier or more content in his life.

Sage completed him.

They'd been invited to dine with the royal family, which he assumed was an olive leaf after their recent conversation.

Or not.

Knowing that Kate and Willow would be present spoke to the former.

At least, he hoped.

But regardless, he had made his decision.

The door opened as they neared, and Brayden greeted them. "Glad you could make it."

"If something happens with Madison, I may have to leave," Sage said, accepting the hug from Willow and lifting a hand to the queen.

It made Ari happy to see her fitting in with his family.

"Ari," Vincent said, shaking his hand.

"How is she doing?" Willow asked as Kate handed Lucas to him.

She was a wise female. She knew how important it was for him to spend time with his new great nephew.

They all walked to the living area and got comfortable.

Ari sat on the sofa with Sage beside him and bounced Lucas on his knee. "He grows more every day."

"And poops," Vincent said.

Ari shot the king a grin. "I remember when you did the same thing."

Sage let out a laugh.

"I forget how old you are sometimes." She laughed, pushing her finger between the baby's squished up hand.

"It is astonishing. Even for me, who was born a vampire," Kate said, taking Lucas. "It's time for his bed. I kept him up so you could say hello."

"Thank you." He smiled at the queen.

Willow nodded. "Trust me, it's best if he goes now before he starts howling like his father."

Vincent snorted.

"Get used to it, princess. Your own howler is coming soon," the king replied.

Ari had noticed the two often bickered, but he'd been alive long enough to know it was just the way the two connected. He suspected the king knew Willow respected him, but it was her way of dealing with being part of a monarchy after living in a free society.

Of sorts.

Free was probably a stretch these days. Humanity had a long road ahead of them.

As did vampires.

"Drink?" Brayden asked, holding up a crystal decanter of what Ari suspected was whiskey.

Ari nodded and spread his arm out behind Sage.

"*Mia stellina*, what will you have?" He still called her his little star.

"Do you have wine?" Sage asked.

"Pinot grigio?" Willow asked, standing.

Sage nodded as Lucas' nanny appeared and took the child from Kate.

Then the queen joined them, sitting on the sofa opposite. Vincent sat in an armchair beside her.

"Dinner will be served in about twenty minutes," Kate said, then glanced at the king. Vincent emptied his glass and placed it on the table in front of them. He leaned back in his chair and studied Ari.

So they were diving straight into the heavy conversation then, were they?

Ari rubbed Sage's shoulder to comfort her, as her hand slid between his thighs. Partnership, he realized. She was doing the same to him.

They were still learning so much about being mates.

Ari wanted her to have a big family.

She would lose her family in a few years now she was a vampire, although her sister was now a vampire living in Seattle with them after mating his new head assassin, Oliver. But her parents were human and in a decade at best they would be wondering why she hadn't aged.

For him, he had been alone for many centuries. If this was goodbye, and they were to leave and start their own dynasty, then he would.

Brayden handed them their drinks.

"I wanted everyone here for this discussion," Vincent said, direct as always. "Hence the dinner."

"I wanted pizza with pickles," Willow said. "But it was vetoed."

Sage giggled. "Not unhappy about that, I will tell you."

"You should have seen her lunch," Kate said. "I never ate that weird."

Vincent snorted. "Macaroni and sardines is not normal, Kate. Never has been. Never will be."

Ari cringed.

Kate shrugged.

"Don't worry, our chef, who is *not* pregnant, has been in charge of the menu," Vincent said. "But we digress, thank you Willow,"

She shrugged and sipped on a pink drink of some kind.

"I'm sure it will be delicious." Ari knew the king's chef had followed him around the world and was trained by some of the best chefs in Italy.

Vincent nodded.

"I want you to know that you were heard when we last spoke," the king said, reaching to fill his glass. "It was important to me to consult my family before responding."

Ari was not surprised, and yet he was.

Perhaps the winds of change were finally here. The king's father and grandfather had acted from fear. Vincent appeared to be using his damn brain.

Hallelujah.

Ari nodded. "I respect that."

"Of course, I told him how I felt," Willow said.

"Willow," Brayden growled softly and Ari couldn't help but smile.

Sage did the same.

"Filter Willow. Please. Just once," Vincent said, shaking his head.

"Once?" she asked, cheekily.

"Christ," the king replied, shaking his head. "And to think there is going to be a mini me walking around one day soon."

"Hey!" she cried. "Brayden—"

The prince shook his head. "I'm sick of defending you. If you want to poke the bear, you need to accept the consequences." Vincent fought a grin. "However, leave my child out of it, brother. That was a low blow."

The grin faded.

"You're right. I apologize," Vincent said, then added, "Brayden."

Willow rolled her eyes.

Kate shook her head, glancing across the table at him. "Life is not boring here, Ari. It's like I have three children."

He smirked.

"I can see that. But tell me, Vincent, what was the consensus?" Ari asked, eager to move the conversation on. "Of the discussion."

He felt Sage's body, which was leaning against his, tense. It was likely he was doing the same thing.

"We acknowledge you as a Moretti uncle," Brayden said, warmth in his eyes. "Inside and outside these walls."

The two had always been close, and he suspected the prince was happy to be the one to share the outcome.

Vincent nodded when his gaze moved to Ari's.

"You are free to announce it, or we can do it together. Whenever you are ready," Vincent said. "I agree it is better we are friends, not foes. This will bring change to all our lives over time, and I make no secret of being concerned. But the fact remains, you are family. You are a Moretti and I have no right to stop you from making that publicly known."

Ari nodded.

"This is also about correcting wrongs made by the kings before me. As regretful as that is to say," Vincent said.

Ari couldn't speak.

He'd waited fifteen hundred years to have his twin brother's ancestral line acknowledge him as a true Moretti.

It had taken him to stand up and demand it.

As with everything in life, nothing was handed to you. You had to speak up.

He hadn't given Vincent a choice. In reality, there never was one. It had been him stepping to the side to accommodate unreasonable fear and demands on him.

The three enormous vampires in the room all knew that.

But today the wrongs had been righted.

Time could not be changed, but they could move forward.

"You are Gio's children. I loved my twin brother, despite his actions and decisions. And I have always loved both of you. Now I can do that openly and our race can know you are my nephews."

Sage wiped tears from her eyes, and Willow pulled tissues from the box on the coffee table.

"Damn hormones," she muttered.

"I hope we will continue to work together," Vincent said. "These are troubling times, and your support has been invaluable."

"We are family, Vincent," Ari said. "Nothing changes in that regard. It may be your bloodline, but Sage and I wish to remain a part of this family and ensure the race is protected."

"Absolutely," Brayden said as the king and queen nodded.

"Sage and I," he tucked her further under his arm, "will create our own line one day. We cannot produce at the rate Gio did in the beginning of our race, so you should not fear this."

"And we will welcome your offspring with joy when they arrive," Kate said, her hands politely sitting on her lap.

Willow beamed at them.

Brayden stretched his arm behind her and clasped his hand over her mouth. It had Ari turning his head to the king, his eyes following a second later.

"What the princess is dying to ask, and knows she cannot," Vincent said, shooting her an arched brow. "Is that we would like to extend an invitation to you both. To hold your wedding here at the Moretti Castle."

"Should you choose?" Kate added.

Sage had asked for a human wedding. He'd agreed after taking her humanity without permission. Not only that, but he had been human once, so it had been an easy choice.

That and he'd do anything for his mate.

He'd waited fifteen hundred years for her, after all.

"Yes!" Sage shouted. Then her own hand covered her mouth as she turned to him in surprise. "Oops. Sorry."

Ari let out a laugh.

"I think that is a yes," he said, nodding his thanks to the king over her head as Sage threw her arms around him.

"Yes!" Willow said. "We're having a wedding."

Later that morning, they lay in bed, Sage sprawled over his chest after he'd made love to her.

"Do you think Piper will want to have a double wedding?" she asked.

Ari ran his hands over her hair and down her body, cupping her ass, then ran it up her back. On repeat.

"She might. But I don't." He answered her honestly. "I want this to be our day. I have waited a long time, *mia stellina*." He half sat, cupping her face. "I have to share you with so many people every day. I want this for us."

Sage smiled. Her eyes filled with love.

"I want that too." She kissed him. "I suppose I thought it was best to bring it up, as I know Piper will ask. You know what she's like. Like a bull in a china shop."

Ari nodded and raised his brows, getting a laugh from his beautiful mate.

"Remind her the honor has been offered to us because we are family. Piper is my sister-in-law, but she is not a Moretti, darling."

Sage lay down, and he drew circles over her breasts.

"Piper is a different bloodline to me."

He nodded.

"All vampires are," Ari explained. "You have the original Moretti blood running through your veins."

As a scientist, he knew she'd be working out the importance of his words.

"As do the king, prince, queen and princess." She tilted her head.

"Yes, but their blood was diluted by his mate. She was a vampire."

"Isn't that incest?" she gasped, and he laughed.

"No. By that point, hundreds of years into our existence, the parentage was far enough away. Then Frances mated Guiliana, and they had Vincent and Brayden. Giuliana, the queen, was changed and had a complete blood transfusion as you did, so they inherited Frances' blood without any further dilution."

"But I have your blood."

"Yes. The pure original Moretti blood," Ari said, running his fingers over her collarbone.

"What does that mean?" she asked, holding his eyes.

"That I am the most powerful vampire on earth. Vincent would have worked it out, but I made it clear," Ari said, his fingers tracing one of her eyebrows. "While our line, when we create life, will never be as large as Gio's, it will be more powerful."

"Oh."

He smiled at her expression.

"You are a female, so do not go beating up the others," he teased, kissing her lips.

"Never going to happen."

"Good. You're not a warrior, Sage. This simply means we're not the inferior extended family in this story. The House of Moretti will be powerful and able to stand in its own right and have a strong voice."

Something he had always wanted.

"I want you to find out how Willow got pregnant so quickly. It's unusual." He pulled her under him.

"Eager to knock me up?" She laughed.

"Yes, mate. I am. I want to see you swollen with our child," he said, as her legs wrapped around him and his cock slid inside.

"Yes," she gasped. "Do it."

"Over and over, my darling *stellina*. Now scream for me."

CHAPTER TWENTY-FOUR

Mate.

His worst fucking nightmare.

It was like a damn mating pandemic around here these days. After hundreds of years as single males holding orgies and being playboys, they were all dropping like flies.

Not that his friends looked unhappy.

Pathetic maybe.

Not unhappy.

Most vampires would be happy.

But not Kurt.

Others hadn't had the kind of childhood he'd endured. His father had been a violent and evil vampire. He had abused his mother regularly and Kurt had grown up knowing it was wrong, but thinking it was normal.

The worst part was his mother had healed fast, so no one knew. No one ever suspected a thing. He had been so little and powerless. Even then, his father had threatened to send him out into the sunlight if he so much as uttered a word to anyone.

Who would he tell?

It was just his mom, his dad, and him. And he was so young and scared.

As he grew, he realized how wrong it was. He became angry and counted the days until he was big and bad enough to do something about it.

When he was young, Kurt didn't understand about mates and how they couldn't be separated. Even when he did, he was still angry with his mother for allowing it. Still, what could she do? His father had been a huge vampire.

Which meant Kurt would grow into one.

And he did.

He grew into a strong alpha vampire who, one day, found the courage to tell his father to leave his mother alone.

The male had stood and walked toward Kurt. But he had been ready and building his fighting skills. His father threw the first punch, which he'd caught in his fist, and pushed him back against the wall.

"Think you're an alpha now, do you son?" he had said, then laughed. "Give it your best shot."

Kurt had taken a step back and warned him. "Touch her again and I will do more than stop you."

Afterwards his mother had said, "He wasn't like this when I met him." She'd said those words to him dozens of times throughout his life.

He'd begun spending less and less time at home by this point, so it took a few months until one day he caught him with his fists, and knees, on her again.

How could his father treat her so badly? She was meant to be the love of his life. His mate. A treasured female.

Females were revered in their race.

Still, it wasn't just his mother who had suffered.

Kurt had been punched, kicked, and spat on since his earliest memories. He had been a tiny child. Completely incapable of defending himself. His mother had howled from the doorway as his father lifted him up the wall, spat into his face, dropped him, and booted him across the room.

He couldn't remember what he'd done wrong. Or if he even had.

That first time had changed him. He had been terrified of his father. The man who should have been the one to protect him, keep him safe, and teach him how to be a good male.

And one day, mate.

Life had suddenly become terrifying. Nowhere felt safe anymore.

He'd withdrawn.

Even his mother had let him down by not protecting him.

Kurt knew his past had led him to become a warrior. He'd grown up with violence and had no doubt he could become like his father.

Instead, he used his fists and power to defend and protect those who couldn't help themselves.

And kill the fuckers who hurt them.

That last day, he'd heard his mother's cries from outside their house. He was a full-grown vampire by then. Larger than his father. He'd long stopped the violence against him, but not his mate. He was just clever enough to not do it when he was around.

That day he'd fucked up.

Kurt had seen red. He'd clenched his fists and without a second thought he vamp-sped inside, ripped his father off her, slid him up the wall and growled.

"I told you to keep your fucking fists off her."

When his father had spat back in his face, all the memories from his younger years had come flooding back.

"Go to hell," Kurt had roared, pulled out a dagger and sunk it into his father's chest.

Behind him, his mother screamed and clawed at his legs. He dropped the man's body to the ground as his life bled away.

The monster was dead.

There were two ways to destroy a vampire. A stab to the heart—or you could rip the thing from their chest.
Same-same.
Or good old vitamin D. Sunshine.
When he had turned, his mother had beat at his chest calling him a raft of names, asking why he'd done it. Which was just laughable.
He'd ripped her off him and put her on the bed, staring down at her and shaking his head.
"You never protected me from him, Mom. Never."
"He loved you," she said, as tears had poured down her face. "He just didn't know how. He wasn't like this when I met him."
It had taken a lot of effort not to scream or slap her in that moment. Never once had she apologized to him or comforted him. She never would.
Kurt realized he had to leave.
Watching her grieve a man who'd been violent and terrorized his childhood, was not something he was willing to do.
She would not last long without her mate. She may have been a victim, but so was he. His own mother had stood by year after year, from the time he was a toddler, and let his father beat him time and time again.
He needed to go and live his life.
Kurt had already been training to be a warrior and years later he'd been recruited by Craig into the Moretti royal army.
Choosing to use his violent tendencies for good, not evil, was something he reminded himself of every day. He was a powerful vampire. He simply chose to protect and serve.
That didn't mean he was suitable for a romantic relationship.

There was no way he would risk mating with a female and turning into his father. Those behaviors lived in his genes and could trigger at any moment.

Few vampires could stop him—with the exception of Craig and Brayden, and probably Ari Moretti.

If he harmed a female. And if they ever managed to find out.

Just like his mother, Madison would heal. She was his mate. He could never do that to her.

And there was a small window available to him to save her.

From himself.

The time between meeting your mate and bonding, where the connection was locked in, was short.

They had to find Callan and get Madison home and out of his life. Or if she was staying at the castle, then he would leave the king's army.

His entire life.

But he wouldn't become his father.

He'd rather boost his vitamin D.

Still, he couldn't deny his feelings for Madison were already increasing at a rapid rate. Watching her collapse, hearing her bones crack for no fucking reason, had messed with his brain. He'd felt useless and furious as he'd sat there doing absolutely nothing.

It was the same feeling he'd felt watching his mother be smacked around like a ragdoll by his father. Or when he'd gone deep within his mind as his father's boots had plowed into his little body.

He lay his arm over his head.

Madison made little sounds beside him as she slept. She had fallen asleep plastered over his chest after they'd spent hours pleasuring each other.

He ran his hand gently over her hair and gazed down at her beautiful, creamy skin.

She was perfection.
His mate was spicy, smart, sassy, and gorgeous.
If only he wasn't such a danger to her, Kurt would love to spend his immortal life with Madison. But the risk was too high.
After what she had been through already, she deserved to go back to her life and get on with her plans. Whatever they were. Kurt still knew very little about his mate. And it was better it stayed that way.
The interesting thing had been, Madison hadn't reacted to him as a mate.
Oh, she had been pleasured, but while he was fighting to keep his fangs in place, she had not.
Despite his need to flee, Kurt's need for her to acknowledge him was fighting against it.
He tightened his arm around her and sunk his face into her hair.

An hour later, Kurt had risen, as was chugging down some plasma in Madison's kitchen while she continued to snooze. He walked into the bedroom and leaned against the doorjamb, watching her lips wobble as she breathed.
It was adorable.
Her arm was tucked under her head, but he could see her sexy butterfly tattoo on the inside of her arm and for some reason that thing just hit him in the cock every damn time.
His phone beeped loudly, and she woke with a start.
"Whaaa-what the, where…" Madison mumbled, half sitting up and then flopping back down.
He smirked, then walked over to the side of the bed and sat. He grabbed the phone but didn't check the message.
"I've got to go to work." He ran his fingers over that damn tattoo. "Sleep. Rest."

"Hey," she replied with a sexy smile.

"Thank you," Kurt said, knowing this was a kind of goodbye.

She narrowed her eyes at him. "Thank you?"

Crap.

"Yeah. You know. For today. It was good."

"Good?" She sat up and ran her hand through her blonde curls, which looked sexy as fuck in all their chaos.

"You know what I mean. We've wanted to do that for weeks. I'm glad we did."

She shook her head at him and frowned.

"Right. So, thanks for the good sex. Are you going to leave a tip on the counter?"

His eyes widened. "Don't do that."

Shit, he had to go.

He hated seeing the pain on her face, but they were a hell of a lot better than bruises and blood. Madison would never know he was protecting her, and he had to be okay with that.

"I've got to go," Kurt said. He checked the message on his phone. It was from Craig.

Urgent. Get to the meeting room now!

Shit.

What the hell was that about?

Madison flopped back down on the bed and shook her head. "Fine, Kurt. Whatever. I should have known you were *that* guy."

"What the hell does that mean?" he asked, glaring at her.

She was the one showing no fucking acknowledgment of their mating bond. *He* was trying to do the right thing.

Mazzarelli, where the fuck are you? Get over here now. Teleport in. Craig telepathed to him.

What's going on?

Callan and a few of his friends just showed up.

Callan.

Callan?

The rogue vampire?

God damn it.

"Shit!" He growled, and Madison sat up in shock at his response. "Not you. Work emergency. I have to go." Then he held her eyes. "We will talk. After."

"Don't bother." She gave him the stink eye and flopped back down. The last thing Kurt heard was her mumble *ass* as he teleported out.

Yeah, he probably deserved that.

But he would bother. He just couldn't seem to walk away.

Fuck it.

CHAPTER TWENTY-FIVE

Callan, Ava, Noah, and Liam all sat in a sparse-looking meeting room waiting for someone to come and speak to them.

Callan felt like he was about to have a business meeting, not announce to the royal family that, oops, he was now a big fucking wolf.

Not by choice.

Those fucking scientists had done this to him.

He was still in a state of shock, but he'd been driven by pure fear and determination to get to the royal family.

After he'd changed, he'd clawed at the door while the others had argued about letting him out. Eventually, Noah had ripped it open and let him run.

And how he'd run.

For miles.

His thinking was different as a wolf than when in his vamp form. It was less about words than it was pictures. He still thought some words, but not as many.

And he felt.

A lot.

He felt the earth and the moon—God, how he'd felt the moon—and the ocean and the trees. He was one with nature.

Callan had a strong suspicion that the moon had triggered his change. But what did he know?

It could have been coincidence.

Liam and Ava were the only two now having mild pains. Noah was showing no signs. Other than the heightened sex drive.

They were quite sure after a long discussion on the bus that it was going to happen to them all.

Eventually.

God, he felt like a complete asshole.

But then again, he was even more of a victim than all of them. He'd been tortured and experimented on for months, and after *finally* escaping, he turned into a fucking wolf.

Had they shoved a bunch of canine DNA inside him? How the hell did that work?

Why had it taken so long for him to change?

The only thing stopping him from going a little insane was the sense of wonder and power he'd felt in his new form. *And* that he'd been able to shift back easily enough.

They'd arrived at the Moretti castle late evening and after answering a bunch of really uncomfortable questions and having to stand around waiting while the security officers talked to a bunch of vampires in their communications devices, they'd finally been escorted inside to this meeting room.

Someone had brought them a tray of fresh blood, which they'd all quickly consumed.

Callan wasn't sure what he'd been expecting, but they hadn't been turned away. Nor was there a red carpet.

He was about to drop a huge bomb on the royal family and all of them were worried about how it was going to be received.

Ava wriggled in her seat.

Callan shot her a look.

"What?" she asked, defensively. "Noah has an erection," she added, her eyes darting to his pants.

"Zip it, Ava." Noah growled, his voice low and serious.

"Just try to curb that," Callan waved his hand about, "Because it doesn't help any of us."

"I told you I needed some relief before we got here." She shrugged.

Liam groaned.

"Jesus, I—" Noah began.

"Stop," Callan said, hearing boots fast approaching.

Then the door opened and in walked three, no four, enormous Moretti warriors.

Including Brayden Moretti.

"Oh, my God," Ava gasped.

CHAPTER TWENTY-SIX

Kurt teleported to just outside the meeting room. He had no idea who was in there and there was an etiquette to these things.

Not to mention the real risk of landing on someone.

They didn't talk about that sort of shit on all those vampire movies.

He snorted to himself, then stepped into the room.

The room went quiet for a moment as Craig, Brayden, and Marcus acknowledged his presence with a range of glances, nods, and chin lifts.

Kurt froze for a moment as his eyes landed on Callan. The likeness compared to the sketch their team had done was spot on. But that wasn't what had stopped him.

He had three other vampires with him.

The tallest and largest male was Callan. Part of him wanted to fly across the room and rip the fucker's head off.

He'd hurt his Madison.

Craig's wide-legged stance and dark look gave him pause. And the fact Callan was just as much, if not more, of a victim. Plus, the male had clearly come to them for help.

If he put his feelings for his mate aside, Kurt found he had access to the compassion he'd always felt for the guy.

The others were interesting: a young female and two strong looking males of different heights. Not nearly as big as a Moretti soldier, but still sizeable males.

And they all looked a little like they were deer in the headlights.

He didn't blame them. The powerful vampires seated around them were the most intimidating on the planet.

"You've done the right thing by coming here, Callan," Brayden said. "We've been looking for you for nearly six weeks."

Callan rubbed the back of his neck. "I wish I had come sooner. It was a confusing and honestly terrifying experience," he said. "As soon as I opened the door and had my freedom, I just ran."

"I don't blame you, man," Craig said. "I echo the prince. We're glad you're here."

"But we have a lot of questions," Kurt said, crossing his arms.

The female let out a small, dry laugh. "Same."

They all stared at her for a long moment, and she didn't say anymore. Instead, she turned to Callan, who appeared to be the spokesperson for the group.

"So, you've introduced us to your friends," Brayden said and repeated them, so Kurt was up to date. He nodded his thanks. "Are they here in support?"

Callan shook his head.

"No," he said, shaking his head. "We're here for your help, but the truth is, I don't think you're going to be able to."

Ava, Noah, and Liam, as he now knew them, looked down. They were concerned.

"I think you better start talking, son," Craig said, seconds before Kurt was about to say *fucking spill it*.

He leaned against the wall and lifted the sole of his boot against it. Ready to move if he had to but getting comfortable in the meantime.

Callan ran a hand over his face and let out a sigh.

"When I left the science lab, I was on the run. Hiding. I needed blood, like all vampires, so found some clothes and acquired some money. I'm ashamed, but I stole because I didn't want to go home or anywhere familiar so those fuckers couldn't trace me."

A few of them nodded, understanding.

"Smart move," Kurt said, impressed with the guy's survival instincts. Even if it had made it difficult for *them* to find him.

Or rather, impossible. Because they hadn't.

Callan continued. "Then I found willing participants and bit them." He glanced at the three vampires sitting along the side of the board table. "These are three of them."

Three?

How many had he bitten?

Well, he'd been on the run for over a month, so potentially many more.

"As one would do for sustenance to survive," Brayden said, but what he wasn't doing was asking more questions.

Kurt knew Brayden. He was waiting for Callan to share his story.

But they were all wound up. He could feel the tension thick in the air as they reflected on Madison's infected bite.

They were about to get their answers, and likely a ton more questions with it.

A shiver ran over his body.

God, if Kurt hadn't met Madison that night, her neck may have healed, and she'd be out there on her own with no support. But then again, he wouldn't be fighting the pull of the bond he felt.

One to which she seemed fucking oblivious.

Which could be a gift. But is that what he wanted? To not have Madison in his life?

Isn't that your plan, douchebag?

Perhaps she would soon. He'd seen some vampires—males and females—need the truth of a mate thrust in their face before they'd see or accept it.

So he had a choice.

He could keep away from her now or tell her.

Heck, they'd enjoyed an amazing day of passion.

It had been more than *good,* but he wasn't sure he could bond with her and ensure he didn't become the same male his father was.

Madison was pissed with him.

That was better than her being stuck in a lifelong bond with someone hurting her.

As in him.

"There are others. At least a dozen. We need to find them. Urgently," Callan said.

They waited for him to say more and elaborate, but he didn't. Just as Brayden went to speak, the little female let out a growl.

"God, just say it," Ava cried. "He's a wolf!"

The room went deathly silent.

What the fuck?

"I'm sorry, what did you say?" Craig asked, tilting his bigass head.

Kurt dropped his foot as his jaw gaped open.

"A what now?" Brayden asked, stiffening. He was straddling a chair and leaned back, shocked. "A wolf? Did you say an actual wolf?"

Callan nodded, looking pale.

Liam rubbed his arm, looking super uncomfortable.

"Ava, fucking hell," Noah said, shaking his head. "He changed last night for the first time in front of us."

"Jesus." Kurt cursed, planting his hands on his hips and shaking his head.

"Holy shit," Marcus said, his eyes nearly falling out of his head.

They shared a look.

One that said, *is this what will happen to Madison? Or him?*

"On the full moon," Ava said, ignoring Noah. "It began happening a few days before and then he changed right on the exact full moon hour. We've all had the same pains Callan had leading up to it."

Pains?

What kind of pain?

"It's likely to be a coincidence," Noah said, earning him a dark look from Ava.

"We don't know," Callan said. "We have no idea what BioZen did to me. The other *side effect* is an extremely high sex drive."

Brayden shot Kurt a look.

She's my mate. He telepathed the prince, knowing he was reflecting back on his claims a few days ago. The attraction was from their bond. He assumed.

Brayden nodded.

But now, a seed of doubt had been planted, and he wasn't sure.

Had he been wrong?

Was Madison infected with whatever this was? Is that why she wasn't reacting to what he'd perceived as a vampire mate call?

"Tell us about the pain," Kurt said, crossing his arms as everyone continued staring at the four vampires in disbelief.

Putting his own concerns aside, he needed to know if the pain Madison had been experiencing was the same as Callan and the others.

The cracking.

The pain.

The collapse.

Could Madison become a damn werewolf?

He shook his head.

"Do you mean to tell me you're a vampire *and* a wolf? And that you can change between the two?" Brayden asked, shaking his head as he spoke. "Because you are sitting in front of me as a vampire, but Ava just said you shifted into a wolf."

Callan ran his hand through his hair, leaving it all mussed up.

"Apparently. Fuck, I don't know. It just happened. Those scientists… they did a lot of horrific things to me," Callan said, standing and beginning to pace. "That's why I'm here. I figured my body was changing about a week ago and that I may have hurt others."

He glanced at his three traveling companions.

"I retraced my steps and found those I could, convincing them to come with me," Callan added. "Shit, I was just trying to do the right thing here. I need help. So do they."

"Jesus," Brayden said, standing up behind the chair and spinning it. He pushed it under the table and ran a hand through his dark locks.

Kurt had never seen the prince so shocked. Then again, his own face probably mirrored it.

Craig and Brayden shared a look, and he suspected they were telepathing.

"How long were you…well, how long did you remain in wolf form?" Marcus asked.

Callan shrugged and glanced at the others.

"It was about two hours," Liam said. "When he came back—"

"Back?" Craig asked, his brows shooting up. "From where?"

"I had to run," Callan said. "Like needing blood, the urge to run was natural. Then when I returned, it took me a little while to will my body back to this state. Honestly, I wasn't sure it would."
    Everyone just kept staring at one another in disbelief.
    "There's something else," Noah said.
    All eyes fell on him.
    "When Callan returned, it was daylight."
    Holy shit.

Kurt kept pace with the prince, Craig on his other side as they headed to the medical center.
    "This isn't good," Brayden muttered. "So not fucking good."
    "No. It's fucking not," Craig said.
    "I need to tell Madison," Kurt said.
    "Let's speak to Sage and Anna first," Brayden said. An order, not a request.
    They'd left Marcus with Callan and Co. He was arranging security in the meeting room for the time being. They were being provided with more food, drinks, and other comforts until they worked out how they were going to proceed.
    "We'll need to turn the old rehab center into accommodation for them and keep them somewhat isolated," Brayden said.
    "We didn't isolate Madison." Kurt frowned, trying to push away his fears.
    Could she be a fucking wolf? As in, she might be undergoing some type of DNA change, like Callan had.
    All of them could.
    He was just trying to ignore the possibility.
    And... the fact she may not be his mate.

"We didn't know she was possibly going to turn into a fucking wolf," the prince replied. "She'll need to go into isolation as well."

Brayden was right.

"And we need to find the other people he bit," Craig said. "Fuck me."

On that… while Madison and he had still not shared blood, he had another confession to make.

Which meant he would be joining them in isolation.

This so wasn't working out as he'd planned.

CHAPTER TWENTY-SEVEN

"Good? I'll fucking *good* you. Stupid big sexy vampire," Madison muttered as she blow-dried her hair.

How dare he *thank* her? As if she'd ironed his shirt or baked him a damn cake.

"Good? It was fucking amazing!" she continued ranting.

What was Kurt scared of?

That she was going to pack her bags and move into his place and change her surname?

She wasn't a human female.

He needed to chill the damn hell out.

"Stupid muscly gorgeous incredibly hot damn male."

Not that she was intensely attracted to him or anything. Or that she felt things she'd never felt for anyone before.

She wasn't falling for him.

Not at all.

Okay, fine, she was.

But since waking, she had felt a strange pull she couldn't describe. From elsewhere. Was it home?

No.

Something different.

Madison flipped her hair over. It was hard not to admit that she felt a strong sense of belonging and being cared for by Kurt. But this new sensation felt at odds with that.

Then again, the frustratingly handsome vampire had made those flippant comments as if she was a hooker, so she was not going to tell him how she felt.

Ugh.

Her anger was back.

"Maybe I should've made him leave a nice grand on the bench." She snarled as the hair dryer roared.

She flicked her head back and let out a scream.

"The hell?" she cried out.

Kurt smirked.

"How long have you been standing there?" she asked, dropping the dryer.

"Long enough to know the going rate."

She huffed and walked off. "Go away Kurt. I am not interested in your dirty talk anymore."

His silence had her turning as she reached the kitchenette. It wasn't like him to not bite back. When she saw his expression, she slowed.

A chill ran down her spine.

"What?"

"Callan is here," Kurt said.

Her jaw dropped.

He was here?

Had they found him?

"That's... that's good, isn't it?" she asked. "Why don't you look like this is a good thing? Wait, is he dead?"

Her heart began pounding as Kurt slowly walked toward her.

"Callan is alive. He's brought some friends with him. Others he bit, as he did you."

"Oh."

"Sit, Madison," Kurt said, leading her to the sofa.

She frowned, sitting when he let go of her and watching him sit across from her.

"Why do I need to sit for this? You said he's alive."

Kurt's head bobbed up and down, then he scrubbed the back of his head, making her feel even more nervous at his obvious discomfort.

"We are moving them into the old rehab center. Now known as the serenity center. You and I need to go into a quarantine of sorts. We can stay in the center *or* in our own quarters. A guard will be on our doors," Kurt explained, as her mouth dropped open even further.

"Why? I've been here for weeks," she gasped.

"New information has come to light." Kurt leaned forward, his elbows on his knees. "Madison, the sensations in your body. We think we know what it is."

She stared at him, her body beginning to shake.

"Callan and his team have had them, as well."

She swallowed.

"Last night, at what appears to be the same time you collapsed, Callan... Callan... *fuck*. He shifted into a wolf."

What?

She let out a laugh. One of those *you're joking, right,* laughs. He didn't laugh. He just kept staring at her, looking pained.

Madison leaped to her feet. "Wolf?"

She stared down at him while he nodded.

"What does that...? Wolf? But... he's a vampire. I'm a vampire."

Kurt nodded, letting it sink in.

And it did.

Her mind whirled with all the discussions she'd had with Sage and Anna over the past weeks about how they had data showing Callan's DNA had been altered. They didn't know how it would manifest or if it was contagious.

In fact, they leaned heavily on it, not being anything that could be passed on to another.

Why would they?

Unless it was an animal bite.

Even then, as a vampire, she should have been able to heal.

Unless her genes were being altered by something in his blood? Hell, she wasn't a scientist.

She'd watched too many zombie shows, obviously.

"And everyone thinks it will happen to me?" She plonked back down as Kurt confirmed her question with another nod, shock spiraling through her.

Oh, my God.

She was going to become a wolf.

"Is he still a wolf?" she asked, feeling nauseous.

Kurt shook his head. "No, he was able to change back. At this point, he said he hasn't tried to shift back into his wolf, so these are the things the team will be looking at."

Madison gripped her stomach.

"What's wrong?" Kurt asked, sitting up.

She stared at him like he was a moron.

Er, I might be a fucking wolf.

What the hell did he think was going on? That she'd eaten bad chicken?

This was bad. Really bad.

Fear flooded every part of her body, and she started shaking.

"I'm going to throw up."

Kurt lay on the bed with Madison tucked under his arm.

It wasn't the position he was planning on being in when he left her earlier this evening. Nor when he told the commander he'd update Madison on the situation and then return to his own quarters to begin isolation.

Yet here he was, with her in his damn arms again.

He had comforted her after she'd thrown up and then broken down into tears of panic.

Understandably.

"Will I ever be able to see my mom again?" she had asked, tears drenching his t-shirt.

He had no answers about anything yet, and she knew that. Hell, what did he know about vampires turning into another sub-species?

Zip.

That's what.

Suddenly, he had a small insight into how humans felt when they learned their mate was a vampire and they had to give up their humanity.

Sage said it was unlikely he would shift. They had assumed at this point the infection was passed on by blood transfer—in this case the vampire bite.

Something they'd not done.

He'd been pretty unpopular when he told the team he'd fucked Madison today, but he didn't care. He'd also confessed she was his mate, and that Madison was unaware at this point.

What he didn't say was that he was now doubting that. His eyes hadn't changed—which was the confirmation of a bond. A black ring would appear around his pupils.

It didn't mean she wasn't. That usually happened right at the end of the mating dance, so to speak.

But learning that enhanced sexual desire was a side effect had given him pause.

A great big fucking pause.

It looked like Madison would be staying in the castle indefinitely until they had answers, and that could take months. If she was going to shift, she would do it soon.

"You'll see your mom. I promise," he had replied.

Liar. You can't promise shit.

"Did Callan say it hurt?" she asked now as he ran his thumb over her tattoo.

He tilted her head so he could look into her eyes.

"Maddy, you know it's going to hurt. You've felt the pain already. Do you want to move into the serenity center with them? It might help. You could ask them questions."

She sat up on her elbow. "Is that what you want to do?"

He shook his head.

She blinked at him, then began to move away, but he held her hip. "Where are you going?"

"That's your plan? Comfort me and move me in with the others? Then carry on with your life."

He growled low in his throat.

"If I wanted you in the center, I would simply order you there." He gripped her chin and tilted it so she was looking at him. "Fuck, I am trying to work out this insane situation just like you. Just like all of us."

The more he thought about her in there with all those other males, Kurt realized it wasn't what he wanted at all. Not with that increased sexual desire they mentioned.

As his mate—*probably*—Madison shouldn't, and couldn't, be interested in anyone else, but these were wolves, and he had no idea what that meant.

Had the rules changed?

Still, he wasn't keeping her from them. She deserved answers, and meeting them may help.

He didn't have a clue what this would mean for them if Maddy *was* his mate and she changed into a wolf.

Would the mate bond disappear?

It was one thing to know he had the choice to leave and protect her. It was another to think she didn't want to bond with him and would take another male.

Yes, he realized how fucked up and selfish that was.

Her entire biology could be changing and with it all the rules. Wolves lived in packs.

Kurt tugged her closer, pulling her up to his lips.

"I'm sorry. I'm just scared," he confessed.

Glistening eyes gazed at him, full of lust and adoration. He felt the mating bond.

Or at least he thought he did. Was it her wolf that hadn't yet surfaced just wanting fulfillment?

Kurt gripped her bottom and tugged her against his hard cock.

If she was his mate, this was the open door for him to exit and never bond again. Maddy could connect with the pack, and he could remain with the king's army.

Or he could fight and make her his.

But it didn't resolve his lifelong concern that he wouldn't turn into a violent mate like his father.

He wasn't like this when I met him.

Those words haunted him.

"I need you," she whispered.

Kurt pulled her skirt up and ripped her panties off, as Maddy climbed on his lap and undid his jeans.

His cock free, he lifted her and slid his fingers through her flesh as she held onto his chest.

God in heaven, she was slippery and ready.

She tried to press down.

"No," he said, moving toward her. "Hold the headboard."

"Oh, Christ," she cried as he positioned her over his face and began to lick her pussy. Her fingers dug into her thighs as she worked his tongue.

Lapping and circling, he dialed into her clitoris with vamp speed and relished as her cries filled the room.

"Kurt, fuck, oh my God."

Her orgasm struck, freezing her limbs in place as it vibrated through her.

"Come here," he ordered, lifting her down his body and over his now extremely damn hard cock. The look on her face was one of absolute pleasure. "You okay?"

"Yes," she said with a little laugh. "I've had worse moments in life."

He growled playfully and pulled her mouth to his with his hand on the back of her head.

"Take me inside, you little vampire," he said against her lips.

Madison's pussy gripped his cock the moment they connected, and slowly she slid down until he was deep within her.

"Now ride me. Ride me hard," he ordered, lifting her so he could suckle on her breast.

She sat up and flung her head back as her hot body stroked him fast and tight. He held her around the waist, his hands swallowing her petite frame as he let her control the speed and angle.

And hell, she did it well.

Then he needed to take charge.

He flipped them, pulling her underneath, and plowing back inside her.

"Hang on, little one, I am going to fuck you like I've wanted to since the moment I saw you." He thrust with all he had. "Scream for me, Maddy. Scream my name."

And as he slammed into her over and over, his body tightening, pleasure sliced down his spine, and spread to his balls.

Then he filled her with the essence of his desire.

Which only belonged to her.

Dammit.

Because if she wasn't his, he was fucked.

CHAPTER TWENTY-EIGHT

"There are plenty of rooms in here, so take whichever one you want," Marcus said as he opened the door to the serenity center.

Callan led the way, with the rest of his crew following closely behind him. This space was more modern-looking than the rest of the castle. At first glance, he noticed two living areas with a large TV screen, pool table and bean bags.

He wondered what it had been used for prior to their arrival.

"This main door will be locked, but we don't want you to consider yourself prisoners. That's not what this is," Craig Giordano, the king's commander, said.

God, he was a huge vampire.

"If I change again, I'll need to run," Callan said. "I'm not going to force it, but the desire was overwhelming. I can't say what will happen if I don't."

Craig nodded, crossing his arms. "I'll get one of the tech guys to install an emergency button. If that happens, press it and someone will teleport in."

"I'll get them on it now," Marcus said, putting his mobile phone to his ear.

Callan nodded his thanks and noticed the others had disappeared into their chosen bedrooms. He went to do the same when the commander spoke again.

"Look, man, for what it's worth, what they did to you. It's fucked up. We've been looking for you. As soon as we found out. Then when you ran, we still never stopped looking."

Emotion poured through him, making him close his eyes and look away.

Knowing that made a difference.

Marcus ended the call.

"Thank you. For all of this," Callan said.

"We'll do whatever we can to reverse this or deal with whatever it is, however we can. You are still a Moretti vampire. Never doubt that," Brayden said, joining them.

"Shit." He lay his arm across his eyes really hard. When he removed it, all three of them were standing there holding the space for him.

"I didn't know whether to come here. I hoped you'd help, but you could have told us to leave." He tucked his bag tighter under his arm.

Brayden shook his head, his hands tucked into his jacket pocket.

"Never. Our job is to protect this race and see it thrive. As the commander said, we never stopped looking for you. We will do our best to find the others, so we'll have our teams speak with you in a few hours once you're settled."

Two vampires entered the room behind them and when they unpacked some tools, he realized they were here to install the button Craig had promised.

"Wow. You work fast," he said to Marcus.

The vampire smirked. "You'd be surprised what we can do when we know there's a big scary wolf in the building."

Callan stared at him for a second and then cracked up laughing.

It was the comedic break he needed after all those feels. And hell, the vampires standing around him were all huge. He wasn't a small guy at all, but these males had height and width on him. And massive power. He felt it rolling off them.

He had no idea of the power of his wolf yet. All he'd done was run. But he had no doubt these vampires would be able to restrain him, even then.

Not that his wolf felt violent.

"Thanks." He grinned at Marcus. "I needed that."

"Callan," Brayden called as he turned to go. "We have another vampire here, who you bit about a month ago. Her name is Madison."

Callan searched his memory for the name, but it didn't ring a bell. He didn't necessarily know all the names of the humans or vampires he'd bitten along the way. The same could be said for any vampire or human out for a one-night stand or similar.

But it explained the feeling he'd been sensing since they'd arrived. He was still trying to understand it. Yet the name meant nothing to him, so he shook his head.

"Sorry, I don't know the name, but I'd like to meet her."

"Worked as a bartender in Seattle. Short blonde wavy hair," Marcus said.

"Oh yeah. Little cutie," he replied, nodding.

"Might want to keep those thoughts to yourself now. Looks like she could be the mate of Kurt Mazzarelli."

Oh fuck.

"That is why he looked like he wanted to rip my head off?"

"No, that's his resting warrior face." Marcus grinned.

Good to know.

The guy was as big as these vampires, but a little rougher around the edges. None of them were strangers to him. Their images were all over VampNet and they were famous for being the king's warriors.

"She might join you in the serenity center. Kurt is with her now," Craig said. "The decision is theirs."

Theirs?

Because he was her mate.

"Has Kurt bonded with her? Bitten her?" Callan asked, his eyes wide.

Jesus, if he had infected an SLC and the guy changed into a wolf, that would not be good.

Kurt was a well-liked—and by that he meant all the females crushed on the guy—senior member of the king's army. That was the last thing he needed on his conscience.

"No," Brayden said, then quieter. "At least not that he's fucking admitted to."

Craig cursed and shook his head. "I'll fucking kill him if he has."

"He hasn't," Marcus said. "I'd know."

The prince stared at Marcus for a long moment and then nodded. Callan figured Marcus and Kurt were close.

Obviously, they all hoped he was right.

"No one is going to blame you, Callan. This is BioZen's fucked up mess. Not yours," Marcus said, clearly seeing the way his thought pattern was headed. "Kurt will be protective of Madison, but that's normal."

Callan knew he was right, but it didn't lesson the guilt. There were so many things going on in his head.

He was a wolf.

He was under the king's roof.

He had potentially infected over a dozen others who may turn into wolves. Before they found him.

And they were out there feeding on others.

What would all of this mean for his future? Could he return to live amongst humans? Or had that time passed now?

Would he die earlier?

Was he still immortal?

Could he go outside in daylight in his vampire form or just as a wolf?

So many questions.

"We have a veterinary nurse here who we'd like to examine you," Brayden said. "Also, do you recall the woman who helped you escape?"

Callan nodded.

"Her face is etched into my memory. I owe her everything," he replied. "I owe all of you."

Brayden nodded once, a small smile on his face.

"Her name is Sage. She's now a vampire."

Whoa.

"Isn't she a scientist at BioZen?" he asked.

"Was," Craig answered.

"She mated with one of ours and is visiting from Seattle," Brayden said. "Looks like she will be staying a while now that you have all arrived. She'll accompany Anna, the vet, along with a medical doctor who is arriving tomorrow. They will work as a team to do what they can to help you."

Who knew the Moretti vampires had so many medical people on their team?

Especially given they never got sick.

"Get settled in and I'll bring the medical team over tomorrow," Marcus said. "That noticeboard over there gives you instructions on all the facilities in the center. You can order food from the kitchen twenty-four-seven."

As the three vampires left, along with the tech team who had quickly installed the promised emergency button, Craig pointed to it.

"Press it. Emergencies only. One of us will come," Craig said, and the door closed behind them.

Not a prisoner, he reminded himself.

This was necessary. Not to stop them getting out, but others coming in, until they learned more about what he was, and how he'd affected others.

And *fuck me*, he'd gone and bitten the mate of a goddamn SLC.

Just his luck.

CHAPTER TWENTY-NINE

"Poor fucking guy," Marcus said as they made their way back through the castle.

Brayden nodded and mumbled his agreement as he pressed his thumb against the scanner, let Craig and Marcus enter the operations room, then the door shut behind him.

The king sat at his desk, with his feet on the desk.

"Comfortable?" Brayden asked.

"I could do with a coffee," Vincent responded sarcastically. Then the conversation turned serious. "They secure?"

Brayden nodded, staying across the room. "Yup."

"You've all been exposed to him?" Vincent asked.

Brayden nodded as Ari and Sage entered the room, and sat near Tom, Lance and Ben, who were tapping away on their laptops.

Marcus sat and put his feet up on another chair. "We all have in one way or another."

"Marcus is right," Sage said. "I don't believe we need to treat this as an airborne or saliva-spreading contagion, because we know it's not."

Brayden nodded.

"His DNA was altered after weeks of treatment when he was with BioZen," she explained. "Our saliva doesn't turn a human vampire, but our blood does. I believe this is the same thing."

The king tilted his head. "So, the blood transfer is through the fangs during a bite."

It made sense. While the bite was more about tasting and imbibing blood, fangs excreted blood at the same time.

"Yes," Sage said. "The result from our overnight testing shows Kurt's bloods are normal. Madison's are showing a slight abnormality."

Interesting.

"I still recommend he stay in quarantine for now as time does seem to play a part in this," Sage added.

"And the priority should shift to finding the remainder of Callan's victims," Ari said.

They all cringed at the term, but it was accurate.

Ari stretched out his legs and Brayden decided to sit down for a change. He preferred to lean, but this was one of those take-a-load-off kind of conversations.

The whole fucking night had been.

"I never thought I'd see the day," Ari said, shaking his head.

While it was shocking for them to learn of a vampire shifting into a wolf, Brayden had no doubt Ari, as the sole remaining original, was the most surprised.

"You and me both," Vincent said.

"I feel for the guy," Craig said. "He never asked for this. None of them did."

There wasn't a head in the room not shaking in disbelief.

"So, what are we doing? We going to blow these fuckers up or what?" Marcus asked, and Craig's lips shifted into a smile.

Yeah, Brayden knew the commander wanted to eliminate them. He doubted the king would ever approve of it because of the relationships he was building with global leaders. It would just prove they were dangerous predators and not to be trusted.

They *were* predators, but they weren't animals. They used their heads... and sometimes weapons.

"We need to find a way to get hold of the rest of the data," Sage said. "With more information, we can help these vampires. Or it's just going to take longer to gather our own research."

Vincent let out a sigh and stood. "So, what's obvious is they are going to be here for the long haul."

"Yes," Sage said, although it wasn't a question.

"Can we trust they won't bite anyone else?" the king asked.

Sage shook her head. "No. No one can promise that. They told the prince and his team they were all experiencing increased sexual desire, which would explain why Madison and Kurt were unable to follow instructions to keep their hands to themselves."

Brayden fought a smile.

The little blonde was sexy as hell. Even as a mated male, he could see that. Kurt had no fighting chance.

His smile faded quickly. There was a long road ahead for those two. If she shifted into a wolf, who knew what that would mean for the bond, or if she would still want him?

He'd seen the worry on Kurt's face.

It was a serious situation.

If they bonded and she rejected him, that was the end. He knew Kurt—he wouldn't survive the loss.

The large vampire was one of his best soldiers. It was why he was an SLC. Brayden had never lost one of his males and if BioZen was the reason he did now, maybe Brayden would go all terminator on them and blow the fuckers up himself.

"Well, for now, they'll have to remain in the serenity center," Vincent said, and Sage nodded her agreement.

Vincent stared at everyone in the room. "Brayden, can we have a word? Ari, I invite you to join us."

Five minutes later, Ari and Brayden followed the king down to his office, Sage teleporting away.

"She's getting good." Brayden smiled at his uncle.

"She may have landed in the shower," Ari smirked. "I cannot remember having difficulty, but there was much more space in the year AD 500."

Brayden couldn't imagine the world that long ago. Then again, he was born just over five hundred years later.

They were all old as fuck.

Vincent didn't even sit when they closed the door to his office. The three vampires took up all the space despite it being a large office.

"This is difficult for me to voice, but I think we need to discuss it," Vincent began.

A chill ran through Brayden's body.

"Don't say it," Ari said, shaking his head.

"It's my fucking job to protect every vampire on this planet, Ari. I have to."

Brayden cursed and took a few steps away, and ran his hand through his hair. "I gave Callan my word that we would protect him," he said. "Don't make me a liar."

Vincent walked to his desk and sat in his large black leather chair, leaning back, then let out a long loud sigh.

"Bray…" the king started, then cursed.

Ari and Brayden exchanged a look which said nothing and everything.

"Just say it so we can all vote against it," Brayden said.

"Why does everyone think this is a democracy all of a sudden?" Vincent asked with a frown.

Brayden nearly smiled. "Then why invite us?"

"Because as the prince of this family, you're one of my advisors," Vincent snapped.

"Then I *advise* you not to even speak the damn words." Brayden growled.

Please don't say them out loud.

First and foremost, those vampires were Moretti vampires. End of story, as far as he was concerned.

Callan had endured months of cruel treatment only to escape and then find his way back to them.

If the Moretti royals were to turn their back on them, or worse...

"Think about it. This isn't going to stop with these four vampires unless we keep them locked up. And we know there are more. Now, I'm no scientist, but I doubt there is a cure," Vincent said. "There's no cure for being a vampire, and there won't be for a hybrid shifter."

Ari sat in one of the large chairs.

"Uncle?" Brayden asked.

The vampire shook his head. "This is why we never wanted humans to know about our species. They get a hint of power and there's always a bad outcome."

They all let that sink in.

"They don't deserve to die," he added.

Vincent's eyes moved to his.

"I'm not killing them. Nor will my males." Brayden spoke firmly, crossing his arms. "You want them dead? You will have to do it."

Vincent glared at him.

"Don't treat me like I'm a monster. I'm thinking about the big picture here," Vincent said darkly. "Like it or not, we are facing the start of a new species. When, or if, we release them, there will be more. A lot more."

Ari nodded. "There will."

"And fast. Not from procreation, but from being bitten," Vincent said. "We don't know how powerful Callan is or how other vampires will react to these new abilities."

Brayden pressed his lips together.

The king was right. There was so much to consider, and it had come as a big damn shock.

"Okay, yes, you're right. One the humans don't know about. Some of them know about us—your pals in *Operation Daylight*—but they don't know about the shifters. Yet."

"Good point," Vincent said. "We could use it as an advantage."

Ari nodded continuously. "Yes. Smart thinking, Brayden. As I said earlier, we need to prioritize finding the others. Then contain and control the spread."

All of them shared their agreement.

"Okay, I'll keep one of our teams on Tomassi, who is now back in Seattle, and the communications team will put out a notice on VampNet to bring these others in," Brayden said. "I know we have your support, Ari, but you have a business, and The Institute cannot keep backing us up."

Ari nodded.

"We need to increase the size of our teams. Especially the SLCs. Our senior team."

And God, he hoped he wouldn't lose Kurt.

"You do. I've approved it, so just do whatever you need to do," Vincent said.

Ari turned to him. "Why don't we run the Warrior Games like we did a few years ago?"

Brayden snorted. "You mean around nine hundred years ago?"

His uncle laughed. "Yes."

"What a great idea," Vincent said. "I recall those, even though Brayden and I were young vamps. They were legendary."

Brayden grinned. "They were indeed."

Everyone had aspired to win one of the coveted senior lieutenant positions in the king's army. To qualify, you had to be serving the king and do a physical test. If you passed, you became a participant in the Games where they competed with others.

Never had they run the competition for an SLC position, but as life threw out more challenges, Brayden believed Ari's idea would be a great way to bring more powerful vampires into his most senior team.

"Are you returning to Seattle?" Brayden asked his uncle, knowing the answer. No male left his mate.

"I'll stay with Sage. I can run The Institute remotely with Oliver and Travis' assistance. Would you like me to help run the Games?"

Brayden smiled. "Very much."

Ari nodded.

Craig was going to be love this. When he first joined the Moretti army, he had heard a lot about them and often shared his disappointment at never seeing them.

They were a mix of gladiator-style and Olympic Games. Challenging, yet far more humane.

"Okay fine. The wolves live. Keep an eye on Tomassi and you can have three more SLCs," Vincent said.

Brayden glanced down, shaking his head at words they had all left unspoken.

He would never have let his brother dispose of the wolf shifters. And frankly, he doubted Vincent was capable of it. The king's job was hard. Brayden knew it was Vincent's job to consider these things, but it didn't mean he had to like it or agree.

"Let's keep this conversation private," Vincent added.

"Indeed," Ari said, standing and nodding his farewell. "Ciao, nephews."

As Brayden turned to follow, Vincent stopped him. "Why don't we bring Xander Tomassi in? If you have him in your sights, it could be easier than getting inside his labs."

Brayden let out a dry laugh. "Sure, but if Kurt doesn't kill the guy first, Craig will."

Vincent smirked. "Well, if you get the information we need, that's one life I'm happy for them to take."

Brayden marched back down to the ops room to update his team.

He was pretty sure they were all going to be happy.

Especially Craig.

CHAPTER THIRTY

"That was Sage," Kurt said, slipping his phone back in his pocket, and leaning against the bathroom doorway to watch Madison slip on her panties.

He'd had worse moments in his life.

Although removing them from her might be even nicer.

She lifted her eyes to his as she fitted them around her hips.

"Hit me with it," Madison said. "Am I a wolf? A giraffe? What?"

He snorted and took a few steps, cupping her breasts.

"Pretty sure giraffes don't have these puppies."

"Argh, enough with the canine analogies." She groaned. *Oops.*

That had just fallen out.

"My bad." His thumb slipped over one of her nipples. "Sage said we're cleared to go to and from the center and our rooms."

"Uh, huh," Madison said, her hands roaming over his biceps as he started on her other nipple.

"I've got some meetings to attend while we're there, while you meet and talk to the others. Get to know them. Or you can stay here." He lifted her onto the counter and replaced his fingers with his mouth.

Madison groaned, and her legs parted as he pressed between them.

Fuck, he wished he hadn't dressed in such a hurry.

"Are you always this wet so fast?" he asked, his voice husky.

"No. I don't know. Maybe," she replied. "Touch me more."

He smiled and licked his way up her arched throat.

Dangerous.

He was itching to bite her. Instead, he gripped her face tightly and slammed his mouth onto hers, his tongue diving inside and taking ownership.

She tasted like toothpaste and fresh blood.

"More," she begged as his fingers lazily danced across her flesh.

Kurt took a step back and undid his fly. While he wanted to play, he had a meeting to attend via video conference with Callan in the center. But he had a few minutes.

He took his hard cock in his hand and stroked it a few times before lining it up at her creamy slick core.

"Ask and you shall receive, sexy." He pressed the head of his cock inside her.

Madison's body arched as she moaned out her pleasure.

His own desire roared through his body as he sunk deep inside her, thrusting and gripping her hips while she clung to his arms.

"Oh, fuck." She cried as he pounded over and over.

"Grip me with your pussy," he ordered her. "Yes, that's, oh, yeah, fuckkk."

He lifted her off the counter and carried her into the bedroom, then sat down on the bed. Madison stretched out her legs behind him, brushing the hair from her face.

"Fuck me, big boy." She grinned.

"I'm not a boy, sweetheart." He lifted her up and down his cock.

She grabbed his shoulders. "That's so damn true. Ohhh, shit."

"You like that?" He leaned back to get an even greater angle.

"Oh God, ohgod, ohhhhh." She cried out.

Kurt let her take over and ride his cock as he pressed his thumb against her clit and circled.

Her pussy clamped around his cock and the two of them came simultaneously.

As Kurt cursed, his body jolted, releasing his hot seed inside her.

Fifteen minutes later, he teleported them into the center. Madison stood close beside him, looking around the large space, and spotting a few of their new residents.

He hated how sexy she looked in her black jeans and tight Levi t-shirt. His insistence that she'd be cold and should cover up with a baggy sweater had earned him two eye rolls.

"Hey," Callan said, walking up to them and running his eyes up and down Madison's body.

The male had a death wish.

"How are you settling in?" Kurt asked, opting for polite instead.

For now.

"Good," Callan replied, glancing over his shoulder at the others in the TV room and smirking. "Some more than others."

"I'm Madison." She held out her hand. "Though we've obviously met."

They shook and Kurt glared as their hands touched.

Fucking mating bond.

"I remember you," Callan said. "You were one of the first I felt a stirring with when I bit you."

The fuck did that mean?

No one was stirring anything with his mate.

Kurt stepped closer to her and lay a hand on her lower back. She gave him an odd look, then turned back to Callan.

"Is that why you took off?"

Callan nodded.

Ava came out and reached out her hand. "I'm Ava. This is Noah and Liam," she said, as the others followed.

"Hey," Madison said, shaking their hands. "Nice to meet you all."

"Ask anything you want. It's kind of wild, but I guess we've had a bit more time to accept what's happening."

"I wouldn't say accept," Noah said, studying Madison.

Kurt forced his feet to stay put.

"Did it hurt?" she asked Callan.

He nodded. "A lot. But afterwards, it felt... powerful. Not saying I want this, but being in wolf form is not horrible."

Kurt studied him for a moment.

The male seemed, despite the circumstances, to be a well-rounded guy. It was clear from what he'd observed and heard that Callan wasn't someone who was at risk of doing anything stupid with this new development, but then again, they didn't know how it would evolve.

There was a lot of testing to be done.

"Have any of you had your bones snapping and the pain?" Madison asked as Kurt walked over to the digital screen in the common area and got it ready for their meeting.

"Ava and I have an arthritis-type pain," Liam answered and shot Noah a *fuck you* look. "Which we clearly know isn't that now."

"I blanked out yesterday," Madison said. "The pain was so bad."

Ava nodded.

"The full moon. The night Callan changed," Ava said, then tilted her head. "Have you been extra horny?"

Kurt gritted his teeth.

"Callan," he called out. "Meeting's starting in two minutes."

The vampire glanced up, back at Madison, then wandered over.

Eyes off.

"Yeah. I have." Madison glanced over at Kurt and, as he lifted the remote to the digital screen, he held her stare. "I thought..." she looked back at Ava. "Is it one of the side effects?"

All three of them nodded at her.

Fuck.

"We've been fucking like rabbits," Ava said, "I'm not complaining. I mean, take a look at these guys."

Liam and Noah both tried not to look happy with the compliment, but Kurt was a guy and saw right through their neutral expressions and bright, happy eyes.

He also knew exactly what they were thinking as they stared at Madison.

They had decided she was joining them.

Kurt started back over to the group to straighten that assumption right the fuck up when the screen came to life.

Dammit.

"Mazzarelli," Brayden said in greeting.

"Captain," Kurt replied.

"The doctor, Sage, and Anna are heading to the serenity center shortly. So let's get this underway," Brayden said as Craig and Marcus came into view, along with a handful of officers who would be taking notes and sketches after they took all the information from Callan today.

"We're escalating the search for these bitten vampires," Craig said, stretching his arms out on the table in front of him and gripping his hands.

It was a serious pose for the commander.

"So, let's start from the top and take it day by day as you describe where you went, who you met, and most importantly, who you bit."

Callan nodded.

They both sat down on the seats behind them, and Callan began to talk.

Out of the corner of his eye, Kurt could see Madison sitting in the living area with Liam, Noah, and Ava chatting, laughing, and getting to know her new pack.

All his stupid fucking insecurities were raging in his head.

So much for not wanting his mate.

If she was his mate.

He had started to feel more confident after spending the past day with her. Now his chest tightened with a sensation he'd never experienced.

This whole thing was so fucked up.

Maddy still had no idea she was his mate.

Sage believed he was not at risk as the shifter genes were passed on via blood. Still, they wanted to wait a few more days now the others were in the castle to see how he reacted before allowing him out of isolation.

He'd been happy with that because he wanted to stay close to Madison.

But he was still working, so he tuned back into the conversation on screen.

"Yeah, then I headed out near the park," Callan continued. "She was human. Because I'd run from Madison and not taken much blood, I needed more."

Callan began to describe what the woman and the dog she had been walking looked like.

"Okay, next day," Craig said, nodding at the two vampires taking down sketches while another Kurt hadn't noticed earlier was tapping on a laptop, taking notes and likely tracking locations.

He bet there were a few others in the room, too. Likely Tom, who often directed their tech teams.

Kurt's eyes drifted back to the living area.

The fuck?

His body tensed.

Ava was on her knees, sucking off Liam.

Jesus.

Vampires were sexual beings and yeah, he'd been to too many orgies and parties where this shit was out in the open. But an everyday occurrence, like this?

No.

One look at Madison and his blood turned cold.

She was licking her lips and watching them like she was a damn virgin on heat.

He stood.

Callan stared at him and then turned.

"Oh yeah, don't worry about them. It's part of this whole change, I guess," he said in explanation.

"What's happening?" Craig asked, frowning.

"Blow jobs." Callan shrugged.

Kurt didn't bother looking at the screen. He didn't need to. Craig was in his head.

Everything all right, Kurt?

No. Maddy's my mate. But... is she?

There was silence and then Craig replied. *You'll know. Just be patient. One day you will know one hundred percent.*

And if I want to rip these vampires into shreds because she is looking at them like she should be looking at me?

More silence.

You have to let her choose. This is confusing for everyone. Sit down.

Fuck.

He turned back to the screen and Craig's eyes held an order in them. He sat back down and when he looked again, he couldn't see Madison. She had moved.

His fists clenched as he tried to focus on the meeting.

Madison had more of her questions answered in the last twenty minutes than she'd had in weeks. She was so pleased she had come.

She was pretty sure Ava was topped up on Red Bull. The female seemed to consider this an adventure and, aside from the obvious tension between her and Noah—she wasn't sure if they hated each other or were possible mates—she wasn't at all phased with the fact she might turn into a wolf at any moment.

"What do you think about all this?" Madison asked Noah.

"It's a total mind fuck," he replied. The guy was extremely good looking and had broody down to a fine art. Selena would find him a great challenge. Whether she'd be successful was another thing.

Not that any of that mattered.

It appeared all of them would be off the dating scene for the foreseeable future. Except she'd had incredible sex with Kurt a handful of times today.

Lucky for him, he'd not called it *good* once.

What was confusing was the moment they'd teleported into the center her body had reacted. She likened it to watching porn. Even though she had no interest in any of the vampires, she was wet and her nipples ached.

"What happened when you collapsed?" Liam asked.

"It was the pain that knocked me out," she said. "Then I woke up and felt fine."

"We've all felt better since Callan shifted," Noah said.

"Still horny as hell, though." Liam laughed, rubbing his hand over his cock.

Madison laughed. But it was a nervous laugh. Not helped because she was sitting beside him.

Ava climbed onto his lap.

"Guys, we have company," Noah growled.

"She's one of us," Ava said, as Liam slid his hand under her top and gripped her breast. "You don't mind, do you?"

Um.

What was she supposed to say?

"Nope. Do whatever." Madison waved her hand around.

"Join in, if you want," Ava said. "Noah could do with a—"

"Ava, shut your mouth," Noah replied in a growl.

Okay, definite angry sex vibes happening there.

Ava shot her a grin and slid to her knees, undoing Liam's pants. Her mouth was around his cock before Madison could blink.

Liam let out a pleasurable moan while Noah groaned quietly in the seat beside her.

What the hell should she do?

Her body began to heat with need.

"Do you feel it?" Noah asked, his erection obvious in his pants.

She nodded.

"We've had time to get past the shame," he said, "but if you want to go somewhere more private, we can."

She swallowed. The burning in her body was beyond anything she'd experienced.

The need to fuck.

She needed to be touched.

From where she was sitting, she could see Kurt. He was in his meeting with the prince and helping Callan. Vampires weren't like humans. They didn't do monogamy unless they were mated.

It wasn't like that between them.

Was it?

Madison knew that once she was cleared, he was planning to send her home. There wasn't anything between them.

She nodded to Noah, and he stood, taking her hand and leading her down the hall.

Kurt tapped his hand against his leg over and over and over.

Callan glanced at him. "Everything okay?"

His eyes shot to Callan's. "Yes," he answered darkly.

Kurt turned back to the screen. Listened for about three seconds, then stood.

"No. I need the bathroom." He began to march through the center in search of Madison.

What are you doing?

Fuck off Craig. If she's my mate and fucking one of these vampires...

"Where is he?" He heard Craig's voice from inside the center.

Just great.

Kurt continued past the living area where Liam was moaning out his orgasm.

Jesus Christ.

Noah and Madison were missing. Well, he was now a dead man.

"Mazzarelli!" Craig's voice caught up with him and the vampire's enormous hand landed on his shoulder, stopping him.

"Let go of me." He growled at his commander as he turned.

"Take a breath," Craig said, his voice dark and low. "Think. You don't know how this is affecting either of you."

Yeah, he did.

He was feeling quite murderous.

"And I am not letting you kill anyone," Craig added quietly.

It was true, the commander could stop him. Not with his words. He was an extremely powerful vampire. One of the strongest in the world.

Brayden was considered the most alpha and powerful vampire in existence. So even if Craig had trouble stopping Kurt, the prince would be there in a blink.

In other words, without their permission, the vampire who had his hands on Madison right now would live to see another day.

For now.

"Let me go. Then at least I will fucking know."

Craig stared at him a moment and then nodded. "If I find him dead, consider yourself fired."

Fucking hell.

Words he never thought he'd hear in his life.

"Are you kidding me?" Kurt snarled at him. "He has my mate. Or possible mate. And you're threatening my fucking job."

Craig pushed him up against the wall. "These vampires are victims. You know that. I know you fucking know that. I also know what it's like to be in the haze of bonding with a mate. It makes you dumb as shit."

Kurt blinked.

"Madison may not know, and she may be under the influence of this… whatever the fuck this is," Craig growled.

"What am I under?" Madison asked.

Craig dropped Kurt to the ground, and they both twisted to face her.

"Do I need to stay?" Craig asked Kurt.

The vampire looked mad as hell, and Madison wondered what the hell had gone on. She'd heard her name as she walked toward them.

"No," Kurt said, walking to Madison and laying his hand on her lower back, leading her straight past the commander without looking at him.

Madison stared up at Kurt, but he kept his eyes straight ahead. She turned to see that Craig had disappeared.

He had possibly teleported out.

When they returned to the main area, she saw him sitting back down in his chair on the digital screen.

"What was that about?" she asked Kurt.

"Work stuff," he replied. "How about you join us?"

She stopped walking and had to lay a hand on his chest to stop him from shuffling her along. "I—"

"Did you suck him off?" Kurt asked, and her mouth fell open.

So, he had seen.

"It was too quick to fuck him," he added, and Madison felt anger blend with the sexual desire running through her body.

"Why? Do you need to know for your records? Isn't the medical team arriving soon?" she said, placing her hands on her hips.

He took a step closer.

"Answer the question," Kurt demanded, and she swallowed.

"No, I will not." She jutted out her chin. "What I do with my body is my business."

His eyes flared with fury.

Then the main doors to the center opened. Sage, Anna and, she assumed the tall male was Dr. Abbot who had arrived from Los Angeles, walked in.

"Well talk about this after," Kurt said.

His hand burned as he pressed it possessively against her back and guided her to introduce them.

Madison pressed her lips together.

Confusing damn vampire.

Well, she was over his Jekyll and Hyde routine.

Madison was ready to start making her own decisions.

CHAPTER THIRTY-ONE

Dr. Abbot nodded as he added the notes into his laptop and glanced up at Callan while he talked. Sage and Anna sat on either side of him.

"So, five weeks ago, roughly a week after you left the labs, the pain began?" Dr. Abbot asked.

"Yes, sir," Callan replied.

Sage shot Kurt a look, which he ignored. He knew his friends and colleagues were worried he had been affected or infected—they weren't sure yet—but he couldn't deal with everyone's feelings right now.

His own were all fucked up.

His eyes drifted to Madison, who had walked past the chair he'd held out for her and sat on the opposite side of the table.

Next to fucking Noah.

She had looked directly at him and blinked when he'd dropped into the chair, seething.

What sort of game was she playing?

Granted, she didn't know, *yet,* he was her mate.

Probably.

Jesus, this entire situation was fucked up. As if it wasn't hard enough to know if someone was your mate or not. Now he was dealing with a female with messed-up DNA.

Dr. Abbot looked around the table at the others. "And you've all experienced these same sensations?"

Nods.

"Anna," the doctor said, giving her the floor.

"Thank you, Dr. Abbot. Now we want to talk to you about other side effects and changes that you have been experiencing but perhaps haven't been completely aware of," Anna said. "As you know from the introductions, I'm a vet nurse and have studied animal behaviors."

Kurt's eyes narrowed.

He hadn't seen any of them scratching or sniffing each other's butts. They were still vampires, for damn sakes. Craig was leaning against the wall, and they shared a look. Their earlier encounter was forgotten.

"Can't believe I could be turning into a fucking dog," Noah said, shaking his head.

Callan glanced away and Kurt realized for the first time the vampire carried a lot of guilt. He had no reason to. He was as much a victim in all of this as any of them were.

"Sorry man. If I could turn back time," Callan said.

No fucking way.

Kurt wasn't letting him carry the weight of this.

"You would go back to the moment the assholes took you." He growled, then glanced around the table. "None of this is okay. Blame can be attributed to me if you want to go down that path. As one of the king's warriors, I should have stopped them."

"That's not what I meant," Noah said, shaking his head.

"No, you didn't. But we all feel responsible for this. Including Callan."

"What Kurt is saying is the blame lies with the humans," Craig said firmly. "He's right. And it is our promise that they will pay. With their lives."

Kurt knew Craig couldn't make that promise, although the big guy never said anything he didn't mean. All of them carried a heavy sense of responsibility for every vampire on the planet. It came down from the king whose purpose was to lead and protect their species.

His rulership wasn't about power. It was about service and longevity.

Seeing these beings going through something unspeakable—and hell, he could be joining them, though it was looking doubtful—was painful and frustrating.

"Well, if I end up a big scary wolf, I'm going to hunt them down and bite their asses," Ava said. Madison shot her a smile.

Craig leaned away from the wall and laid a hand on her shoulder. "I appreciate the need for revenge, Ava, but I want you to promise me—all of you—you will keep away from BioZen. They are dangerous and we don't know what weapons they have that can be used against our kind."

Ava swallowed.

"None of you are going near it," Callan said firmly and both Kurt and Craig turned to the vampire, then glanced at each other.

There was strength in his words, which wasn't surprising given his experience being trapped in the labs. Yet there was more to his tone.

It was laced with alpha energy.

When all four of the bitten in the room nodded their agreement, Craig's brows raised slightly. He removed his hand from Ava's shoulder and went back to his leaning spot.

Interesting, Craig said.

Very fucking interesting, Kurt agreed telepathically.

"Okay, so I have a list of questions here and we'll start from the top," Anna began.

"Well, obviously there's the sex drive," Liam said. "It started for me as soon as Callan found me again."

"Same," Ava said.

"Ditto," Noah added.

Madison cleared her throat. "And me."

Anna looked up. "Just today?"

Kurt stared at Madison across the table, but she wouldn't look at him.

"Yes, when I arrived in the center and met them."

Anna tapped her pen on her chin.

"Does the heat go away when Callan is not present?" she asked the other three.

They all shrugged. "We haven't really been apart. Not in great distance," Ava said.

"So it's a pack thing?" Anna half asked. Everyone stared at her, so she continued. "Wolves. They live in packs. There's an alpha who is the dominant. A little like vampires, but there is only one."

Craig cursed from across the room.

"Can... so... will we all have to live in the pack?" Madison asked, and this time she did glance at Kurt for a quick second.

The fuck she will.

"They're also vampires," Kurt growled. "Not just wolves."

"These are just questions, Kurt. So we can determine facts as they unfold. We don't know," Sage said, giving him a small smile full of pity.

Fuck that.

He stood and walked a few paces, then joined Craig against the wall. Madison shot him a look which he didn't understand. She looked lost, but mad at him. Did she want him to support her or leave her alone?

God, he was so fucking confused.

"The answer is we don't know," Anna said. "As Sage said, we'll be learning as this unfolds. Not all of you may shift as Callan has."

Madison nodded, turning to glance at him again. He hated the lost look in her eyes. He gave her a wink, and she blushed.

He wanted to be more supportive and understanding, but he was fighting the need to possess her as a mate. All the while he kept wondering *if* she even was his. Or this was just some wolf crap he was a side effect of.

And speaking of alphas...Maddy needed to understand he was very alpha.

All the SLCs were.

It was why Brayden and Craig had selected them. It had taken them a while to find their balance with each other due to the overwhelming dominance they all desired. But nature's way of things ruled.

Brayden was the prince and the most alpha fucking vampire he'd ever met.

Craig, a close second.

They'd all worked out their place over time, but that was centuries ago. Now they were a tight team full of powerful males who held great respect for one another.

When it came to females, and the vulnerable, they were very protective.

He let out a long, quiet sigh.

Which brought him back to his personal issue. He couldn't guarantee she would be safe with him as his mate.

So, did he walk away?

Did he demand she know she was his mate?

Or, who knows, it could be that she had been emitting some magical wolf sex scent that made him want her.

Madison Michaelson might not be his.

CHAPTER THIRTY-TWO

"Hey girl," Brooke said as she answered the phone. "How's castle life with all the hotties?"

Ugh.

Less fun that it had been.

"Great," Madison replied, and it sounded fake even to her ears.

"Okay no. I'm not buying that," Brooke replied, her voice firm and caring. "What's happened?"

Well, I just found out I'm probably going to turn into a wolf. The vampire I have been fucking is hot and cold... mostly hot... and I have no idea why I even care because it's not like he's my mate.

Right?

Because why were they reacting like this to one another? Most vampires shagged. Then shagged some more if they enjoyed it a lot. But with no strings attached.

Kurt was acting like she belonged to him.

Do I want to belong to him?

Now she was being crazy!

Oh, and then I met my... pack mates. And I want to fuck all of them. Like, I need to go back now and do all the things with them.

Madison grabbed a cushion from beside her on the sofa and hugged it. As if it was a substitute for an orgasm.

Which was unnecessary.

She could return if she wanted. Everyone had made it clear if she'd wanted to visit or move into the center, she could.

When she'd replied that she'd think about it, Kurt had almost snarled at her before teleporting her back to her room. Then he left.

Just left.

Okay, sure he said he'd check in on her tomorrow.

Fucking tomorrow?

So, he fucked her a handful of times. She found out she could be a damn wolf shifter. And a vampire. A hybrid of some kind… whatever… and Kurt just left.

Ass. Hole.

She couldn't go home to her mom. She couldn't talk to her friends about it. She was alone.

Again.

But she did have one option. Going back to the center.

What Anna said had been a surprise, but the more she thought about it, the more real it had felt. Madison had watched the others and seen the look in their eyes.

They all sensed it.

Though she hated to admit it, there was a connection between them. Perhaps it was because of what they were going through, but she didn't think so.

When Kurt had teleported her home, she'd felt a separation and pull that was new. The same feeling she'd felt when they had arrived at the center, not that she'd known then, but this time it was stronger.

She returned her focus to her friend. "Just problems with the project I'm here for."

"And you still can't tell me what it is?" Brooke asked.

"No. Sorry," Madison said. "I'm making friends though."

"That's good. Although I wish you were coming home," Brooke replied. "We miss you."

"Same." Madison meant it. So much was changing in her life. All she wanted was to sleep in her bed and pretend none of it was happening.

Well, mostly.

Despite her feelings, she knew she'd miss Kurt.

Lying in his arms yesterday, she'd never felt so safe, secure, and wanted. Even if it wasn't true.

He'd held her like she meant something.

"Selena is checking on your mom this week. I'll go in a few days," Brooke said. "I'm pretty sure I've put on ten pounds from all her baking."

Madison grinned.

That was about right. Her mom's love language was food.

"Do you think she's okay?" she asked. "It's hard to tell on the phone."

"I think so. She talks about you and your dad. But she's joined a Facebook group on cake decorating and that's keeping her busy. The kitchen looks like a MasterChef show."

She had?

That made her heart happy. "And you're reaping the delicious benefits."

"Yes, ma'am. It's a tough job." Brooke laughed. "Oh, my Uber is here. I better fly. Call me tomorrow."

"I will. Hugs," Madison said, feeling sad their time was up so quickly. "Love you."

"Love you back!" Brooke said as she ended their call.

Madison flopped back onto the sofa and tried to ignore the burning between her legs.

And failed.

Well, Kurt had made his statement loud and clear by leaving her, so it was time she made some decisions of her own.

CHAPTER THIRTY-THREE

Kurt teleported into Madison's room. "I apologize for—"

He looked around the empty living room and listened for the shower.

Silence.

Five steps and he was in her bedroom. It was empty.

Fuck.

There was only one place she could be. The only place she was allowed to go. The serenity center.

Craig had been right. She needed him.

God damn it!

The commander had knocked on his door an hour ago and invited himself in. Not that Kurt would ever turn Craig away. He may be his superior, but he considered him a friend. In fact, they were all family. A different kind than the traditional, but family, nevertheless.

"Look, I'm no therapist," Craig had said, putting his boots up on the coffee table.

Kurt had nearly laughed. The huge alpha vampire was as far from Dr. Phil as anyone could get. How his mate, Brianna, handled the brute was beyond all of them. But she had him wrapped around her little finger.

"But I've been instructed to speak to you."

Ah.

"Brianna sent you." Kurt smirked.

Craig nodded and rubbed his forehead.

"Look I'm okay, man," Kurt said, "I over reacted—"

"Yeah. You did," Craig said, his commanding tone returning. "However, as someone who went through a lot of confusion figuring out Brianna was mine, I get it."

God, that had been hell for all of them.

Craig and Brianna had been forced to fake their relationship when she was still human, so she could attend Willow and Brayden's mating ceremony.

The sexual tension had been obvious to them all, while the two denied their connection. In saying that, watching the fiery redhead drive the commander to near submission was highly entertaining for them all.

The problem was, Craig believed he'd met his mate hundreds of years earlier.

Turns out he hadn't.

Now Kurt was beginning to understand the anguish he would have gone through.

"It's all so fucked up. I never wanted to be mated. Never," Kurt said. He had never told anyone about his family and didn't want to dig through the past. "But in that moment when I thought another male had his hands on Madison, I was out for blood."

Craig nodded at him slowly. Knowingly.

"I can't claim her."

"You could talk to her," Craig said. "At least that's what Bri said I had to say."

Kurt shot him an amused look, despite the seriousness of their conversation.

"Yeah, I could. But what sort of asshole would I be? Any day she could turn into a fucking wolf. She had four vampires in there—one a hybrid—wanting to fuck her. Madison doesn't need me claiming to be her mate, when all it could be is a reaction to her over-enhanced sex drive."

Craig shrugged.

Yeah, not Dr. Phil.

"Or you are, and you give Madison the opportunity to tell you what she's thinking."

Jesus. Maybe Bri was rubbing off on him.

He had a point. But... "Then what? I say, great, we're mates and oh, by the way, I'm moving to Antarctica."

Oh.

Crap.

That had slipped out.

Craig frowned and leaned forward. "The fuck you are."

He didn't understand.

If he did, Craig would ship him over there himself. None of the males under the castle roof would tolerate a vampire who harmed females. And Kurt wouldn't risk it.

"It's easier this way," he said. "I'm not mate material."

Craig snorted.

"You think I am? I demand a lot in all ways. I'm controlling, possessive, protective and demanding. And she makes me be all considerate and shit."

Kurt let out a dry laugh and stood, running his hand over his head.

Watching him and Bri together was amazing to him. He'd never seen two people more in love. Okay, perhaps Ari and Sage. But that vampire had waited fifteen hundred years for love. It made sense the male loved his little scientist like she was the last female on earth.

And she was. To him.

Was that how he felt about Madison?

He'd been so focused on planning his escape, while trying to figure out if she was his, he'd not stopped to think.

He knew he'd kill for her.

And that was it. The truth of his nature.

Violent.

"You're a good man, Craig Giordano, but don't bullshit me. We're not the same. You know who I am. I'm dangerous and not someone who should be in a relationship with a female."

Craig's boots dropped to the ground.

"Okay, I'm out of my depth here, but you sound crazy. Do you think you'd be on my goddamn team if I thought you had the ability to harm a female? Or a human woman? Fuck that. You offend me and the prince by even thinking that." Craig growled.

Ah, no.

That's not what this was about.

Christ, how had this gotten so turned around?

Fucking hell.

"You don't understand, Craig." God damn it. The need to explain himself, forcing the words from deep within him. "My father… he hurt people. My mother. Me."

Craig went silent.

His commander's eyes bored into him, full of questions. Then Craig let out a curse and shook his head. "You never told me this."

Kurt shrugged.

They stared at one another for a long moment as the reality of what he'd shared sunk in.

It felt strange to share something he'd kept hidden from every living being for so long.

The shame, the anger, the fear of the little boy inside who had been so defenseless all rose to the surface. And yet, he just stood there, vulnerable and trusting the vampire he had known for so long.

"You killed him," Craig said, without question.

"Yes," Kurt said. "Eventually."

The enormous vampire sat and nodded at the other chair. Kurt flopped into it, knowing he was being ordered to share more. And strangely, he was okay to do it. As if he'd ripped the scab off and now needed to get it all out.

Not that it was easy.

Just that it was way past time that he did.

He leaned on his knees and shook his head, staring at the floor.

"It started when I was little. Barely walking. There was never a reason. He was just an asshole. My mother watched and never stopped him."

Craig just listened, but he could see the fire of fury in his eyes. The one all the warriors got whenever they heard of an innocent being harmed.

"I lay in my bed, day after day, listening to him hurt her while I grew taller and stronger," Kurt said. "Then I stabbed him. Right in his cold fucken heart."

"Good."

Kurt looked up.

He wasn't concerned the commander would question his act of murder, but there had been something else in his voice.

"You are not him," Craig said firmly.

"I don't know that, nor do you," Kurt said, shaking his head.

"Yeah, I do. This is bullshit projection. Its fear," Craig said standing. "Now, go talk to your girl. Because even if she isn't your mate, she's your friend. I reckon she probably needs one right now."

He blew out a long breath.

"And if I hear you say you're going to fucking Antarctica again, I'll knock your fucking teeth out."

Kurt grunted out a laugh.

They both knew his teeth would grow back.

"By the way. The doctor said you can probably resume work tomorrow. He just wants to review the bloods with Sage but looks positive," Craig said.

"Good."

"So don't be late." He teleported away.

Kurt let out a laugh and leaned back in the chair.

It had taken him ten minutes to decide Craig had some valid points.

Maybe.

He still wasn't sure he was capable of being a good mate.

He wasn't like that when I first met him.

Those damn words haunted him.

But he was Maddy's friend, and he hated that he'd left her alone. So, he'd teleported to Madison's, and she was fucking gone.

Kurt knew where she was, and the fact she had gone to them spoke volumes.

Suddenly, he didn't feel at all like her friend, and completely like a jealous and furious mate.

CHAPTER THIRTY-FOUR

Brayden rubbed his hands together and grinned. "Not going to lie. I'm fucking excited about this."

"Hell yeah!" Craig said, slamming his hands on his hips and stepping up the front of the room beside the prince. "Let's get this fucker."

All the SLCs, except Kurt, were crowded around awaiting instructions and this was one directive Brayden was excited to be giving.

"Obviously, our priority right now is finding the remainder of Callan's bite victims. The communications team are currently fielding calls from the posts they've put on Vamp-Net, so until we get strong leads, we can't act on anything," Brayden said. "Which means today we're bringing Xander in for questioning."

The sounds of '*Fuck yes*' filled the room.

They had eyes on Xander Tomassi, who was currently dining out with a group of people in central Seattle. The Moretti soldiers had the place surrounded and were ready to move in.

He might not be the only head of the snake, but Xander was one of them, and they were about to remove him.

Permanently.

"Ben, we are ready to go in T-minus thirty minutes. Let your boys know on the ground in Seattle we will have live camera feed and be operational ready at nine p.m. local time," Brayden said.

"Yes, sir." Ben nodded and pulled out his mobile device.

"Lance, the jet is firing up so get your team and head to Seattle to escort our new guest home," Bray instructed. "You'll bring the team back with you. Which team is it? The red or black team, Marcus?"

Their tactical teams were broken down into red, orange and black.

Marcus spoke up. "Red."

"Four of them will remain in Seattle on surveillance unless we want to outsource to The Institute."

Brayden shot Craig a questioning look.

"No, keep our guys on it," Craig confirmed. "Let's get a cell prepared." Craig nodded at Tom.

"Got it." Tom nodded back.

"Right, let's go. Tom, get your officers in here and let's get these screens fired up," Brayden said, as everyone moved into action.

And it was about damn time.

They'd played cat and mouse with this human for long enough. Now Xander was coming in and facing the dangerous vampires he'd been stupidly taunting.

"Need some help?" Ari said, stepping into the room.

Brayden grinned.

"No, but you can take a seat and enjoy the show."

Ari's lips stretched into a smile as he lowered onto a desk and crossed his arms.

Go time.

CHAPTER THIRTY-FIVE

Nikolay used one hand to swirl the clear, distilled liquor around in the crystal decanter. His other arm lay heavily on the table.

He was surrounded by members of his family and security—men less dangerous than him, giving the impression he was protected.

Laughable really.

His body was covered in weapons. A gun tucked in the back of his pants, a slim knife inside his shirt sleeve, his ankle pistol and one inside his jacket.

It was his reputation, one well-earned, which was his true weapon.

Nikolay Mikhailov rarely hesitated.

The only thing that had given him pause recently was the gorgeous black woman standing on the tarmac yesterday.

Elizabeth.

The moment he'd seen her, desire had rushed through his body straight to his cock. Her eyes had slid to his and the mix of fear and arousal had fueled the filthy thoughts percolating in his mind.

And those full lips of hers were so tantalizing he could barely look away. Her breasts would wrap perfectly around his cock as he slid through them.

Then she'd surprised him by asking his name.

Nikolay knew he scared women. Good girls crossed the street even as they desired his tall, muscular body, strong jaw and thick, long cock.

Elizabeth had shown in that moment a tiny glimpse of the spice that lay cleverly hidden behind her façade. She might be able to fool other people, but he was a master of the game.

He had played his father, Boris Mikhailov, who'd been the head of the Russian mob for decades. Nikolay saw what others didn't and it had been his wining hand.

Yes, he saw the naughty girl beneath Elizabeth's corporate attire, which is why he'd ordered her to wear red.

It was the first step in their journey together where he would force her to expose herself. She would be uncomfortable, and he would challenge every one of her boundaries.

He couldn't wait.

It had been a long time since he was this excited.

Nikolay was going to break her and fuck her.

And she would enjoy it.

As would he.

But first, he would make her wait.

Nikolay lifted the glass to his lips again as Xander Tomassi walked into the private dining area with his three bodyguards. They were skilled individuals, and he was impressed with their backgrounds.

Because, yes, he'd had them all checked out.

"Good evening," Xander said, taking a seat.

"Where is your team?" Nikolay asked, anger lacing his words. He had been expecting Elizabeth and the BioZen director.

If his demands had been ignored, someone would pay.

The man sitting beside him would be a good start.

He had zero interest in dining with Tomassi. After spending hours with him yesterday, he'd had quite enough of the man's inflated ego. The Italian pharmaceutical executive thought himself, incorrectly, quite powerful.

All he'd done was discover a new race—yes, Nikolay could admit that was quite a big deal—and undertake research on them without being caught. He also had some powerful customers, including him.

Who the other customers were, was of great interest to Nikolay.

It was obvious many of them were governments. Who else had millions for enhanced humans? Who else would have need for them?

Perhaps the Italian mob.

These were the things he needed to know. And which governments would be receiving delivery?

Either way, he would receive Kane in a few hours, and that put him ahead of the game.

"Elizabeth insisted she meet us here," Xander replied. *Likely so she didn't have to endure your slippery fingers during the ride over.* "As did the director. He has... concerns about meeting."

Nikolay raised his brows and affected a bored expression.

"He can explain. He'll be here soon," Xander said and lifted a glass of whiskey, which had just arrived, to his lips. "I understand Kane is ready for collection."

"Yes," he said, offering no more information.

Xander nodded and perused the menu. "Will you be heading back to Russia now?"

Nikolay's eyes lifted as Elizabeth walked across the floor to the table.

In a sexy-as-hell red dress.

"No," Nikolay answered, his eyes never leaving her body. "I have other business to attend to while I am in America."

The man kept talking but he blanked Tomassi out as he stood and greeted Elizabeth.

"Good evening," he purred, taking her hand.

'Ciao, Nikolay." She blushed.

She greeted Xander briefly as Nikolay led her around the table to sit on the other side of him. When she sat, he leaned into her sleek black bob and whispered, "You have pleased me with your dress choice."

Her head turned as he straightened, and their eyes met momentarily.

When he returned to his seat at the head of the table, he lifted his tumbler and watched her take in her surroundings. His eyes dropped to the heart-shaped neckline, showing off her ample breasts and slim waistline. The skirt of the dress had fallen just shy of her knees, but the slit up the side had told him all he needed to know about her mindset this evening.

If he was a gambling man, he'd put ten thousand dollars on Elizabeth having no panties on underneath. Which meant she could keep the dress on as she sat on his face later.

But he wasn't going to move that fast with her.

She would be begging him before he let her have the release she would crave.

His men kept Xander busy with idle conversation while he focused on Elizabeth. They were trained to observe and ensure his needs were met. Nikolay had made no secret of his interest in her, and that he planned to make her his.

He would know if Tomassi had touched her again.

"This is a very nice restaurant," Elizabeth said, filling in the silence. "Is this your first visit to the United States?"

"No." He smirked. "I have been here many times. In fact, I own property here."

"Oh," she replied, surprise in her eyes. "I moved over recently. I was offered a promotion within BioZen. I was living in Rome before this."

Clearly, Xander had brought her to America to continue as his mistress. He was surprised she had agreed.

Perhaps she liked being dominated.

Nikolay would enjoy finding out. He listened as he watched her plump lips move. They would be perfect.

Around his cock.

But strangely, he found himself enjoying her innocence.

Because, while he strongly suspected she would like his darker sexual tastes, she *was* innocent. To his way of life.

He wondered for a moment, as he glanced down the table full of people, if Elizabeth deserved to have that stolen from her.

Then when he turned back to her, the fire in her eyes nearly took his breath away. Was she playing with him?

He wasn't sure.

And he was never unsure.

A low growl slid from his throat as a need to dominate her overwhelmed him. A waiter poured Crystal champagne into her glass as he held those fiery eyes.

"I thought this might be something you would enjoy." He lifted his tumbler in a toast.

"*Grazie*," she replied and their glasses touched.

"*Saluti*," Tomassi said, reaching over the table with his own glass. "To partnerships and valuable employees."

Then the man made a big error. He winked at Elizabeth, and it sent a sliver of anger through Nikolay. Fortunately for Tomassi, they were interrupted.

A man in a hat, coat, and dark prescription glasses walked into the room. Nikolay knew the dark-skinned man was the director.

Who didn't wear glasses.

"Please, take a seat," Nikolay said, as the man began to remove his layers.

Cash Whitmore sat while one of his team poured him a glass of red wine.

"It is not safe for me to be here," Whitmore said, narrowing his eyes when he saw Elizabeth. "What is she doing here?"

Nikolay held his stare for a few beats and then turned to Elizabeth, who looked very uncomfortable. The man was a director of the company that employed her, after all.

His attitude was unacceptable.

"Perhaps you could powder your nose for a moment while we have a short discussion, Elizabeth," Nikolay said, standing and pulling out her chair.

It wasn't a request.

Her eyes darted everywhere.

Before she walked away, he lay his land on her back. "Elizabeth is my guest. When she returns, I demand she be treated with respect."

Whitmore raised a brow and shot a look of disbelief at Xander.

When Elizabeth disappeared, Nikolay sat back down.

"Let's talk then," he said, his tone turning dark and forceful.

"The board has approved the manufacture of a vaccine despite their shock at learning about the vampire race. However, we have a greater problem. Members of the US government have gotten wind of the work we're doing and news of the vampires," the director said.

Xander cursed.

"Who?" Nikolay demanded.

"That is none of your concern," the director responded, and Nikolay's trigger finger began to itch. He saw Alexi, his second in command, raise his brows, and he gave an almost imperceptible shake of his head.

"As I said, it is not safe for me to be here. I'm being watched. This changes everything. Not everyone in the White House is happy with what we're doing and there will be resistance. We need to proceed carefully, but with speed now."

Speed he was fine with.

"We need to control the narrative so we can release the vaccine and ensure we are profitable." Xander said, stress tightening his eyes.

The director nodded. "We may have to do that earlier than expected. I'm expanding the team. You will remain a senior member, but we need more people to get this done faster."

"I..." Xander began, looking incredibly displeased by his sudden demotion.

Nikolay nearly laughed.

"We will discuss this another time, Xander. Now, I must go." The director stood. "I understand you want to be prioritized, Mikhailov, but we have other clients with just as many guns pointing at our heads."

Nikolay watched the man pull on his coat.

"I'm not used to hearing the word no, Mr. Whitmore." He also wasn't used to being dismissed, but if the man was being followed by US agents it was in all their best interests to wrap up this meeting.

Fucking Tomassi. He should have given them a heads-up.

Damn amateur.

"I run a pharmaceutical company, Nikolay. Forgive me if I don't know the rules when dealing with corrupt government officials and gang members," the director said.

A few of his men sniggered as a smirk of his own let loose.

"Then let me share my best tip," Nikolay replied, swirling his vodka around in his glass. "There is no one more dangerous than the *Bratva*. I recommend you proceed wisely when deciding who receives your first shipment of the vaccine."

The director held his eyes while Nikolay drank the rest of his vodka, enjoying the fear he saw within them.

"Jesus fucking Christ," Xander cursed, shaking his head.

The director slapped his hat on and lay a hand on Xander's shoulders. "Call me tomorrow. We will talk."

"Yes, sir."

A large man who had been standing in the shadows stepped out and directed Cash Whitmore toward what appeared to be the back of the restaurant.

Then they were gone.

Nikolay stared into his glass for a moment, thinking. When he looked up, Xander was tipping his own drink up to his lips, before placing it on the table.

"When Elizabeth returns, we will leave," Tomassi announced.

Nikolay shook his head at the man's stupidity. It was like he *wanted* to stop breathing.

"She stays. You need to leave. I will be staying in my penthouse in New York awaiting news of the vaccine. You might want to find yourself a new finance manager."

"The fuck, Mikhailov. You can't just take her," Xander said, standing. A bunch of metal clunked as two of his men stood, guns at their side, and Xander's men stepped in, their own weapons lifted. "Fuck."

"Think carefully before you make another move," Nikolay said, leaning back in his chair. "She will have a choice. I'm not a monster."

Well, that was debatable.

"Ah, here she is." He gave all the men a sharp glance and the metal disappeared. Even the BioZen security did as he said.

"Oh," Elizabeth said as if sensing the tension at the table and not sure how to react.

Nikolay stood and moved behind her, protectively. Possessively.

"Your employer is leaving. It appears our party has shrunk. Shall we dine elsewhere? I know a good spot nearby."

Before she could answer, they all began to move out of the dining room at his nod. Xander moved with them.

"I need to grab my coat," Elizabeth said, stopping by the counter and signaling to a server.

"Xander. We shall speak again soon," Nikolay said, slowing to wait with her. Two of his men took a step forward, nearing the door as Xander's team exited the restaurant. Tomassi shot him a nod, turned, and followed his security outside.

"Boss, we've spotted snipers in the vicinity." Nikolay's head security guy spoke, his finger on his ear. They had men outside the restaurant, too, and he had obviously just received a message from one of them.

"Let's move," Alexis said from his other side. Nikolay nodded.

"Then let's go."

"What's happening?" Elizabeth asked, her coat slipping onto her shoulders.

"Put your head down and follow me," Nikolay said, wrapping an arm around her shoulder. The second they stepped out of the door, the world spun into action.

It happened so fast

Shots sounded out.

Fuck.

Xander was thrown to the floor as half a dozen men surrounded both of their security teams. Then they disarmed them with a skill that impressed Nikolay.

Something that was not easy to do.

Impress him, that is.

From the look on their faces, the highly trained former military men who'd been employed to guard Tomassi, and his own Russian team, were shocked.

And on their asses.

Then all Nikolay saw before the men disappeared with inhuman speed, taking Xander Tomassi with them, were black uniforms, huge guns and... teeth.

Fuck.

They weren't teeth. They were fangs.

These were fucking vampires.

"Oh, my God. They have Xander!" Elizabeth cried. "Call the police. We need to call the police."

"Let's move," he ordered his team, and directed her into his waiting Cadillac. When the door shut behind them, he sat, his heart thumping. "Straight to the airfield," he ordered, and the vehicle began moving.

"We have to help him," Elizabeth cried, shaking, and trying to open her purse—he presumed to get out her phone.

Nikolay lay a hand over hers.

"He's a dead man, Elizabeth. There's nothing we can do," he said. "Do you know about the project he is working on?"

She nodded. Her eyes were wide with fear.

"Were they..." she started.

"Yes. I can protect you, but you need to come with me now. To New York. There's no going back there now. Do you understand that?" Nikolay cupped her cheek as she nodded. "One way or another, I was going to make you mine."

He let that sink in for a minute, then continued.

"Say yes and I guarantee your protection and... pleasure."

Color returned to her cheeks as visible arousal spread across her body. Nikolay didn't wait for her answer. He knew that was a yes.

"Good girl."

He turned his head and stared out the window, grinning.

Game on.

These vampires were going to be a fun adversary to play with. Especially now he had Kane.

And while it was unfolding, Elizabeth could ease his appetite for subservient pussy.

CHAPTER THIRTY-SIX

Madison curled her legs under her and listened as Callan shared his story with her. She'd felt all the emotions over the past hour. Anger, shock, empathy, and sadness for what he'd experienced during his time in captivity at BioZen.

Now the tall vampire was coming to terms with the fact they'd changed the very essence of who he was.

He was no longer a vampire.

He was what everyone was now calling, a hybrid shifter. Who the hell did that to a living being?

Monsters—that's who!

She wanted to get in a car and drive over to the BioZen head office herself and rip them to pieces.

But she could be next.

"So Kurt found you?" Callan asked.

She nodded. "In the bar. We kind of hooked up."

"You didn't bite him?"

"No. So hopefully he won't shift."

"Madison, I think there's a strong chance you might become a hybrid, too. If that happens, and I do end up the alpha of the pack, I want you to know I will do everything I can to protect you. All of you."

Jesus.

"Wow. It's a lot," she said.

"Tell me about it." He laughed dryly. "But here's the thing. After being held captive and tortured—well, you just heard it all—and being freed, all I want to do is live my life."

He had a point.

"I can't change what they've done, but as long as I'm free, I'm going to make the most of it. If that means I change into a wolf from time to time, or whenever I want, then so be it. Those fuckers aren't going to control me anymore."

She blinked back the emotion that rushed at her.

"You are so strong, Callan."

He reached out and squeezed her hand. It was comforting and warm. A tear ran down her cheek.

"I hate they did this to you." She sniffed, wiping her cheek.

"Come here." He pulled her against him and wrapped big strong arms around her.

Madison felt safe and warm, something she'd been searching for forever. She'd felt it with Kurt, but there was always a sense it was impermanent with him.

Callan had just promised he would always be there. But there was something else. An underlying sexual buzz that she got from all the vampires in the center.

It was impossible to ignore, and a part of her didn't want to. Yet, her feelings for Kurt were equally dominant.

"You are a young vampire," Callan said, pulling back to glance down at her.

"Yes. How did you know?"

He frowned. "Not sure. I can... wow, I guess I can sense you."

She pulled back. "Like a mate?"

Was Callan her mate?

"I don't think so. I've felt something similar with the others, but not necessarily picked up the same thing."

"So, a new ability, maybe?"

He shrugged. "Perhaps."

She settled under his arm and rested back into the sofa, putting her feet up on the coffee table. "I wish I could go home. My dad died a year ago and Mom won't last long on her own." She suddenly wished she could talk to Kurt like this.

"That's a valid concern," Callan replied. "It's unlikely she has much longer, though. A year is a long time to live without your mate."

Madison knew that. It's why she had been planning her future. Now she had no idea what it would be.

"Yeah. I know. So, if we all become wolves, we'll be living in a pack? Here?" she asked.

His hand rubbed her arm.

"I don't think we can stay here. Not because we aren't welcome. Rather, it doesn't feel the right thing to do. I have some ideas, but I'm still working it out. We'll all talk about it as a group when the time comes." Callan shrugged.

She liked how inclusive he was.

She felt his strength and alpha vibes, but rather than deciding their future for them, he was going to include all of them in the decision-making. That was new.

Madison smiled and leaned her head on his shoulder, then bolted back up when her eyes lifted to the doorway.

Shit.

How long had he been there?

"Comfortable?" Kurt asked.

CHAPTER THIRTY-SEVEN

Kurt wanted to be mad with her. He really did.
And he was.
Mad and fucking jealous.
He'd teleported in and heard their conversation. Not on purpose. His vampire hearing had allowed him to overhear as he walked down the hallway.

Hearing Madison open up and talk about her life had been a surprise. Why the hell hadn't she told him about her mom being on her own? Or her dad dying?

Why didn't you ask, douchebag?

All they'd done was banter and fuck. He'd spent most of the time worrying if she was or wasn't his mate, not really hearing when she did try to tell him how scared and vulnerable she was feeling.

He'd heard the fear in her voice and had felt it deep in his chest.

Then, when he'd walked down the hall and seen the two of them curled up together in an intimate hug on the sofa, he'd seen red. His jaw had locked, and fists curled, but he'd forced himself to stay put.

It had taken Madison a few seconds longer than Callan to notice him.

"Comfortable?" he'd asked.

Her eyes flew open and the head she had rested on the hybrid's shoulder lifted.

"I thought you were working?" she asked, only moving slightly away from Callan.

Interesting.

Kurt was trying really hard not to jump to any conclusions. *Really* fucking hard.

"I thought you were at home," he responded, and noticed Callan was staying very quiet and just observing them.

Smart vampire.

"You left," Madison said.

He nodded.

"Yes," Kurt replied, his eyes shifting to the hand that was lying on her arm. He looked back at her and held her large blue eyes firmly. "We should talk."

Madison chewed her lip for a moment, and he wondered if she was going to reject him.

His heart skipped a beat.

Was she going to choose the pack? Or rather, was he right, and she wasn't his mate?

Soon, she would shift. They were all sure of it, and the male with his arm protectively around her could take her from him.

Permanently.

The wolf in her could be interfering, or completely interrupting, their mating bond. That was the other option.

If that was the case, he would need to fight for her.

But is that what he wanted?

Of all the vampires in the world for this to happen to, it was him. In theory, it was perfect. He'd met his mate and had the opportunity to walk away. He'd never have to face the possibility that he was like his father.

He could step away before a decision was made for the new pack's life and then return, never having bonded.

Craig would just have to accept his choice. And fine, he could break his fingers or whatever.

Like he'd give a fuck at that point.

His heart pounded as she watched him, full of doubt. If she was his, had he bonded with her more than he was admitting to himself? Because right now he felt really fucking uncomfortable.

Sounds of pleasure hit him from the other vampires down the hall. Kurt's head turned and then moved back to her, wondering if she had been participating in the orgy before he'd arrived?

Regret began to settle throughout his body.

She wasn't sure about him.

Fair enough, he'd given her no reason to believe she could rely on him. But Kurt suddenly wanted to be the male to comfort her, to make her feel safe and heard. He didn't want anyone else to be providing that for her.

Fuck it.

He took a few steps and held out his hand. "Come."

His alpha dominance pushed through his words, demanding she come to him.

If she was his, she would.

He wasn't sure who moved first, but Callan removed his arm and Madison stood, taking his hand.

"Enjoy the rest of your night," he said to Callan, giving the vampire a nod of respect.

Madison glanced over her shoulder at the hybrid. "Thank you for listening."

"You're welcome," Callan replied. "Anytime."

Not if I have any say in the matter.

Then again, Kurt was happy she had someone to go to if he ended up being a useless piece of shit like his father.

They walked out into the hall, and Madison stared up at him, her eyes full of hurt.

"You left."

"I won't make that mistake again. Unless you want me to." He lowered his mouth to hers, and teleported them back to his place.

CHAPTER THIRTY-EIGHT

"Good to have you back, Kurt." Brayden walked into the ops room the next night.

Craig had texted him to confirm the medical team had cleared him for work with one instruction: Don't bite anyone.

They were confident enough now, after reviewing weeks of his tests and the information gleaned from Callan and the others, that the change was passed via blood.

So, not airborne.

As long as he kept his fangs to himself, he could get back to work. And thank fuck, because Xander was now locked up in one of the castle cells.

His fellow SLCs grinned, and back-slapped him like he'd been away on a tropical island holiday for a month.

Unlikely.

"So does that mean I get to interrogate the science fucker first?" He smirked, sitting his ass on the edge of a desk.

"No. But nice try," Brayden said.

Kurt had read the latest team report. Priority one was finding the missing vampires. Next on the list was keeping their eyes on the BioZen locations for any changes.

But someone was going to be doing the interrogations, and they were all lined up for it.

"We need to find out who Xander was meeting the night we took him. One of the team involved with the extraction believes they were Russians," Brayden said. "Ari and his team found evidence that the head of the Russian mob, Bratva, are involved."

Oh, those mother-fucking Russians.

"The same fuckers who injected me when I was working with Oliver." Kurt cursed.

Brayden nodded. "Yes. Nikolay Mikhailov is a dangerous enemy. The interrogation is going to be important. Xander is a suit, not a warrior. He'll talk," Brayden said. "But I might just drag it out a little, after all the suffering he's caused our vampires."

Hell yes.

"Now, as we recently discussed, there's a lot happening, and our team is stretched. We need to grow the Moretti army."

Kurt could see why. The challenges they were facing now were more dangerous than ever before. Not only did they always have the vampire rebellion in the shadows wanting to take over the crown and create a democracy—which, if they knew what was going on behind the scenes, they would realize that was a *really* bad idea—they now had humans to deal with.

And they were a much greater threat.

They knew BioZen was going to do something with what they had learned from their research on Callan.

When or what was unknown.

Did they know what they were doing to Callan?

Did they have more vampires?

So many fucking questions.

Hopefully Brayden was right and Tomassi would talk because they had to get ahead of this. And more senior team members would be a great step in having the resources to act fast and pivot where they needed.

"You will have all heard about the Moretti games held in the early past of the last millennia. Recently, Ari reminded me of the trials the king and I used to watch as young vamps." Brayden grinned at the room, full of suddenly-excited faces staring back at him. They all shuffled in their seats, murmuring their knowledge. Only from rumors, as they were all younger than the two Moretti royals. "Qualifying vampires compete for one of the revered positions. We are looking for three more SLCs."

Kurt grinned.

They had stopped holding their annual ball after the rebellion had breached the castle security. Something like this was just what the wider team needed.

VampNet would be on fire, voting for winners and choosing their favorites.

"Ari has offered to run the games for us while Sage remains in the castle working with Dr. Abbot."

"Will you share the qualifying requirements?" Marcus asked.

Brayden nodded. "Ari will. Each of you will identify the vampires you believe could be contenders. My guess is most of them will already be in the Moretti army, but it's not a requirement."

Kurt watched as Marcus nodded slowly. He knew exactly who he was thinking about.

Charlotte.

This was going to be trouble.

"Females?" Marcus asked.

Oh hell. There it was.

"Everyone. I don't give a fuck what's between their legs," Craig said. "This is about skill and strength."

As it should be.

Their jobs were hard and dangerous and were getting more complex every day.

"It's not just SLCs we need. Vincent and I are reviewing the structure of our wider teams to see what other skills we need," Brayden said. "You know, like fucking medical people."

They all let out a bunch of dry laughs.

Because it was laugh or cry. Who the hell ever heard of vampires needing medical treatment?

Becoming an SLC had saved his life. It had been his goal as a young vamp, and when Craig had recruited him, he'd been able to be the warrior he'd trained to be and put it to good use.

Now he was beginning to see that he wasn't like his father after all. Just the thought of harming Madison made him sick. There was no way he would do it.

Perhaps there really was a chance for him.

For them.

As the meeting broke up, Brayden called him back.

"We're meeting with Callan and Dr. Abbot in a few minutes. I'd like you to join us."

"Sure."

"Callan requested the meeting," Brayden added, and now he had Kurt's attention.

"Do you know what he wants to talk about?"

"No, but I suspect it's about their future. Think about it. Would you sit in that center and let others make decisions for you?"

"Fuck no." He crossed his arms. "But what the hell does he think is going to happen? They can't leave."

Brayden put the cap on a whiteboard marker he'd been writing with. "No. It's likely he's been doing a lot of thinking and worrying. It's just a conversation. I think you should be there, given your relationship with Madison. I'd like your perspective."

Craig sat and kicked his feet out, crossing his ankles. "The guy is smart and more alpha than I think we are aware of, yet."

Kurt thought that too.

"Oh yeah, he's smart, all right." Brayden yanked a couple of weapons out of the back of his waistband and sat down. "So we work with him, not against him."

Kurt shrugged.

"He doesn't deserve to have his freedom removed because of this, but a world with vampires and hybrids? Fuck, it's pushing our luck to think we can contain that from humans."

They all nodded and sat with their thoughts for a moment.

"Yeah. Let's take it one day at a time. He deserves to be heard. Then we take it to the king," Brayden said. "Let's go."

Then they all teleported to the center.

CHAPTER THIRTY-NINE

Callan lay on the bed with Noah's mouth around his cock, Ava straddling his face, and Liam pumping into Noah from behind.

It wasn't a terrible way to spend a few hours.

"Yesyesyes," Ava cried as he dug his fingers into her hips and ground her pussy down and lapped at her.

Jesus, Noah could suck like a pro. He shot his hips up as the guy cupped his balls, but the strong vampire pushed him down. Callan could have thrown them all off him, but why the hell would he do that?

Ava pressed into his face, his tongue slipping inside her as the sounds of Liam slapping against Noah's ass filled the room, along with their moans.

As she cried out her orgasm, Callan cupped her breasts and pinched her nipples. She loved that.

His thighs widened as he felt his own orgasm building closer.

Talking to the medical team, especially Anna, was helping him understand what was happening to him. After shifting into his wolf and settling into the center, he had found himself becoming protective on a completely new level.

Was it the pack alpha kicking in?

He didn't know.

What he did know was he wanted Madison with them.

Sexually? Hell yes. She was gorgeous.

There was something holding her back.

Kurt, obviously.

Still, he couldn't sense a mating bond between them.

What he did sense was her desire to join in their sexual activity. With him and the other pack members. The heat was there in her eyes, but the relationship with the alpha vampire clearly stopped her.

Noah slipped off his cock and Ava spun and slid her mouth and hand around him, finishing him off.

"Come here," he ordered Noah, and the guy stood and walked to the side of the bed. Callan took his cock in his hand and stroked it.

"Suck me." Noah's voice was gruff as he pressed into Callan's hand.

"Say please," Callan smirked, then gasped as Ava began licking the end of his cock playfully. He was ready to come, and he needed to be deep down her throat.

Noah groaned. "Fucking please."

Callan leaned forward, knowing how much the male hated to beg. He was dominant, but he was instinctually learning how important it was to ensure there was a hierarchy in their group.

Pack.

He watched Liam pick Ava up and spin her around so he could fuck her from behind.

Excellent. This would get her deep-throating him.

"Fuck, that's good." Noah groaned.

"Ohmomnodnd," Ava said around his cock as another orgasm built within her.

Callan's brain was on fire. With Noah's cock in his mouth, Ava's mouth on his, he was losing concentration.

He wanted more.

Lifting off Noah, he reached for Ava. "On my dick now."

Liam pulled out and Callan slid down onto the bed. "In her ass."

Liam smiled and lined up on the bed as he positioned Ava on his cock.

Hell, yes. She slid onto him and placed her hands on his chest as Liam slowly entered her rear.

"Shittttt." She cried out, her eyes on his. "So glad you bit me."

He let out a half laugh as pleasure shot through his shaft and then he took Noah back in his mouth.

They didn't usually all fuck together like this, but the arousal had been building all evening and it had just kind of happened.

Callan was not complaining.

It was hot as hell.

Then they all began to come. He felt Noah go off and pulled off the guy—swallowing come was not his bag—and the vampire pressed into Ava's mouth to finish off.

They all knew each other now, so it was automatic.

Watching them while she rode his cock set Callan off. He gripped her hips and sat watching the sex show as he filled her with his own cream.

Liam growled out his orgasm, collapsing over her, and when Noah fell out of her mouth, she flopped onto his chest.

Fucking hell.

This was definitely one great side effect of their situation.

Would they all feel the same when their wolf kicked in?

Because somehow Callan knew it was going to happen.

Sooner or later.

And he wanted to be prepared for it to happen.

When Craig, Brayden, and Kurt teleported into the center, Callan was showered and ready to meet with the huge vampires.

He hadn't expected Kurt to join them, so this was going to make the conversation a little more awkward, but this was his future, and it was important he speak up.

"My lord," he said, greeting the prince.

"No need for that," Brayden said, slapping him on the arm and leading him further into the center. "Let's head down to the large meeting room."

Craig and Kurt followed closely behind.

"How are things going in here?" Brayden asked when the door closed. All three of them sat with their chairs pushed out from the table to accommodate their big forms.

"No one else has shifted yet, but my need to do so is growing. I spoke to Dr. Abbot about the urge last night," Callan said. "I'll need to go tonight."

Brayden nodded.

"The grounds are huge. You are welcome to go whenever you like. That button is always there, so you can call on us."

He'd learned it was programmed to alert all the SLCs and so if he pushed it, one of them would teleport in. Which was fine, but Callan didn't want to hold his wolf back. He needed to let it free.

When he chose.

Not as an emergency, but as a way of life.

When he said as much, they all nodded. Vampires were as much animals and predators as a wolf. Same but different.

"I appreciate your need to keep us contained in here, so no one bites anyone. I do. But I want to talk about the longer term."

Kurt shifted uncomfortably and Callan was very conscious of the way the vampire was watching him.

Whether he knew it or not.

"Carry on. You are free to speak your mind," Brayden said to him.

One thing he was beginning to appreciate about the Moretti prince was his pragmatic mind. He was a powerful warrior, but also smart and he used commonsense, from what Callan had seen so far.

"We can't stay here." Callan held up a hand, so the others knew to keep listening. It was a bold move in front of three powerful alphas. "I know we are welcome, and I cannot express my gratitude enough. But when the numbers grow, and they will as you find them, and their wolves appear, we will need space."

A lot of space.

The need to run and be in nature was stronger now.

"We need our own place to figure out who we are without risking others, any restraint *or* judgment."

Brayden had held his gaze the entire time and he could see his mind ticking over.

"Not to hide or contain us, but to allow us to thrive in our own world. To learn what we are," Callan said. "These vampires feel like they belong to me, and I know that's a hard thing to hear as my prince, but I want to be honest with you."

Craig cursed under his breath.

Callan pressed his lips together, but didn't apologize.

Kurt glared at the hybrid across the room.

No fucking way.

He was basically claiming Madison was his.

Like fuck she was.

"They are Moretti vampires," Kurt said. "Nothing will change that."

Callan turned to him. "Perhaps. Or maybe it already has?"

"Bullshit," Kurt replied. "The king—"

Brayden lifted his hand and they all fell silent.

"Kurt is right. This conversation is for the king," he said. "I hear what you're saying, but we all know this is uncharted territory. If this is how you feel, then we need to address it. But when it comes to staking claim on a vampire, the king or a mate are the *only* ones able to do that."

Yes. And Madison was *his*.

The problem was, she hadn't indicated she felt that way, and he still hadn't told her he suspected she was his mate. He didn't want to put that on her while she was dealing with the possibility of shifting into a wolf.

Like, one fucking big life change was enough for her, surely.

But he also hadn't asked her if she had engaged in sexual activities with the wolves and it had been eating at him. Now, hearing Callan claim Madison—and sure, all of them—were his, he snapped.

Kurt stood and planted his hands on the table.

"Tell me hybrid, have you fucked my…" *Fuck.* "Madison?"

Kurt hated that he was being disloyal, but he had to know. He had to hear it from Callan. If the male confirmed he had, Kurt wasn't sure exactly how he would react, but the look on Craig and Brayden's faces told him they wouldn't let him do it.

Fury burned through his veins as he waited for Callan to answer.

"Has she not told you?" Callan asked.

Oh, the fucker.

His brows lowered as his fangs edged out of his gums.

"Answer the fucking question." He growled.

"I'm not betraying her trust if she hasn't told you." Callan stood. "You need to speak to Madison."

Turns out he hadn't snapped before.

Now he did.

He leaped across the table, fangs out.

The world around them exploded. Craig jumped up and grabbed him. The prince stood, and the fucking hybrid began to shift into a damn wolf.

A loud howl filled the room as chairs flew in all directions. All three of them went into full-blown warrior mode.

"Stand down," Brayden roared loudly. A blast of his Moretti energy dominated them all.

Callan shook his head and growled at them.

"Jesus," Craig said. "Do you have a death wish?"

"One more warning, Callan. Stand the fuck down." Brayden growled even louder, taking a step forward and holding the hybrid's huge blue eyes.

Jesus.

It was rare to see Brayden in his full-blown alpha mode, but this was off the fucking charts. The air was throbbing with power and energy, challenging all of them to their knees.

Kurt took in the big black wolf in front of them and wasn't ashamed to admit how spectacular he was. The shift had happened so damn fast, there had been no warning.

Callan stomped his paws at Brayden, but wisely took a small step back, his tail wagging vigorously.

Brayden shot a look over his shoulder at Kurt. "You. Leave. Teleport right now."

Kurt raised a brow and glanced back at the wolf, shooting him an angry look.

"Last warning, Mazzarelli." Brayden growled.

The last thing he heard was Craig cursing.

Then he teleported to Madison's.

Her head shot up, surprised to see him arrive in her living room.

"You and I need to talk," he said, his voice on edge.

"What's wrong?" she asked, standing up, then her legs buckled under her as her body exploded and began to shift.

This time Kurt knew exactly what was happening. He'd just witnessed it.

Game over.

He'd lost his sexy little vampire.

CHAPTER FORTY

Callan stood as the king entered the meeting room. Which had just been put back together after shifting back into his vampire state.

Brayden had teleported away and returned with the king a few minutes later.

This was his first-time meeting with the Moretti king and while the male wasn't any larger than the prince, in fact slightly less broad in the chest—yet still fucking massive—there was an energy about him which left absolutely no question he held the absolute power of their race.

Callan could feel it like an energetic force rolling off him.

And that was off the back of facing Brayden Moretti head on.

Something he would never forget in his life.

"Your Majesty," he said, lowering his head.

"Sit," the king said, and he did. Now, being in the king's presence, he was becoming well aware of his place in the food chain. Not that he'd ever questioned it before, but the need to take a leadership role with those he'd changed was something he couldn't ignore.

"Before we start, I want to express my displeasure at what happened to you," Vincent said. "I know the prince has shared that you have our full support in whatever you need to recover. But I want to reiterate it."

Well, this was a good start.

"Thank you, Your Majesty," he replied.

"We're also committed to finding the others. Our team is on it full time as a priority. Obviously, we don't want them out biting others or feeling lost and alone," Vincent said.

Callan could feel them. As odd as that sounded, he could feel all of them.

He wanted them all together.

In fact, he sensed, if could just leave, he may be able to find them now.

"Brayden has also told me of your request," Vincent said, his eyes looking less happy now. "You wish to leave us and set up in a new location?"

"Yes, sir."

"And will you still consider yourself part of the vampire race? Part of my race?" the king asked.

Callan had to think about that.

"Are we?" he returned the question. "Do you acknowledge us?"

The king leaned back in his chair and nodded. "You would not be here right now if I did not."

Brayden, who had been standing, sat down in a chair.

"The medical team shared that you might want to form a pack and lead as their alpha. This would be natural," Brayden said. "Yet we need to establish a clear structure. You are still a vampire, and of our bloodline."

"I am also a wolf with, as you say, a need to protect and lead them. I mean no disrespect, but I cannot ignore my new instincts."

"Yet they are my vampires," the king said, power in his voice. "And that is not something I take lightly, nor would I simply turn my back on them and hand them over."

Callan thought about that and slowly nodded. "I highly respect and appreciate that as one of your vampires," he replied. "So then, can it not be both?"

As the two Moretti royals stared back at him, Callan suddenly felt a cold shiver run through him.

His head shot up.

"Something has happened." He jumped to his feet. "One of the..." His eyes darted to Brayden. "Someone has shifted."

The prince narrowed his eyes. "How do you know that?"

"It's Madison," Craig said, as he stood away from the wall he was leaning against at the rear of the room. "Kurt just telepathed."

"You're coming with me," Brayden said, taking Callan's arm.

The king stood.

"We'll resume this conversation after I've had time to think. Keep me updated." He teleported away.

"Let's go," Craig said, and a second later they were standing in a living room staring at a small white wolf and a crazed-looking Kurt.

"Hey, little wolf," Callan said, crouching.

Madison padded across the floor and rubbed up against his legs. "You're absolutely stunning."

"Mother fucker." Kurt cursed, but Callan was completely focused on his new pack member.

CHAPTER FORTY-ONE

Madison leaned into Callan's legs, finally feeling safe. He ran his hands through her fur, and she closed her eyes, finding comfort in the sensation.

Home.
Family.
Safe.

Then she heard Kurt curse and lifted her eyes to his.

He was hurt. But her wolf shied away from his anger and sunk further into Callan's warmth and soft words.

She had felt the moment her body shifted into a wolf. Of course she had.

It had been painful and terrifying.

Yet it wasn't the breaking and shifting of her bones, the sudden growth of hair, her head and face which completely contorted and reshaped, or the four paws which had been the shock. It was the feeling of being instructed to change, as if she had no choice, which was most frightening.

She hadn't known or had any warning she was about to shift; it had just *happened* to her.

Suddenly and without choice.

As the pain had dissipated, Madison had stood, panting, becoming aware she was a wolf.

Holy fucking hell.

She'd known this was a possibility and the past few days her body had given all the signs it was going to happen, but experiencing it was quite different.

She had blinked, trying to clear her eyes before realizing her vision was altered in this form.

Kurt had taken a step toward her, and she backed away, growling.

Why did I growl at him?

For some reason she hadn't wanted Kurt touching her. The male she'd been so vulnerable and intimate with over the past few days.

"Madison. It's me," he had growled.

She hadn't liked his growl. He was scaring her.

Kurt had teleported into her room, angry, just before she had changed, and her wolf did not like it.

She was sure he had triggered her shift.

"You need to calm down," Callan said, crouching beside her and lifting his face to Kurt. "Her wolf is submissive."

She glanced up and saw fury on Kurt's face. The vampire in her understood his frustration, but the wolf in her wanted him to stop.

She took a few steps away, behind Callan.

"It's okay, Maddy." He soothed her.

"Her name is fucking Madison." Kurt growled.

"Dude, I think you should listen to him," Craig said, crouching down as well.

They all stared at her for a while as Callan continued to run his hand through her fur and calm her. Her heart rate settled and her rump lowered to a sitting position.

"Good girl," Callan said, and she liked that. Her head butted his knees, nearly sending him flying, and he laughed.

A giggle lodged in her throat, but she didn't know how to laugh as a wolf.

She was starting to enjoy this.

Her eyes found Kurt's. He had sat down on the coffee table. She wanted to go to him, but the judgment in his eyes kept her at Callan's side.

She let out a little bark at him and his eyebrows raised.

"What is she saying?" he asked.

"I don't speak wolf," Callan said, laughing. "Maybe if I shifted, I would."

She tilted her head at him, wondering how she could understand him.

"Did your shift trigger her?" Brayden asked and nodded a greeting at Dr. Abbot and Anna, who had just teleported in.

Madison leaned against Callan and his strong hand landed on her back, providing the comfort she was looking for. The doctor asked as he and Anna crouched down in front of her.

"Oh wow. You are beautiful," Anna said. "I hope you can understand me. You're white and fluffy with pretty green eyes."

"She is beautiful," Kurt said softly, and her eyes lifted to his, her heart thudding in reaction to his words.

Would he accept her?

He looked unhappy.

Her heart sunk and when he stood and walked away, a whimper escaped her throat. She lowered to the floor.

"Jesus," she heard Callan say. "What an asshole."

Perhaps he was.

An hour later, after the doctor and Anna had observed her and she let them touch her a few times, with Callan there as protection, she was coaxed back into her vampire form.

Anna quickly covered her with a blanket and she burst into tears.

"Oh, God." Anna ran her hand up and down Madison's arm. "Are you okay? That must have been terrifying."

She nodded, as she felt Callan's hand on her back.

"You all right?" he asked.

Her head just kept bobbing as concern surrounded her.

"Why did I change?" she asked, even though she had heard all their conversations.

"We were hoping you could answer that," Dr. Abbot said. "Was there anything that triggered it?"

"Kurt teleported into the room angry. My wolf got scared."

"You were protecting yourself," Callan said.

She looked around, even though she knew Kurt had disappeared. He had told her he wouldn't leave her again, and he had.

"Can you give us a minute?" Callan asked, and she realized Brayden and Craig were still there.

"We can go to my bedroom," she said.

Brayden stood. "No, we'll leave you alone. We will be back later."

All four vampires teleported away. They walked to the sofa and sat really close. It shouldn't have felt wrong after she'd been rubbing up against him as a wolf. But now she was a vampire, it didn't feel right.

So that was confusing as hell.

"Buzzy, right?" Callan said, referring to the shift.

"Yeah," she said, letting out a laugh. "Painful, crazy, but one of the most amazing feelings in the world."

"You didn't want to run."

"No." She shook her head. "I just wanted to stay beside you. Obviously. God, what a dumb wolf I am."

Callan grunted out a laugh, but she didn't feel his judgment.

"I don't think you're dumb. It's scary. You were surrounded by some of the most powerful predators on earth while shifting into a little wolf. And you were little Madison. My wolf is about four times your size."

She raised her brows at him.

He shrugged. "I'm just saying you shouldn't be ashamed of how you reacted."

Madison tugged the blanket around her. She wasn't necessarily ashamed, more surprised. She could hold her own around them as a vampire and yet she'd become so submissive as a wolf.

Worse, she'd been scared of Kurt.

"I didn't like it. I should have bitten him or something," she said.

Callan laughed. "You and me both."

He didn't even ask who. It had been obvious.

Tears filled her eyes.

"Is he your mate?" Callan asked softly.

"No. I wondered if he might be, but if he was, surely he would never have been able to leave me so vulnerable with other males. You and I both know that," she said, a tear sliding down her cheek.

He wiped it with his thumb and cupped her face.

"You aren't alone. I want you to know that," he said. "I am speaking to the king about our pack moving away from the castle."

Our pack.

"Somewhere safe where we can run in nature and discover who and what we are now."

She nodded.

"Will you come with us?"

Did she no longer belong with the vampires? Fear sliced through her as her world wobbled on its axis. If Kurt wasn't her mate, and she was no longer just a vampire, then did she have a choice?

Although she wasn't sure, she nodded.

Because perhaps it was the right path to take and would soon feel right. After she grieved the loss of the vampire she had begun to believe, in the last day or so, might be her mate.

Callan smiled.

Then his eyes dipped to her lips and his mouth lowered, laying a gentle kiss on her mouth.

Madison closed her eyes as her mouth opened to his and his arms wrapped around her.

"I've been waiting patiently for you," he said, "We can return to the others, or it can just be us."

Her body reacted to his words, her pussy flooding, and the need rising once more. Callan tugged the blanket and she let it fall, exposing her breasts. His mouth dropped and began to suckle on her nipple.

She moaned.

God, it felt great. She had been drawn to him sexually, and all the members of the pack, for days. Yet, as his hand ran down her side and made its way between her legs, she froze.

Madison pulled away.

No, this was wrong.

"I can't." She tugged at the blanket and covered herself.

"You need time." He stood, nodding. "I get it. You thought he was your mate."

She shook her head.

Not because he was wrong, but because she was confused.

She wanted Callan to touch her. She wanted Kurt to love her.

Why couldn't it be both?

Why was the need for both pulling her in opposite directions?

And did it really matter?

Kurt had walked away, in front of everyone, and made it clear he didn't want her.

He didn't claim her.

Eventually she would have to go with the pack. That was now becoming obvious, but she needed time.

"Give me a few days. I need to speak to my mom. Call my friends," she said. "Then I'll… I guess I'll make a decision."

"Take your time." He took a step forward and kissed her once more.

She closed her eyes, enjoying the taste of him and yet, it just didn't completely feel right.

Not wrong.

Just not right.

And that was confusing.

CHAPTER FORTY-TWO

"So, that happened," Brayden said, as he and Craig took a seat in Vincent's office.

Craig shook his head. "Never fucking thought I'd see that."

Brayden snorted. Never in a million years. "No, what a mind fuck. Still, she is a beautiful wolf."

Craig just kept shaking his head.

Vincent walked over and sat on the arm of a chair and crossed his arms.

"Callan is right. We can't have this happening in front of other vampires." He looked up as Ari walked in. "Oh good. I felt you should be in on this conversation, given the circumstances."

Ari had been updated on the evening's event.

"Is Madison okay?" Ari asked before sitting on the sofa beside him.

"Yes. She's in shock, but she's being looked after," Brayden replied. They had left Callan with her, but he planned to return after their meeting to check on her.

"Not by Kurt," Craig muttered. "Fucking idiot."

Yeah, that needed to be sorted out. His behavior was clearly that of a mate, but he wasn't claiming her. To leave Madison with all the males around her was strange at best.

"He doesn't believe she's his mate," Craig said, as if hearing his thoughts. "I know we were all stupid when it came to figuring out our mates—"

"Speak for yourself." Ari grinned.

It was true. Out of all of them, Ari had been the least stupid. Craig and Vincent were equal contenders for first place. At least, as far as Brayden was concerned.

"Kurt thinks the wolf pack is creating the sexual attraction, not a vampire bond," Craig continued.

"Is it?" Vincent asked. "He might have a point."

Brayden shook his head.

Not after the way Kurt had attempted to attack Callan. He had known Kurt for too many years to know the cool, calm and collected vampire would react like that over a female.

The guy had a female fan club full of choices.

Madison was his mate. No doubt.

"No. No way," Brayden said.

"There's history. Family shit," Craig said. "I won't break his confidence. But let me talk to him."

They all nodded.

"Now," Vincent said. "Let's discuss the future of what appears to be a vampire-wolf hybrid race. Jesus, like I don't have enough on my plate."

Ari shot him an amused glance.

"I'm sure they are sorry for the inconvenience, brother," Brayden said, rolling his eyes.

Vincent updated Ari on the request from the pack leader, as they were now calling Callan, and they bandied back and forth on the pros and cons.

In the end, it was decided Vincent was right.

"I agree. Having them shift into wolves while we are learning more about them in the castle isn't wise," Ari said. "And you can't keep them locked up. It's been a week and already Callan wants out. That says it all."

Vincent nodded.

"We have that property in Greenwood. The house is big enough for at least thirty people. The surrounding land is enormous," Brayden said. "Plus, it's just under two hours' drive away."

"True. It's close enough that we can visit regularly to keep an eye on their progress and provide any regular medical care," Craig said. "Makes sense."

The property was set up for the royal family to escape to if their race was exposed to humans. Well, that had happened when they were in Italy last year and they had moved to the Tuscany property.

Now they had a different strategy.

Vincent had a relationship with world leaders, ensuring their militaries would not be rushing to eliminate the vampires.

At least, that was the theory.

They had other properties nearby if needed, and the one he was recommending was the better one for the shifters. It was large and had miles of forest land surrounding it, making it secure and private.

"Sounds perfect," Ari said.

"We will need to put some rules in place," Vincent said. "They are still Moretti vampires. I appreciate the nature of a wolf is to form a pack, but I want to speak to Callan again before they leave to make sure he is clear I am still the king."

They all nodded.

"I'll go break the news. Craig, you go sort out lover boy," Brayden said. "Then we're going to visit Xander in his cell."

It was time to get that asshole talking.

CHAPTER FORTY-THREE

Kurt ran along the lake, the same path he'd run with Madison just a few days ago.

She wasn't his.

She had been terrified of him and run—padded—to Callan when she had sought out protection.

Fuck.

He leaped over a fallen trunk and flew along the path.

Fucking fuck.

"Jesus!" He yelled, his feet nearly smoking as he came to an abrupt halt.

Craig stood in his path.

Kurt froze. "What's wrong? Is she okay?"

There was no need to ask who.

"No. Her fucking mate just walked out on her. She's not okay." Craig growled.

Kurt frowned. "Callan left her?" His fists clenched as his breathing began to regulate after his run.

"Can you be more of an idiot?" Craig said, rolling his eyes. "You! You damn moron."

He shook his head and began to walk away.

So, this was an intervention.

Kurt had been part of these many times in his life when he'd seen a fellow vampire lose his path in bonding with his mate.

"Madison is not my mate. We all saw that," Kurt growled.

And yeah, he'd been hurt and embarrassed.

For starters, females didn't reject him and they certainly didn't cower from him. For fuck's sake.

He wasn't his fucking father.

He'd made damn sure of that.

And yet, watching her hide behind Callan had been too fucking much.

It was everything he'd never wanted to see on a female's face. One he... loved.

Loved?

Did he love Madison?

Christ.

He stopped.

"Oh good. The idiot has worked it out," Craig said.

Kurt turned and stared at the commander.

"Callan left her?"

"Okay, let's start from the top." Craig rubbed his face. "*You* are Madison's mate. *Callan* is still with her. *You* left. Now, get your ass back to her and start groveling."

Kurt blinked.

Craig just told him to grovel. To a female?

"I know. Don't tell anyone I said that. It's just easier. Saves time. Trust me on this." Craig nodded.

He loved Madison.

Callan was with her?

Alone.

"They're alone?" he asked.

Craig nodded.

"Fuck." His eyes widened. That fucker was with his mate.

"Go," Craig said. "And Kurt?"

He looked the commander directly in the eye. "Bite her. Forget the medical people, forget the risk. If she's your mate? Bite her. I have a strong feeling about this."

Kurt only half took in his words, but nodded, and muttered some kind of agreement. Then he teleported outside her room and knocked

.

CHAPTER FORTY-FOUR

Brayden walked up to the cell doors and stared at the pathetic human cowering on the bed.

"You can't keep me here. I don't care that you aren't human. This is illegal," Xander yelled at him.

Brayden reached up with his arm and leaned against the bars.

"Are you fucking kidding me?" He laughed. "You kidnapped our vampires and kept them in laboratories so you could do research on them. Often torturing them."

"You are lucky you aren't dead," Craig said from beside him. "If I let you out, you'd last ten minutes before someone ripped your fucking head off, Tomassi."

"So I should be grateful?"

"You should enjoy the act of breathing while you still can," Brayden said.

"Are you keeping me here so you can threaten me every day, or are you going to kill me?"

Craig shrugged. "Undecided."

"Animals." Tomassi spat.

"Speaking of," Brayden said. "You have been playing God with my vampires. Do you know what you have done?"

"Yes." He sat on the edge of the bed. "It cannot be undone, if that's what you want to know."

Brayden wanted to rip open the cell and rip the fucking monster's head off.

"Dangerous games you're playing," he said instead. "But your days are numbered."

Can we kill him yet?

Not yet. He answered Craig.

"Lucky I've left behind a legacy, then," Xander said. "And the events already underway are going to change the world."

"I look forward to you telling us all about it." Craig grinned. "Because, human, you will talk. You will tell us everything. If you think what you did to our vampires was painful, I will let you wonder about all the things I'm going to do to you."

Brayden watched the narcissistic asshole as he tried to remain calm. His breathing and heart rate—both of which they could hear—increased rapidly.

They knew he wasn't going to spill all the information on their first visit.

But eventually, he would talk.

Meanwhile, they would let him simmer in Craig's threat.

Brayden might even let the commander follow through with some of his ideas.

God knows he would enjoy watching it.

Vincent sat, shaking his head.

"A fucking what?"

"Some kind of super soldier," James Calder, POTUS, said.

He wasn't about to tell the president about their hybrids, but now he was finding out the fuckers from BioZen had mixed their vampire DNA with human soldiers and created… super fucking soldiers.

Jesus.

This wasn't good.

"What do we know about them? the king asked.

"Very little. The leak came from inside BioZen. From the top. Once we learn more, I will let you know."

Vincent tapped his pen.

"We have Xander Tomassi. I know that wasn't the agreement, but we brought him in," he shared.

James stared back at him.

"He's unharmed. And will remain that way if he talks," he added.

James nodded.

"Then I'd like to talk to him. Have my people speak to him," James said.

Vincent sat back in his chair and stared at the screen.

"Yes, all right. We need to keep all of this out of *Operation Daylight*," he said. "This is escalating quickly. The less they know, the better."

"Agreed," James said. "I will fly over in a few days' time. Keep him alive."

He'd do his best.

But his vampire warriors were mad.

And he didn't blame them.

They'd be even more furious once they learned of this new information.

Fucking super soldiers.

These scientists were the true monsters and needed to be stopped.

"James, my patience is slipping. If we don't stop these people, they will change the world as we know it, far more than we ever have in fifteen hundred years. You must see that," Vincent said. "This world is our home, too."

The president sighed.

"I have ten million vampires relying on me. You have hundreds of millions," he continued.

"We need to flesh out the true beast. If we jump in and destroy the tail, you know it will grow back stronger," James said. "BioZen might be the supplier but who are the customers? That's what we need to find out."

Humans.

That's who the customers were.

But he couldn't say that.

There was a lot the president didn't know. He'd have to decide what he shared with him when he arrived in Maine.

Until then, he hoped Brayden and Craig could get as much information from Xander Tomassi as possible.

While the guy kept breathing.

Not that he deserved it.

"See you when you arrive." Vincent said, and closed the lid on his laptop.

He cursed and swiveled in his chair so he could look outside into the moonlight.

Be the king, his father said. It's fun.

Yeah, right.

Okay, he hadn't actually said that.

But no one could have predicted the shit they were dealing with right now.

Not in a million years.

CHAPTER FORTY-FIVE

"Oh, I thought you were Brayden." Madison blushed when she opened the door. Her hair was wet, and he could smell the coconut and vanilla body wash she used in the shower.

"Can I come in?" Kurt asked.

"Why would you want to?" Madison asked back.

Fair question.

Because I love you.

Because you are my mate.

"I want to explain why I left," he said, his arm on the top of the door frame.

"No need. You do it so much I'm used to it."

Ouch.

But again, fair.

"Maddy, please," Kurt said, begging for the first time in his adult life. He had begged his father to stop hurting him millions of times as a child and promised himself he'd never beg anyone again. But for her, he would. "Let me say the things I need to say and if you want me to leave afterwards, I will."

And he would.

"Five minutes." She turned away.

That was all he needed. He closed the door behind him.

"First, tell me how you're feeling." He stood as close to her as she would allow.

She shrugged.

"Fine, physically. Mentally I'm fucked up," she admitted. "Emotionally about the same."

He could see the layers of sadness and confusion in her eyes and wanted to pull her into his arms.

"You were terrified of me." He stared down at her. "I fucking hated that."

She swallowed.

"You are never scared of me. You snap back. You sass me," Kurt said. "Why? I need to understand."

Madison shrugged. "I know. I can't explain it."

"Do you think I would hurt you?" he asked, his chest tight in anticipation of her answer.

She lifted her eyes to him and nodded. "As a wolf, the threat felt real. You're a really powerful vampire, Kurt. I felt your energy far more intently in that form. Your anger was directed at me and got stronger when I moved away."

He cursed.

"Because you fucking moved away from me and cuddled up to Callan," he ground out, trying not to get angry.

"He felt safe." She spoke softly.

He cursed again, and took a few steps away.

"I'm sorry," Madison said, and he turned.

"Don't apologize. Shit." He stared at her.

If he didn't explain why he'd left, she would never understand. After a lifetime of never telling a soul about his childhood, he was about to tell a second person in a matter of days.

"My father beat my mother," he said. "Repeatedly."

Her mouth fell open.

Violence in a bonded relationship was rare in their species, unlike humans. It happened, but it was rare.

"And me," Kurt added. "He beat me when I was a tiny vampire. So I killed him."

Madison nodded. Her eyes moistened.

"I swore to never mate. Ever. I didn't want to be like him."

"You wouldn't be." She breathed hard. "Never."

He walked to her.

"Yet you cowered from me." His voice was thick. "It nearly fucking broke me to see you like that. Terrified, as if I would ever harm you."

Her eyes filled.

"You leaving hurt me more than these muscles could." She stepped up and lay her hands on his pecs. "You promised you wouldn't."

Jesus, she knew.

Madison knew he was her mate.

"Maddy," he said, cupping her face. "You fucking know. How long have you known?"

She sniffed.

"I'm still not sure. I'm drawn to the pack, to Callan, but not like this." Madison leaned into him. "It feels safe and like home with them. But with you I feel alive, except there's no solid footing."

Kurt closed his eyes.

He knew why she felt like that. And it was his fucking fault. He hadn't been fully committed to the bonding. He'd constantly been looking for a way to escape it, question it, and deny it.

Yet at the same time, he'd been angry when Madison was showing signs of her own doubts. One that was not of her choosing. The pack.

"That's my fault." He ran his thumb over her cheek. "But how about we change that?"

Big green eyes stared up at him, full of hope.

Full of emotion he'd been ignoring.

She loved him. He saw it now.

"Madison Michaelson, you're mine. You are my mate." He smiled as she gasped and pulled her tight against him. "If you will have me, I will never let you out of my sight again."

"Do you mean that?" she asked. "I'm a shifter. Part wolf."

He scooped her up and carried her into the bedroom.

"The most beautiful wolf I've ever seen." He lowered her on to the bed. "I love you."

Her hand found his face as he lay beside her, tugging her against him.

"I love you too." A tear slid down her face. "But what if this other part of me won't allow us to bond?"

He had been wondering that too, but Craig's words came flooding back.

Bite her. Trust me on this one.

"I'm willing to take a chance on this. Will you?" He propped himself up on his elbow and gazed down at her. "You're mine, Maddy, and I am *not* going to stop fighting for this. You have to know that about me. I let my stupid childhood beliefs get in the way and that is not fucking happening again."

Madison's hand ran along his biceps as if studying him for the first time, and his body shivered.

"I feel a pull from you both. I need it to end or it's like I will be torn in two." Her eyes met his. "I want you, Kurt. I've always wanted you."

"Then let me claim you, sweetheart. Because, and I'll say this every day for the rest of our lives, *you are mine.*"

His mouth slammed down on hers as she wrapped her arms around him. Without care, he ripped their clothes off and covered her with his body.

"We can take our time afterwards, but I need this," Kurt demanded.

"Yes," she cried as his mouth harshly sucked her nipple.

He wrapped her legs around his body and slid his hand between them to prepare her. Circling her clit, she soon was wet enough to accept him inside her.

He thrust inside to their combined screams.

"Fuck." He tucked his hand under her ass and pounded into her.

Mine.

Kurt felt the mating bond roar to life.

Fin-a-fucking-ly.

She gasped, her hand going to his face, and he knew what she was seeing. His eyes had changed to reflect the mating bond—a dark ring around his pupils would be there for life now.

Hers would appear very soon.

His fangs ripped out of his gums.

"You can't." She cried out.

"Yeah, baby. I can. If you'll let me?" He wanted and needed her consent for this. She wasn't human, but even vampire mates had the right for refusal.

"You might... shift."

"Trust our bond," he asked of her, his cock sliding slowly in and out of her. "Trust me."

Madison nodded. Then he lowered his head to her neck and pierced the skin as his fangs sunk in.

Power suddenly erupted between them.

"Oh, shit." She cried out.

A taste so delicious it had to have come from the gods filled his mouth as her blood combined with his. His body roared with heat and fire as his orgasm struck, filling her with every thrust while he drew from her vein.

Mine.

As Madison panted and caught her breath, Kurt rested on one of his forearms and smiled down at her.

"Hello, mate." Sparkling eyes blinked back at him, and then her face broke into a huge smile.

She gripped his face. "It's gone."

Kurt frowned.

"What's gone?" he asked, lifting up a few inches.

"The tug from Callan. It's gone. All I can feel is you," she said, glowing.

Thank fuck.

His mouth descended on hers and as their tongues playfully circled one another's, he felt a sense of joy and peace deep inside that had never been there before.

Love.

Mate.

Family.

CHAPTER FORTY-SIX

Five days later

Kurt stood with his arm wrapped loosely around Madison's lower back as she leaned into him.

It was a strange thing to not want to be physically away from someone. If he could strap her to him, he would. Felt a little co-dependent but, a) he didn't give a fuck what anyone thought, and b) now he understood why his colleagues and friends had lost their goddamn minds over their mates.

As he had.

Having the complication of the wolf in the mix had thrown them both. As if mating wasn't hard enough as it was.

Now, at least he could telepath and feel her through their mating bond.

Madison glanced up at him and tip-toed to kiss him. He pulled her against his chest as she palmed his pecs, and his body reacted immediately to her touch.

"Sexy vampire," she said.

"Don't you forget it." He smirked and got a full-blown eye roll for his efforts.

They were standing outside the castle doors as a large van was being loaded with supplies. Over the past few days, there had been a lot of conversations. The king had approved Callan's request to move to another location, which they all agreed was a good decision.

Several of the vampires and humans he'd infected had been located and were being escorted to the castle by Alex, one of the assassins at The Institute who lived in Seattle—the city where Callan had been.

Today they were leaving.

"Can't believe Ava has shifted already," Madison said. "I'm glad she did while she was still here. Her wolf is so pretty."

"Not as beautiful as yours," Kurt replied. Ava was a little bigger than Madison in wolf form and had a full brown coat of fur.

"You're biased," Madison replied.

Callan lifted a box into the van and then turned, spotting them on the steps.

"Nearly done?" Kurt asked.

Callan nodded. "Think so. We have more than enough supplies to last a year. The king has been very generous."

"You're a Moretti blooded vampire. And wolf. No one is turning their back on you," Kurt said. "I will be out to visit once you're settled."

Kurt had been appointed the senior wolf liaison. After bonding with Madison, and they had exhausted themselves with pleasure, they had gone to see Callan.

He had sensed her bond to him snapping.

The medical team had spent hours asking all of them questions for their records so they could learn more.

He had shaken hands with the hybrid shifter and a peace between them was formed.

Callan had kept Madison safe, and only followed his instincts. He'd made it clear to the male that he knew what had taken place between them before he'd returned for her. Maddy had told him everything. While it had infuriated him, Kurt had to accept it was a confusing situation for all of them.

He had walked away when he shouldn't have.

He would never do it again.

Now Madison was his mate, and she would want no other. Nor would he.

It made sense for him to take on the new role. The king trusted him, and Madison would need, and want, to visit the pack village. This way, they could go together.

He would still remain an SLC, but these would be additional responsibilities.

Another reason they needed more vampires on their team. Life was changing.

"Thank you," Callan said, shaking his hand, and then turning to Madison. She reached up and gave him a tight hug. It was a brotherly hug of sorts. One that told him the wolf was her family and always would be now.

"See you soon."

Madison turned to him, and they walked back inside the castle.

"There's still a connection with them all," she said. "I can't explain it. Before, the thought of them leaving would have created a type of panic, but that's gone now. It's kind of like family leaving. You don't want them to, but you know you'll see each other soon."

"Are you sure?" he asked, needing to know she would be okay.

Madison nodded. "Yes. I will need to visit regularly, though. I know that."

As they walked through the castle, Kurt thought about her words. "So you can be in your wolf state and run?"

"Yes. But just to remain connected to their energy."

They had agreed with the king she would keep her wolf hidden from the inhabitants of the castle for now. It wouldn't always be possible, but there would be no shifting and running through the halls.

"We'll find a space for you to shift here on the grounds," Kurt said, opening the door to their home. "Discreetly. Expecting you to keep your wolf contained is not right."

He recognized the need to keep the information contained for now, but he suspected there would be a side effect to not shifting regularly and the medical team agreed with him.

Pick your battles.

Everyone was adjusting to this new world of theirs, including the king. So he would work on his rules one day at a time. To be fair, Vincent had been more than accommodating to the pack and over time, their lives would evolve.

"The great news is you can go out during the daylight," Kurt said, lifting her onto the kitchen bench and spreading her thighs so he could step between them, closer to her.

"I was excited about it, but nervous," Madison said. She had yet to go out into the sun and he totally understood it.

"I'm envious," Kurt said. "While the sun is our enemy, there is a natural curiosity about how the heat feels on the skin."

"Well, I don't have skin in my wolf form. I have fur, so I guess I won't be finding out anytime soon," she said. "I need to ring my mom and tell her I won't be returning to Seattle."

There had been many tears over the past few days as Madison came to grips with all the changes in her world.

She had phoned her friends, Selena and Brooke, and they were going to come out and visit soon. Selena sounded like trouble, and he was pretty sure a few of the males would be quite happy to have her around.

As for her mom, she still hadn't made a decision.

"The offer still stands to move her to Maine. Either in the castle or somewhere local, if that's what she wants," Kurt said, running his fingers through her hair.

Madison sighed. "She won't move."

He let the emotions settle as her eyes shadowed.

"She will be happy her daughter has bonded," he said. "Leaving you alone would be hard. It might... and I say *might...*" It was highly likely, and they both knew it. "Be what's keeping her alive after your dad died."

Mates didn't live long when the other passed. A year was an extremely impressive effort. It showed how much she loved her daughter. For vampires, this was the natural way of life, and Madison knew that.

"I'll call her tomorrow," she said. "One day at a time."

"One day at a time." He repeated their mantra and ran his hands over her hips and nudged her into his body.

"If she does decide to move, lets work it so we can take that holiday. I promised I'd take you to Italy, and I meant it," Kurt said.

"I'm going to Italy," Madison said breathlessly. "I can't believe it. And with a sexy-as-hell vampire as my guide."

"As your mate. I can't believe only four weeks ago, I was a single vampire who walked into a bar and flirted with a sexy barmaid," Kurt said, shaking his head and nipping at her neck. "Now I'm mated."

"Can I confess something?" Maddy asked.

"Always," he replied.

"I had a crush on you when I was a young vamp."

His lips spread into a huge grin. "Yeah?"

She nodded and blushed. "I had a poster of you on my wall."

Kurt tried to rein it in but failed.

He laughed.

She slapped him playfully. "Don't laugh at me."

"I'm sorry. The whole fan girl thing just doesn't seem like something you'd do," he said. "You have far too much sass for that."

She *was* sassy, but it had become quite apparent through her wolf that she was a submissive, and hell, yeah, that worked in the bedroom.

"I was young."

"You're still young," Kurt said, reminding her she was only fifty-five years to his six hundred and something.

He'd given up counting.

"Well, maybe I still have a crush on you." She teased him, tilting her head.

"Sweetheart, you can crush yourself to me every day and night for the rest of our lives."

"Deal, vampire. Deal," Madison said.

Then he slipped off her panties and crushed his mouth to hers.

Who would have thought?

Kurt Mazzarelli, a mated vampire.

He closed his eyes and lost himself in his beautiful, sexy hybrid mate.

EPILOGUE

Callan teleported back into the center where the entrance was lined with bags and boxes. All of which they had to fit into the van.

"Ready?" He called out to his pack members.

It was funny how quickly everything, including his language, was changing. He felt his wolves through an energy that ran through his body.

Ava had shifted so he could feel her more strongly than the others. He still sensed Madison since she'd mated with Kurt, but not the same.

Liam had half-shifted, which had been painful for him and Callan was concerned. The drive to their new home was only an hour away, so once they got settled, he'd see how he could help the male.

Not that he had any idea what he was doing.

Noah had not shifted. Interestingly, aside from the heightened sexual drive, he'd experienced no other side effects at all.

"Coming," Ava called out.

"You did, in any case." Liam ran past, scooping her up and planting a kiss on her cheek.

"Put her down." Noah growled, pushing him as they all joined up by the bags.

"Don't tell him what to do," Ava snapped. "Just because you missed out…"

Noah turned and crossed his arms. "I didn't *miss out*. I chose not to participate."

"Whatever," Ava said.

Liam shot him a look and rolled his eyes.

Callan smiled.

Their bickering was starting to get on everyone's nerves, but he figured Ava just needed a good run and Noah was probably getting ready to shift.

What the hell did he know?

They were all working out this new life of theirs.

"Grab your things," Callan said. "We have four days to get set up in our new home before the new wolves arrive."

It was weird to think they were never going home.

He had left behind a job and friends, but after being in the BioZen lab for months, he had long given up worrying about his past.

Life had changed forever.

Now they were creating a new future. A hybrid vampire-wolf pack with Moretti blood.

Moretti-blooded wolves.

And he was their alpha.

Turn the page to read the first chapter of **The Vampire Warrior**–Marcus and Charlotte's steamy, wild romantic story.
It also includes Sage and Ari's wedding!

Can't wait that long? Callan's fated mates

romance kicks off in **The Alpha Wolf,** book one of my new series, **Moretti Blood Wolves** based in the **Moretti universe.**

THE VAMPIRE WARRIOR

CHAPTER ONE

"No." Marcus spoke firmly and kept his pace as he walked through the halls of the Moretti castle.

The king had decided they would remain in Portland for the winter. And Christmas, but it wasn't wise to bring that holiday up as the king had an unhealthy dislike of it.

No one was really sure if he actually hated Christmas, or he was doing it to mess with the new princess, Willow. His brother's mate.

Possibly both.

Also, this Christmas there was to be a wedding at the castle. Yes, very human. Ari Moretti, the king's great uncle, was marrying his mate, Sage. A former human. Apparently, he had promised her a big fancy wedding after taking her humanity when he turned her.

So, the king was bound to be in a bad mood this winter with both a wedding *and* Christmas festivities filling the halls.

Except this year there was another event taking place. One Marcus knew he was totally on board with.

The Warrior Games.

And the frustratingly sexy vampire who was keeping stride with him and nagging his damn ear off was a potential candidate.

If she would stop trying to exit from his team.

All because he'd kissed her.

After she had kissed him.

Totally different occasions.

Marcus had hoped planting his mouth on hers would even the playing field so she could get over it and focus on becoming the best she could be.

God knows she trained enough.

Obsessively.

Marcus knew that was what it took sometimes. But he'd been trying to train her on the importance of rest.

They might be vampires, but they were not immortal gods. They were biological bodies that required sustenance, blood, and rest.

But his really dumb plan had not worked.

First, it had just given him a six-week erection that wouldn't go away, no matter how hard he tried. Pun intended. Second, Charlotte could barely look him in the eye.

Unless she was glaring at him.

Then, yeah, then she was all fire and steel.

But he knew better.

He'd felt her hips as he held her firm while his mouth took complete possession. He'd felt her wet lips against his as she opened without hesitation and burst into flames.

He'd seen the glimpse of vulnerability after she'd surprised him with the first kiss. She was nearly as surprised as he was.

They had parted, shocked, their eyes locked as they both processed the electricity swirling between them.

Marcus had moved away first.

She was one of his team members.

He wasn't going to fuck her.

Charlotte had so much potential. They needed to get their sexual attraction for each other under control and get to work so she could qualify for the Games.

Marcus was the best trainer in the Moretti army. He took that part of his job very seriously. Less so than keeping the king alive, but, you know, that was a good thing.

Now, with the Games approaching, he needed Charlotte to lose the attitude—although it was sexy as fuck—and stay in his team.

"No?" Charlotte asked, her voice laced with bewilderment. "Just, no? You can't say no. My question was *why* my request to be transferred has been declined."

He kept walking.

"Marcus!" she said, her voice louder.

He whirled on her.

"That's Senior Lieutenant Commander Vecchia to you." He growled, his face inches from hers.

Finally.

Finally, she'd fucking blanched, surprise in her eyes as she took in a healthy dose of his alpha energy.

Not that he wasn't hard on her, but he'd put up with her sass for long enough.

So she had kissed him.

They both needed to get over it.

He hated how embarrassed she'd been. Especially when it was just as much his fault.

When he looked back.

The time for playing was over.

They needed more senior warriors on their SLC team. Charlotte could be the first female to serve the king directly.

It would take both of them to get her there.

But not if they were fucking on the side.

"Enough with the attitude. Our team meeting is about to start. Get your sexy damn ass in the room. Right now," he said, his hands on his hips. He could have left the sexy bit off. *Fuck.* "I have an announcement to make. After that, you can decide if you still want to transfer."

He'd be mad as fuck if she did.

Not that anyone else couldn't train her.

Just not as good as he could.

"Oh, I'll be transferring." She glared back at him. But he'd seen the little flash of doubt cross her eyes.

He pushed the door open, without looking away, and she narrowed her eyes a second and then stepped into the room.

Stubborn damn female.

When he followed her in and stepped to the front of the room, taking in the black uniform-clad team of strong vampire warriors in front of him, he wondered how many of them would qualify.

Likely very few.

But he was determined to find the right vampires for the king.

Lives depended on it.

The vampire race were depending on them.

They had dangerous enemies and their team of five SLCs was not enough anymore.

The room quietened as some found a seat or wall to lean on.

Marcus crossed his arms.

"Later tonight the king is announcing the first Warrior Games in nine hundred years," he said. "There are about five of you in this team who will qualify."

Excitement filled the room.

"What do we win?" someone asked.

Yeah, he hated the name. It didn't represent the seriousness of the objective.

"One of three Senior Lieutenant Commander positions," Marcus said.

The room went silent as mouths dropped open.

A few *holy shits* dropped.

There were only five SLCs in the king's army. Marcus was one of them. Aside from a recent recruit, no one had been invited to join the SLC team since the mid-1600s.

This was a very fucking big deal.

Marcus gazed around the room until his eyes landed on Charlotte. She was looking at the floor. Whether she had felt him or not, he didn't know, but she slowly lifted her face and their eyes locked.

She swallowed.

The knowledge sunk in.

Unless she chose not to enter, which would be a poor decision on her behalf, she had a very strong chance of becoming one of his colleagues.

And the tug of desire they were both fighting would have to be doused.

Forever.

Marcus and Charlotte's steamy romance is next in The Vampire Warrior. It also includes Sage and Ari's wedding!

Can't wait that long?

Callan's fated mates romance kicks off in **The Alpha Wolf,** book one of my new series, **Moretti**

Blood Wolves based in the **Moretti universe.**

Visit Amazon for the paperback versions of my books, or your favorite online book retailer to grab an eBook version.

ALSO BY JULIETTE N. BANKS

The Moretti Blood Brothers
Steamy paranormal romance

The Vampire Prince
The Vampire Protector
The Vampire Spy
The Vampire's Christmas
The Vampire Assassin
The Vampire Awoken
The Vampire Lover
The Vampire Wolf
The Vampire Warrior

The Moretti Blood Wolves
Steamy paranormal shifter romance
The Alpha Wolf

The Dufort Dynasty
Steamy billionaire romance
Sinful Duty
Forbidden Touch
Total Possession

Realm of the Immortals
Steamy paranormal fantasy romance
The Archangel's Heart
The Archangel's Star
The Archangel's Goddess

LET'S STAY IN TOUCH

To receive information about my new or upcoming releases, new series and free giveaways join my **VIP BOOKCLUB.**

Visit my website www.juliettebanks.com **to join a**nd to find all the links to connect with me on **Instagram, BookBub and Goodreads.**

I'd love to invite you to join my **private Facebook Group.** I'm very active in there and share a lot about my writing process, what's coming up, plus sneaky (and spicy) excerpts from my current manuscripts before they publish! Click the link below to join, answer the group questions and just remember its R18!

www.facebook.com/groups/authorjuliettebanksreaders

Printed in Great Britain
by Amazon